Accidental Vegas Vows

A Silver Fox Boss Romance

Unintentionally Yours

Mia Mara

What happens when you accidentally say, 'I do' to your silver fox boss in Vegas because you're saving yourself for marriage? A baby...

Damien:

I took my gorgeous, feisty intern to the altar - Elvis and all - just to wed and bed her.

I know it was wrong.

I'm old enough to be her father.

But one unforgettable night in Sin City and she has me on my knees.

Now she's the only one who can help this rookie single dad out.

A five-year-old boy has been left on my doorstep.

He's quickly becoming the reason my heart beats.

I'll do anything to stop his crazy aunt taking him away from me.

Even play happy family for the courts.

Olivia insists our arrangement has an expiration date.

But the more heated nights we spend together, the more I forget all the reasons why we have no future.

Vegas might have been a mistake. But I'll fight for the beautiful mistake growing inside her and keep our accidental family together.

Chapter 1

Olivia

I could barely hear the roar of applause or the words spilling from the wiry man's mouth over the incessant, unending thumping of my heartbeat. There were eighteen of us left — interns, all of us, straddling our seats as though they would somehow ground us. One more would be chosen to give their presentation.

And I needed it to be me.

Dear god, I needed it. Needed the attention of the higher-ups, needed the security of a full-time job out the other end of this in three months. And the only way to get that was to be *noticed*. But the chaos of the room, filled to the brim with clients, employees, management, and board members of Blackwood Energy Solutions, was making my anxiety almost too much to bear.

I swallowed down my fear as the intern at the podium stepped down.

To my right, a girl I'd only seen in passing a handful of times crossed her fingers in her lap beneath her binder. The lanyard around her neck clipped into her dangling ID card. *Kelsey Somers.* I'd heard about her, heard of her determina-

1

tion and loudness, and for what might have been the first time in my life, I actively wished for someone else's demise. However badly she needed to be chosen, I needed it more.

My stomach churned. *Okay, Liv. Maybe don't wish for others to fail.*

Sound slowly filtered back in, and in the now deafeningly silent room, the heavy steps by the podium boomed and echoed against all four walls. *Last chance.*

Turning my attention to the sound, though, might have just been the worst thing I could have done.

The large, hulking frame of a man who stepped up to the podium wasn't the same as the one who had been presenting in between interns — no, this was someone new, but someone I recognized, someone who even from here took up far too much space and demanded attention.

Damien Blackwood.

Oh my god, I'm going to be sick. The CEO of the company, the owner, up on the stage, staring straight into the group of interns. My pulse hammered again, blocking out the noise.

He was far, *far* too attractive in person.

His height struck me first. It was something I hadn't been able to glean from the staged photographs in the lobby, but here, in full fucking color, it was obvious — he must have been somewhere between six foot and six foot four. His hair, meticulously styled with little black and gray strands hanging beside his face, was the only true indicator of his age: forty-five, according to Forbes in their January issue. A playboy by nature, according to the tabloids, and the likelihood of him even giving someone like me the time of day was unheard of. He was far too sexy to be running a company. His face should have been plastered on billboards, projected in movie theaters, or printed by fashion houses. But even with all of that, it wasn't the wrinkles beside his eyes, the close-cut facial hair, and the shocking blue of his irises that grabbed my attention.

I was far too focused on his *hands.*

One large, ring-laden hand wrapped around the microphone and for a fleeting moment, I forgot entirely about my project, about my pitch, about everyone else in the room. The light glinted off the watch on his wrist and my breath caught, but not out of fear, not because my mouth had gone dry and my throat was closing in. Instead, my mind drifted far too close to the sun, imagining the way that same hand would look around my wrist, the way it would curve around the swell of my breast, the way two fingers would disappear inside of my—

The eruption of applause yanked me back down to reality so harshly I almost forgot to breathe.

Kelsey stood up beside me, beaming as if the world was her goddamn oyster, and clutched her binder to her chest. *Did I miss something?*

"Excuse me," she said, her knees practically bumping mine as a request to move past.

The others around me clapped with tight lips as I shifted in my seat to allow her through. I joined them almost robotically, the reality of the situation slowly sinking in, forcing bile up my throat to make room for the rocks that filled my stomach.

I wasn't picked.

I wasn't fucking *picked.*

My breathing picked up as I watched her climb the stairs. Mr. Blackwood reached out a hand for her and she took it gleefully, her fingers so small as they rested gently in his palm for leverage in her heels. Her black hair, curled

3

and tucked behind her ears, bounced as she approached the podium.

But I didn't hear the echoing sound of her nails tapping against the microphone, didn't hear the laughter from the crowd when she asked, "Is this thing on?"

Instead, two words pinged around inside of my mind, filling the space, doubling, tripling, quadrupling until the words blurred and became meaningless as they seeped into my bones, becoming me, entangling themselves with me.

I failed.

———

I couldn't get out of my head.

I made a break for it the moment the meeting ended, choosing instead to pour myself back into work instead of hanging around, mingling, and chatting idly with everyone else. At least if I could work on my project and perfect it, I could leave Blackwood knowing I'd given it every goddamn shot I had in me.

Staring at my feet to keep myself from making eye contact with anyone who might want to talk to me, I slipped inside the elevator, my shoes crossing over the metal threshold just as the doors slid shut behind me. Across from me, a larger pair of shoes lingered, polished to a shine, fine leather and tapered slacks—

Oh, fuck.

I couldn't bring myself to look him in the eye as I checked which floor we were on, jamming my finger into the button of the next closest one up, but the light flickered, flashed, and I pressed it again. It didn't even light up at all.

"You're one of the interns, right?"

The elevator came to a screeching halt and so did I. Frozen, unmoving, with my finger jammed into the button for floor eight, all I could do was try to breathe. *Why aren't we moving? Why aren't the doors opening?*

"What the...?"

Turning my head to glance over my shoulder, I stared directly at the center of Damien Blackwood's chest. I wasn't brave enough to look any further north—or south, really— but even that was a mistake. The way his suit clung to him... tailored perfectly to fit the obvious muscles in his arms, his shirt puckering just slightly over what I could only assume were the ripples of abdominal strength in his core.

And his *cologne*.

It permeated the space the longer we lingered, with hints of rum, almonds, and vanilla invading my nostrils and making my head spin.

Fuck, it smelled *heavenly*.

The lights flickered above my head, and I made another mistake and looked up at them, my gaze dragging right across his chiseled, hair-speckled jaw and the high ridges of his cheekbones. Every beat of my heart seemed to amplify behind my eardrums as the lights went out completely.

"Power must be out," Damien mumbled, and a second later, two white emergency lights lit the small metal cube.

"Ironic," I gulped. His piercing blue stare burned into me as I finally dropped my gaze to his, every part of myself heating. "Cause of the... y'know, the solar panels."

Ignoring me completely, his hand slid down his jacket, tendons flexing and two platinum rings catching the light just as his fingers dipped into the pocket. One singular brow rose when I caught his gaze again, and just as quickly as it had appeared, it slipped from his features as he typed furiously at his phone.

The walls were too goddamn close.

Every surface reflected the two of us standing as far apart as we possibly could in the cramped space. Endless realities, endless mirrors, and no matter what, in every single one, he hadn't picked me today.

My throat went dry.

"They're getting the power back on," Damien said, his voice filling and replacing every cubic inch of air. It was rougher than before, a little hoarse, a little angry. "It'll be a few minutes."

I nodded and leaned back against the cool glass of the mirrored wall, letting my head fall against it. "Okay."

The quiet descended, nothing but our heavy breathing and the occasional clunk from outside of the elevator. I tried not to look at him, but the only direction that didn't reflect him a million times was down, and even then I could still see his pristinely polished shoes. I was almost positive his reflection beamed from those, too.

But the silence, the stress, the anger — it was bearing down like gravity, pushing into my shoulders, my head, my bones. *I hadn't been picked.* Someone, likely him, had read through my proposal and didn't think it was worthy of being spoken aloud or presented to the board. I clutched the binder closer to my chest, trying to take a deep breath in, but all I got was that damn cologne and the faint scent of what I could only imagine was shoe polish—

"Why wasn't I picked?"

My stomach sank the moment I realized I'd said the words out loud. Somehow, the silence became thicker, heavier, and I winced as another clang came from somewhere above the elevator box. His jaw tightened, the muscles below his ear sticking out just a hair further.

"I'm sorry—"

"Which one was your proposal?"

The softness of the words caught me off guard. I clutched my binder tighter, my heart pounding behind my ribs, and tried to focus. *Why the fuck did I even bring it up?* "Uh, mine's the..." My words trailed off as one hand, rings glinting, reached for my binder.

"Let me see it," he said, his voice like gravel. His brows knitted as his fingers slipped over the top of the binder, the tips of them ghosting against the top buttons of my blouse and making both my breath and the black fabric catch. I relinquished my binder before he could demand it and loosened my grip on the one thing I'd worked the hardest on since university, watching mindlessly as he pulled it from my chest and flipped it open.

"It's the water purification one," I breathed.

He glanced at me briefly as he skimmed the first page. "You say that as if I should already know," he said, tucking one finger beneath the paper and using it to flip it over the rings of the binder effortlessly.

What the fuck does that mean? "Were you not in charge of choosing who got to present?"

The question hung in the air as he read over my proposal. I watched him like a hawk, taking stock of every shift of his features, every time his brows rose or his nostrils flared. He flipped the page and flipped again, shifting on his feet, studying the words I'd worked so fucking hard on.

I didn't know what to say to him, didn't know if I was *allowed* to say anything at all. But when I'd finally worked up the courage to ask for my binder back after the fourth and fifth clang of the elevator from above us, he spoke before my words could breach my teeth.

"Is this true?"

I blinked. "Is what—"

He flipped the binder in his hands and held it out toward me, one platinum ring glinting as he pointed his forefinger at a single sentence I'd written. *The research team at the Korea Institute of Science and Technology (KIST) and Myongji University have created a membranous fabric capable of filtering water while simultaneously using the current to produce electricity.*

I followed the length of his finger up, my eyes raking over the tanned skin of the back of his hand and the antique-looking wristwatch, up his suit jacket sleeve, and oh god, he was closer now, towering over me—

"Is that true?" he asked again.

I nodded, but fuck, my head was spinning. "Yeah. The filter is dense enough to filter out everything from microplastics to heavy metal particles," I explained, swallowing whatever saliva I could accumulate in my mouth to soothe my raw throat. "Purchasing that technology could be business-changing."

"Yeah. It absolutely could," he mumbled, pulling the binder back toward him. "Do you know if they're offering up their rights to it?"

Blue eyes met mine again, softer almost, and from this close, I could see his age clearer. The crows' feet on either side of his eyes, the faint crease between his brows, the lines of his forehead. What I'd thought was completely black stubble showed hints of gray just like his hair, and the longer I looked, the more it seemed almost taboo to have thought the things that had gone through my head back in the presentation room. He was almost twice my age — forty-five to my twenty-four.

But that didn't stop those images from flashing through my mind again.

"Olivia."

One word, one singular word, *my name*. The way he said it sounded as sweet as honey and just as viscous and thick. I imagined it slipping from his lips over and over as they trailed my bare skin, over my collarbones and further across the swell of my breast, another mumble seeping out as they latched on to my nipple—

"You know my name?" I breathed, reality crashing back in like a screeching banshee.

He blinked at me once before tapping the front of the binder. *Olivia Martin,* it said in big, bold letters. "You're also wearing your name tag."

I gulped. "Right. Yes, they're considering selling the tech."

The elevator shifted as the lights flickered back to life, replacing the bright white emergency ones. For a fleeting, ill-timed second, I almost resented them, resented what it *meant*.

"I'd like to take a closer look at this, if you don't mind," he said, shutting the binder with one hand and tucking it under his arm. The box we stood in moved again, shifting, until it slowly resumed its rise one inch at a time.

"Uh, yeah, sure," I mumbled.

Two seconds later a ding rang out through the small space, announcing our arrival at the closest floor. *So it had registered my button pressing.* The doors opened and he took a single step, his cologne swarming me from the proximity, but quicker than I could register, his eyes met mine in a flash of blue as he paused. God, he was too damn tall.

"I didn't choose who got picked," he said.

I was right.

"I would have chosen you."

Words failed me as he stepped across the threshold of the elevator and exited on floor fourteen — Human Resources and Bookkeeping. The doors shut behind him, leaving me alone in the small reflective box with my racing, debaucherous mind and pounding pulse.

But faced with my reflection in the doors and no binder to cover myself, I couldn't keep my eyes from wandering to my chest where more buttons than I'd intended had been left open.

Three, to be exact.

Enough to see the entirety of my cleavage and the edges of my bra.

Holy fuck!

My cheeks heated as I realized it must have popped open when his fingers had caught on it.

Oh my fucking god.

He saw everything.

Chapter 2

Damien

The view overlooking San Francisco from my office on the top floor of Blackwood Energy Solutions was barely enough to keep my thoughts from wandering back to the elevator and back to that encounter with *her*.

From up here, the cars crossing the Bay Bridge looked miniature and the people on the streets looked like ants — but that wasn't what I focused on. I took in Alcatraz, Treasure Island, and even the Golden Gate Bridge from the floor-to-ceiling windows that wrapped around two-thirds of my office. I stared, imagining the lives of every single person in each location, wondering if any of them were locals or simply passing through. Were they going home after a long day at the office? Were they heading back to their suburban two-story to take out their garbage and mow their lawns?

But even that, even placing myself into the shoes of the people who were literally beneath me, didn't distract me enough from her.

From the moment she'd stepped into the elevator, I'd found her attractive. That wasn't unusual — she was young,

11

beautiful, timid but defiant. It tracked. But the green of her eyes kept haunting me, the way her thick lashes had batted when she was confused, the curve of her plump, pink lips when she'd folded her teeth over them... Her clear skin save for a smattering of freckles, the way her thick hair had fallen over one shoulder as if the chestnut waves had a mind of their own, how the top of her head only reached my shoulder at absolute best.

And her fucking *brain*.

The proposal she'd had was brilliant. I wasn't sure why it wasn't chosen, and every word of it I read only proved to me that at the very least, her proposal trumped each one that had been picked to present today. I'd poured over it the moment I'd returned to my office, taking in every possible use she'd thought of, every business strategy she'd outlined for it. It was far beyond what I'd expected, and she easily deserved a full-time job here, if not something better. I wondered if she was chastising herself for how it went down, wondered if there was something I could do to make it better.

That fucking blouse, though.

The way the sides of it parted when I'd grabbed for her binder.

The peek at what she hid beneath it.

The way they'd practically burst out when I grabbed her.

I policed myself heavily when it came to the women who worked at Blackwood — I didn't need the mess that would inevitably come from sleeping with one. But *fuck*, none of them had made me that desperate to touch my swelling cock in the confines of that goddamn elevator.

I'd resisted coming on to her, of course. I wasn't eager to make an employee uncomfortable or receive an HR complaint on my spotless record. But in the confines of my office with the door locked and nothing to distract me but work, my view, and the binder she'd prepared sitting on my desk, the temptation to jack off was getting harder to beat back.

But just as I was about to give in, a knock sounded on my door.

Fisting the fabric of my slacks and readjusting my throbbing cock, I sank into my leather chair and pressed the buzzer on my desk, begrudgingly unlocking the door.

"I know you're busy, Damien, but I'd like to remind you that I'm a lawyer, not a lackey," Ethan quipped, his glasses shifting on his scrunched nose as he shut the door behind him.

"Sorry. My assistant's out for the day and you were already heading up." I leaned back in my chair, kicking my feet up onto the polished wood of my desk. "Did you bring it?"

His eyes rolled as he rounded the wingback chairs opposite my desk and dropped a handful of papers before me. "Yes, obviously."

I grabbed for the papers, skimming them quickly. The first was a list of names of those joining us on the Vegas trip next week. The second, outlines for how to keep HR happy and content with the Vegas trip. And the third, bundled under the rest, was the employee information for Olivia Martin. "You're a lifesaver."

"I literally just carried paperwork from floor fourteen to floor eighteen, but sure, I'll take it," he said, eyeing me as he slouched into the wingback chair.

Ethan had a point. Although I kept him here at the offices, he wasn't technically an employee of the company. He was Blackwood's lawyer, *my* lawyer, but more than either of those, he was someone I enjoyed the presence of, even if he didn't follow me blindly like the rest. "Well, you were already down in accounting," I said, and his nose crinkled again.

"Do I get a bonus for helping, then?"

"Don't overthink it, Ethan," I grinned.

He was roughly fifteen years my junior, but with the disappointment covering his features, I could have sworn he was my father.

"Fine. You can have a bonus. *Again.*" I flicked through the papers and pulled Olivia's file to the top. "Do you think HR would have an issue with me inviting an intern on the Vegas trip?" I asked.

He stared at me for a moment, his jaw twitching and his glasses shifting. His button-up shirt and slacks instead of a full suit were lackluster, especially for being on my floor, but I looked past it for today. "Do you mean the Martin girl? If she was chosen to present earlier, then I think they'd understand."

I shook my head as I flipped a stapled page over, reviewing the photocopy of her resume. "She wasn't picked."

"Are you inviting the ones that *were?*"

I snorted. "No. They'd cause more trouble than they're worth."

Ethan leaned forward, his elbows resting on his spread knees. "So you're sleeping with her."

I shot him a glare. "You know damn well I don't do that here."

He shrugged.

"I met her today. We got stuck together in the elevator with the power outage," I said, scanning each line of her resume. "She's brilliant. Her proposal should have been top of the damn pile. I've no idea why she wasn't chosen."

I slid Olivia's binder across the desk toward him and he took it willingly, flipping each page as if it wasn't the most interesting thing he'd seen today. "She's not even a full employee, Damien."

"She should be. That proposal is genuinely worth more to Blackwood than all of the interns that presented today put together."

He sighed as he flipped another page, studying it just a little bit closer. "I understand that you see potential," he said, his words hanging as he glanced at me over the top of his glasses. "But you're asking for trouble by bringing along someone that inexperienced to what is likely going to be the most important business trip of the year."

He wasn't wrong. Blackwood Energy Solutions would be pitching to envelop multiple other green initiative businesses into our conglomerate, and if things went well, we'd be leaving with pocketfuls of new income revenues and avenues to scale up green initiatives across the country. It was crucial that we succeed — but I couldn't deny that the idea of having her nearby didn't excite me. Especially when there would be down time. I could tempt myself at least a little, get to know her a bit more.

"I can tell there's ulterior motives here, Damien."

"Okay, yes, I'm attracted to her," I grumbled, slapping the paperwork down on the table. "But that doesn't negate her being a valuable asset. I've already spoken to accounting about offering her a full-time job, so it shouldn't be a hard sell. And I'm more than capable of removing myself from a situation if I'm too... tempted."

"You know, you could try women your own age for

once," Ethan snorted, slamming the binder closed and chucking it back onto my desk.

I turned to my laptop, pulled up my emails, and began drafting one to the company address on file for Olivia. "I would if they weren't so insistent on settling down immediately and using me for my money. Besides, you know damn well what happened with Marissa. It's not my fault that girls Olivia's age are more often up for casual things."

"What are you doing?" he asked, his gaze flicking between me and the back of the screen in front of me.

"Inviting her on the trip."

"I haven't even spoken to HR—"

"You will," I grinned. "And you'll convince them. For me."

He pursed his lips as he slid his phone from the pocket of his slacks. "Can we at least discuss the plan for integrating the new companies?"

I typed furiously, writing down the first words that came to mind. "Yes. In a second."

Olivia,

I want to offer my sincerest apologies that you were not chosen to present in front of the board today. Please know that I'm taking this matter incredibly seriously and will be raising it with the head of your department.

I've read more of your proposal. It's incredibly well done and, honestly, one of the freshest ideas I've seen in years. I've spoken to accounting to ensure you'll be offered a permanent role within Blackwood, so please do not worry about not being on that pipeline by not being chosen today.

That being said:

I'd like to formally invite you to join us next week in Las

Vegas, Nevada for the pitch we'll be doing at the Luxor. There are a few companies we'll hopefully be acquiring and I think it will give you some good experience to see how it all operates. I also think the presentation you prepared for today would go down well if you'd be interested in sharing it in Vegas. Your flight, hotel, and meals will be paid for if you choose to join us.

Have a think and get back to me by the end of the day tomorrow.

Damien Blackwood
Owner and CEO

I read back over the words once, twice, and a third time, contemplating whether I should add the postscript that danced in my mind. With how nervous she'd been around me, the little ways her breath had caught, the blush that had painted her cheeks in a warm pink...

I typed it just to reread it.

P.S. — If you decide to come and present, make sure your attire is as put together as your presentation this time. ;)

I knew it was unprofessional. I knew it didn't come across as well as the rest of my email. But a part of me couldn't shake how flustered I knew it would make her, and the temptation that bit at the back of my skull took over.

I clicked send before I could talk myself out of it. At the very least, she'd get a chuckle out of it, and at the most, she'd know that I was... interested. It could even provoke a response.

Maybe I'd crossed a line.

Maybe I was tempting myself far more than I should. But I couldn't help but find myself addicted to the *if only*, my mind dabbling in how I could handle that with someone from the office, how I could keep her a secret. It broke every rule in my book. It broke my standards. I'd only met her for, what, ten minutes? But there was something about her, something about her mind and her form that plagued me.

I knew that feeling well.

And I knew it might not stop until I got what I wanted out of her.

Chapter 3

Olivia

My stomach turned over as I stared down at Mr. Blackwood's email for what must have been the hundredth time.

Make sure your attire is as put together as your presentation this time.

Every time I remembered just how indecent I'd looked when the elevator doors shut, it was like reliving that mortification over and over again. The little gasp, the heat of my cheeks, the sinking stone in my gut that failed to cease its nauseating tendencies all came back and hit me like a freight train.

I'd already agreed — Mr. Blackwood and I had exchanged fairly civil emails back and forth immediately following it. But I still found myself staring at that initial one time and time again, wondering if he was plainly stating that I needed to *not* allow that to happen at the presentation or if he was insinuating something far different.

Something that made the nausea turn to butterflies.

But that wasn't appropriate.

I stared out the window of the taxi as we passed the

Golden Gate Cemetery, temptation eating away at me. If he meant more than what was written and my potential full-time role counted on me playing along, surely that was something HR needed to be aware of. But it was his company and his alone. He could act the way he pleased no matter what HR said.

There was someone I could speak to about this, though.

I pulled up Sophie's contact on my phone and pressed the call button, lifting my phone to my ear. I'd be at the airport in less than ten minutes with the way traffic was moving, and I needed to know in that ten minutes just how nervous and uncomfortable I would be for the next two days in Vegas.

"Aren't you meant to be getting on a private jet right about now?"

I snorted into the phone. "I doubt Mr. Blackwood went that far."

"*Mr. Blackwood?*" She cackled, the sound quickly becoming muffled. "God, you're so lucky I'm on lunch. The rest of HR would have had a field day with that."

The thought of the entire human resources department laughing at me instead of just Sophie made me cringe. "Should I not call him that?" I asked.

"Christ, no. I think you'd send him to an early grave if you called him that to his face," she chuckled. "And for the record, you *are* flying private. All of the attendees are."

"Jesus," I breathed, directing my attention out the window as we went straight past the entrance to the airport. "I wanted to run something by you real quick if that's okay. Work-related, not friend-related."

"Shoot."

"It's something I, uh, failed to mention a few days ago when I told you about the offer he'd extended," I started. I glanced at the taxi driver in the rearview mirror, tempting fate as his brown eyes met mine briefly. "He added a P.S. at the bottom of the email. He mentioned my... wardrobe malfunction."

"You mean your breasts being in his face?" she laughed.

"They were not *in his face*, Sophie."

"Same difference."

"He said to make sure my attire was as put together as my presentation," I whispered, hoping the taxi driver wouldn't hear me over the car's engine and the faint classical music from his speakers. "Should I... report that? Like, to *you*?"

"Report it?" The slight sound of her chewing filtered down the phone, and her next words were around a mouthful. "I mean, if it made you uncomfortable, go for it."

I bit down on the end of my thumbnail as the taxi turned into the bay labeled *Signature Flight Support*. "I don't know if it did."

"Then don't report it."

"What do you think he meant by it?"

"What do *you* think he meant by it?" she parroted, a little giggle leaking from between bites of her food. "He was probably just giving you a word of warning in case you always walked around with your tits out."

"He put a winky face next to it," I added. I could feel my cheeks heating as the driver's eyes met mine again briefly, crinkling at the edges as if he were grinning.

"Well that changes everything," she drawled, sarcasm thick in every syllable. "Seriously, Liv, you're overthinking it. Maybe he just wants to fuck you."

I nearly choked on my saliva.

"Don't act like you wouldn't want that," Sophie laughed. "You've been talking about him all goddamn week.

Just have fun in Vegas and if his behavior bothers you, I'll note it down and handle it."

"Oh my god," I mumbled.

"Love ya! Have fun!"

The call disconnected the same moment that the driver put the car into park and shoved open his door. I swallowed, my nausea only doubling as I realized there was a very good chance that she was right. Maybe he *did* want to have sex with me.

The idea of telling him no was somehow harder to imagine than every other way I'd pictured him for the past week.

I stumbled out of the car, watching in silence as the taxi driver retrieved my small suitcase from the trunk, and flattened down any hint of a wrinkle on my dress. At least in something that almost reached my knees and covered the entirety of my chest—sans buttons—he couldn't say I was dressing provocatively.

The black fabric was fairly tight, though.

Cursing myself for not picking slacks and a shirt with some kind of blazer, I took my bag from the taxi driver and passed him a ten-dollar bill as a tip before making my way inside.

The interior of the private charter service was ornate and gorgeous, but considering I was already late, I wasn't given a second to appreciate it. My bag was whisked away by workers who took it straight out onto the tarmac, and once I'd given my name and checked in, I too was led out into the abrasive sun.

The jet sat undisturbed around a corner, engine idling, with two pilots milling about by the bottom of the stairs. It looked large enough to seat at least twenty, and from the looks of the people in the windows, most of the twenty people were men.

"You must be Ms. Martin," one of the pilots said, his lips taut as he looked at me. "We've been waiting for you."

"Traffic," I offered as a half-hearted apology.

"It's fine. We're only twenty minutes behind schedule," the other said, passing a slight smile in my direction before gesturing for the stairs. "We should get going."

I climbed the steps to the aircraft, fully expecting some kind of flight attendant to demand to see my ticket at the top and direct me to my seat, but as I rounded the corner, it didn't look like assigned seats were even a thing. There were a handful still available, most taken up by men and a couple of women I'd never met but seen in passing around Black-wood. In the center at a table for five, Damien lounged, hunched over the polished wood table with a glass of amber liquid clutched in his palm.

The second he clocked me, his grin turned wicked.

"Ms. Martin," he said, his voice booming above the others. "Sit wherever you'd like."

I'd never been to Vegas.

The flight had been stressful — I wasn't sure what I'd expected, but Damien spent the entirety of it talking business with the close handful of men that sat at his table, leaving me toward the back alone. I'd spent most of it anxiously going over my notes and trying not to be tempted by the occasional glass of alcohol being passed around the plane.

When we touched down, we headed directly to the conference center in the Luxor. Thrust into negotiations without a single clue what was happening, I found myself huddling toward the back again, listening but not engaging. Damien watched me from a distance, his eyes always lingering, tearing me apart — and when it had been time for me to present to those who had come with us, the internal higher-ups and the handful of board members, he introduced me personally.

Our brightest intern. That's what he called me.

All in all, the presentation went down well. Damien stayed next to me as our group huddled around me, flipping the page for me when I needed it. And afterward, when he presented in front of the other companies, he name dropped me when he mentioned the new and exciting changes that would be coming to Blackwood in the near future. He hovered as I spoke idly to a handful of business owners and local green initiative planners. He stayed close enough that I knew he could hear, but far enough that it left me alone and vulnerable.

I wasn't entirely sure how I felt about that.

But after, as the night progressed and we left the confines of the Luxor and padded down the strip, Damien announced to the twenty-or-so of us that he was treating us to dinner and drinks in celebration of landing the contracts.

That's how I found myself almost at the head of the long table beside Damien in a luxurious cirque-themed restaurant I hadn't caught the name of somewhere inside the Bellagio.

I was two drinks and a main course deep, with a ring and antique wristwatch laden hand far too close to mine on the table. His knee brushed against mine, and my stomach twisted with a hint of butterflies and mostly anxiety. *Was that on purpose?*

My pulse hammered in my ears. He hadn't even said a word to me.

His mouth moved silently as he spoke to the man on his left, his fingers drifting ever so slightly closer to mine on the table. I tried to work out what he was saying, if it had anything to do with me, if the shape of my name crossed his lips — but I couldn't pick apart any of it, not until he turned his attention to me instead.

"They're all impressed with you, you know," he said, his voice low enough that only I could hear it. He sipped at his glass of whiskey, a wry little smile creeping across his lips and puckering the wrinkles beside his eyes.

I needed more alcohol if I was going to survive this. I knocked back the last of my drink before reaching for my third.

Damien's gaze was too much, too lingering, too daring for me to handle without it, and I kept finding myself getting far too lost in the sea of blue and the temptations it held. "Does that include you?"

He chuckled, his eyes locking with mine as his hand crept just an inch closer. *He doesn't want you. That would be insane. He's the CEO, HR would go crazy if they found out.* "Especially me, Olivia. You're already proving my choice to hire you was an excellent one."

Heat invaded my cheeks and the space between my thighs.

This hadn't been what I'd expected when I sent my resume to Blackwood for the internship. I couldn't deny that I was absurdly attracted to him, couldn't deny that I liked the way he talked to me or said my name, and more than anything, couldn't deny that a part of me that I didn't let see the light of day might let him fuck me if he asked. "You can't just say things like that," I breathed. *Oh shit.* The alcohol was making it too easy to speak to him.

"Like what? I was paying you a compliment," he chuckled.

"I..." I reached for my drink, downing almost half of the mojito in a single gulp. *Horrible idea, Liv. Make it easier to say how he's making you feel, why don't you?* "I don't know."

He set his elbow on the table, resting his chin on it and blocking out the man to his left entirely as he gave me his full attention. Somehow, it wasn't intimidating, and I wasn't sure if that was because of the alcohol or if it was because his shields were lowering. "What does that mean?"

"Are you flirting with me?" I asked, the words falling out of me before I could even process them. My cheeks heated further, practically *burning*, and his eyes widened in response.

He took another swig of whiskey. "That would be against HR policy," he said. "But if you're wondering if I'm attracted to you, then yes."

Oh, fuck.

"Does that bother you, Olivia?"

If I wasn't borderline drunk, I would have ran. I would have taken my things and asked him what hotel room I was in, thrown myself onto the bed, and sent in a resignation email.

But I *was* borderline drunk, and he was looking at me like I was the only person in the room. "I don't know," I squeaked. "I'm not... I'm not good at this kind of thing."

He chuckled as he sipped again. "We're just having fun. If you're worried that you need to act a certain way with me or feel okay about this just to get ahead, don't. That's not how things work at Blackwood's." His lower lip tucked between his teeth for a fleeting second as he let his gaze drift just slightly lower down, taking in my neck, my shoulders. *Oh, my god.* "But if you mean you're inexperienced..."

"That one," I blurted, clutching my drink in my grasp like a vice. The alcohol was doing the talking. Admitting that, speaking it out loud, almost felt like I'd walked into the restaurant fucking naked. I was twenty-four for fucks sake, a fully-fledged adult, and because of what I'd promised myself, I still hadn't done *it* with anyone. "That."

His smile widened further and he scrubbed at his lips with his hand to hide it. "Olivia," he mumbled in a low voice, my name sounding like fucking butter in his mouth. "I can guarantee I've got enough experience for both of us."

Jesus fucking Christ. I didn't doubt that for a second, and neither did the space between my thighs. I crossed my legs to dull the ache that blossomed there.

"With flirting, of course," he laughed, one eye closing in a wink.

This man was going to tempt me far too much. "Is this... what you do? I mean, I've heard rumors that you, uh, sleep around."

His unexpected laughter nearly sent his whiskey spraying into his glass. "That's a bit forward."

My face felt like it was on fire. "I'm sorry—"

"No, no, it's fine," he grinned. "You're tipsy. I'm not expecting you to have a filter. But to answer your question, yes. Casual is what I prefer. Not at the office, though. That's off limits for me."

Off limits? Does that mean I'm off limits? "I don't think I could do casual sex," I breathed, hating the words the moment they left my mouth.

"Why?"

27

I blinked at him, trying to weigh up the positives and negatives of speaking the truth, but in the haze of the alcohol and the wild laughter down at the other end of the table, I couldn't find a negative. Screw it. "I'm a bit more conservative when it comes to that kind of thing," I said, my voice a little low, a little quiet.

He leaned just a little bit closer, his eyes sparkling with intrigue. "How conservative, Olivia?"

I swallowed. "Ask me when I'm drunk."

———

At the bar, Damien's hand held me in place on my lower back, my feet feeling far too clumsy in my heels after a further two cocktails. I was in dangerous territory — the kind of drunk where my filter was gone entirely, my inhibitions left behind and dunked in the Bellagio's fountains. He was getting there himself, too. I could see it in the way he looked at me, with his heavy-lidded eyes and the way his mask of authority had slipped entirely. We were tucked away around the corner from the table, just the two of us standing at the side of the bar, and every second we spent here felt like a ticking time bomb.

"You're touching me," I breathed. He'd ushered me forward to order with his hand on my back, and it just hadn't left.

"I am." His eyes met mine from beside me, his hand resting just a little more insistently against me. "Is that a problem, princess?"

Exhaling shakily, I let myself move toward him, let myself get just a little bit closer. "No."

"You can tell me if it is." He gulped down the last of his drink and motioned idly toward the bartender for another, his attention almost entirely on me.

"It isn't," I insisted, and god, why did I *mean* that?

He grinned, turning to lean on the bar with his side as he gratefully accepted the next whiskey. "Well then... Are you drunk enough?"

"Drunk enough?" I asked, struggling to remember through the far thicker haze that clouded every thought. "What do you mean?"

He chuckled as his hand idly began to draw circled on my lower back. "How *conservative* are you, Olivia?"

Oh, shit. *That.*

"You don't have to tell me."

I swallowed, my body naturally inching closer to him. "I want to tell you," I said, my voice so low that I could barely hear it over the chaotic sounds around us. It wasn't a lie — with the alcohol in me and the way his hand felt against me, it was making things too easy.

"Would it be easier if I guessed?" he laughed, lifting the empty glass out of my hand and replacing it with my abandoned replacement.

I grinned. "You can try."

"Okay. I'm going to go out on a limb here and say... you've only dated two men, one in high school and one in college," he said, a little smirk creeping up his lips. "You didn't have sex with the first one, but you lost your virginity to the second. Never had to flirt with a man because you're just that pretty."

"You couldn't be more wrong," I snorted.

"*Really?* Don't tell me you're a virgin."

I paused with my drink halfway to my mouth. "So what if I am?"

"No, absolutely not." He shook his head, his cheeky grin unwavering. "Not a chance."

I swallowed past the little surge of soberness that hit me. "I am, though. I've never slept with someone."

Wide eyes met mine as he sipped at his drink. "Genuinely?"

"Genuinely. No sex till marriage."

His cheeks heated as he sipped at his whiskey. His fingers dug in, pulling me just an inch nearer, just a little bit closer to temptation. "I need to be more careful with you than I thought, then."

My chest was almost flush with his, and I could feel the heat building in the small little gap between us. My heart pounded against my ribs, and in my haze, I just wanted to lean into him, wanted to close the distance. He was my boss, and so what? If HR had a problem with the CEO sleeping with an employee, it wouldn't apply to us. "Why?"

He set his glass of whiskey back down on the counter and closed the gap himself. "Because if I'm being wildly honest, Olivia, I'd like nothing more than to take you back to my room. And now I can't, for *two* reasons."

The chill of his hand that had clutched his glass seeped into my skin as he cupped my cheek in it, his thumb drifting across my lower lip. I had to grip the bar for stability, and as I looked up at him and the intense, overwhelming temptation that face filled me with, I couldn't help but have a flickering want for the same thing as him.

I didn't trust myself with him.

"You'd have to marry me, then," I chuckled, my face burning from the heat he imbued me with.

He leaned a little closer, the scent of whiskey, almonds,

rum, vanilla — everything encapsulating me. He hovered, just an inch from me, just an inch from what I knew he could tell we both wanted.

He glanced around as if to check if anyone could see us. "Fuck it," he rasped.

His fingers dug into the small of my back as his other snaked around the rear of my neck. His lips met mine in an instant.

Heart pounding and head swimming, I let him kiss me, let him have control as he moved his mouth against mine demandingly, roughly, feverishly. His tongue dove between my teeth, ensnaring mine, and I could taste the whiskey on him.

I clutched the front of his suit jacket, far too over-whelmed to know what to do with my hands, but good fucking *god* I wanted more of this, more of whatever he wanted to give. If he wanted sex, there was a part of me that wanted to give that to him regardless of what I'd promised myself.

But even in my drunken stupor, I wouldn't let it happen.

I couldn't.

His mouth devoured me as his fingers slipped up further into my hair, twisting around the tresses of waves, tugging, fisting it. The burn of my scalp was almost enough to cut through the numbing effects of far too much alcohol.

His lips left mine, his chest heaving, his mouth just barely stained from my lip gloss. Those fucking piercing blue eyes met mine, wild now instead of heavy, and when he spoke, I was convinced I didn't hear him correctly.

"We're in Vegas, princess. Marry me."

Chapter 4

Damien

The group filtered out the Bellagio's doors, piling into cars that would take them to the Flamingo where my assistant had booked their rooms. "Incredible job today, everyone!" I called, drunkenly shaking hands with the few who were paying attention. "Enjoy your evenings and I'll see you all tomorrow evening for dinner."

I checked my watch — only just barely past midnight. The night was still young on Vegas time.

A flash of chestnut hair and a tight black dress caught my eye. Olivia stepped through the revolving door behind the last three employees, her cheeks pink and her footsteps slightly uncoordinated. Her mouth parted and her eyes glossy, she locked gazes with a driver.

I moved before I'd even decided to.

Before she could grab his full attention, I caught her by the wrist. "Where do you think you're going?" She blinked as I pulled her back to me, her balance tipping before she caught herself on my chest.

Her eyes searched mine for something, but whatever it

was, she didn't say. "The Flamingo," she said as if it was the most obvious thing in the world.

I narrowed my gaze at her. *Is she really this dense or is it just the alcohol?* "You're not going to the fucking Flamingo just yet," I mumbled. Instinctually, I released her wrist, hoping that her stumble and my insistence didn't come across as anything more than a helping hand to whoever from the office was watching us. I didn't know what had gotten into me over the past week, but there was something about her, something that was so goddamn tempting, that made me lose all sense when she looked at me. It had only amplified with her presence here, and even more when I'd let myself hold her upstairs.

And that fucking *kiss*.

I needed more, but suggesting she marry me for it was probably not the brightest idea or the best way to get what I wanted, even if it would kill two birds with one stone. I'd said it in the heat of the moment, my mind drunk on the idea of burying myself inside of her. I still was, but in the fresh air with the effects of too many drinks starting to wear off little by little, the error of my insistence was blinding.

I wasn't even sure if she remembered what I'd said, but I wouldn't have felt right without saying something. "I'm sorry about what I said upstairs. I wasn't thinking clearly."

She shook her head and covered her lips, a little giggle breaking through. "I don't think I've ever had someone offer to marry me on the spot just to sleep with me," she said. The blush across her cheeks spread further and deepened. She looked so small, so fucking bendable. "It's okay. It was, uh, flattering, I think?"

I wondered if she'd think the positions I'd been imagining her in for days were flattering.

"So... if I'm not going to the Flamingo yet, then what *am*

I doing?" She blinked, the alcohol still thick on her breath as she watched the last employee be driven away. I pulled her to me the moment they were out of eyeshot. "And don't you dare say *you*."

"We're in Vegas, and the night is young," I grinned. "I figured we could spend a little more time together out on the town."

The wind kicked up, forcing her hair over one shoulder as she laughed. "You're like... twice my age, *grandpa*. How are you awake enough to keep going?"

"I'm not nearly old enough to be your grandfather. Maybe your dad, at best."

"My dad, huh?" she grinned, her tongue dragging along the edge of her top teeth as I pulled her toward the waiting car I'd ordered. "Should I call you *daddy* then?"

The idea of that was almost sobering enough to give me pause, but I hauled her into the backseat with me anyway. If she was going to be the death of me this evening, I'd go willingly with whatever she'd give me.

———

No loud parties. No clubs.

Those were her only requests if we were going to keep going into the night, and I was more than happy to oblige — so on the 64th floor of the Delano, out in the open air in their rooftop bar, we truly began our evening.

Overlooking the entirety of the strip, she leaned against the railing, her hair blowing over her shoulders in the warm, early-summer breeze. I almost regretted saying anything

34

about the wardrobe malfunction in my email — at least then she might have worn something slightly more revealing, leaving me more skin to sink my teeth into.

"You're different around them," she said, her fingers ghosting across the back of my hand as she placed her empty glass in my grasp. The way she looked at me was maddening — it was as if she saw a million solutions to questions she desperately wanted answered. "I like this version of you more."

"I have to keep *some* kind of professionalism around them," I laughed.

"And not me?"

"I think we've established that I don't feel a need to with you."

Her blush spread again, and *god,* it was so fucking cute.

"I've already crossed lines with you that I absolutely shouldn't have, even if it's HR compliant," I added. "I can talk to you like a human and not a robot dressed in a business suit."

She bit her lip as I handed her the replacement drink. "Is it bad that I like that you crossed a line with me?" she asked, and instead of taking her drink from me, she grasped the straw with her fucking *tongue* and pulled it into her mouth, sucking at the strong cocktail. The little smirk she gave as she released the straw told me she knew exactly what she was doing. *Tempting me.*

"Christ," I breathed, watching her as those big eyes met mine innocently. I set her glass back down before she could insist on drinking far too quickly. "You say you're a virgin but it doesn't fucking look like it."

"I'm not *that* innocent," she laughed, one hand coming to rest against my chest. "I've watched porn. And movies exist."

Movies and porn. Was that genuinely all she was working with?

I took her face back in my hand, desperate to feel her lip against my thumb again. If I did it again and we did nothing else, I could memorize the way it felt at the least and imagine it elsewhere instead.

"You've never done *anything*?" I asked, lightly brushing my thumb across her mouth, committing it to my mind over and over.

Her lips parted as she leaned into me. "I've had a few boyfriends. Held a guy's dick in my hand once," she laughed. "That's about as far as that went."

I studied her features, watching as they relaxed the more I held her, the more I touched her. The faint music and chatter from the other patrons, the sounds of traffic far below us, and my ever-growing proximity didn't even seem to phase her anymore. "You didn't want to go any further with them?"

She shook her head. "No."

Exhaling shakily, I touched her lips with my thumb again, transfixed by her. So fucking smart, but so *bold* with some drinks in her. "Would you go further with me?" I asked. I regretted it the moment it left my lips — it shouldn't have come out. It should have stayed neatly tucked away with all of my other thoughts of her.

She nodded. Not an ounce of hesitation.

"Do you understand what I *want* from you?" I rasped, my thumb just barely slipping past her lips. Her tongue pressed against it, warm and wet and fucking *soft*, and... I needed to calm down. I needed to not do this with her, but I couldn't find it in me to stop.

She didn't answer me — but the flutter of her lashes, the way she didn't fight me in the slightest as I fisted the fabric at the small of her back, told me she was having the same thoughts as I was. That made it so much worse, so much *harder*. Blood rushed between my hipbones.

I turned her, pressing her back against the railing, crowding her. "I want you," I said, the words coming out as a low growl as I dropped my head beside hers, my lips hovering beside her ear. "In whatever ways you'll give me."

The little noise she made sounded almost like a gulp, but I took it as a confirmation.

I pressed my lips to hers again, testing my luck. She didn't flinch, didn't panic, didn't hesitate — she kissed me back just as eagerly. The heat of her breath, her hand on my chest, the way she lingered when I tried to take a quick breather... I didn't want to stop.

HR policy strictly said that sex with employees who were not in an established, committed relationship already at the time of hire or married to one another was off limits. Her beliefs limited her to similar standings.

But neither had any stipulations on anything *other* than sex.

Throwing one cursory glance over my shoulder to ensure we were alone in our little corner of the rooftop, I decided to test both of our boundaries. A horrible decision, really, but I wanted her too much and she was right there, and if I waited a second longer, she'd need another gulp of her drink to pluck up the confidence to let me touch her.

Shielding her with my body, I kissed her again, this time letting my hands drift. She leaned into it, breaking from my lips only to give me a little gasp and my fingers went lower, and lower, and lower, down along the hem of her black dress. She kissed me demandingly as I lifted the fabric up along her thigh, up over her rear, and exposed what was beneath to only me.

I broke from the kiss, giving her just enough space between our lips to object if she wanted to, and glanced down where my hand rested against the top of her black, lacy underwear and the bare flesh of her thighs and hips. Fluttering lashes hid bright green eyes as I dragged my gaze back to her, and before I could even ask, she spoke.

"Touch me," she breathed.

Fuck. We were screwed. "Spread your legs, Olivia," I ordered.

One shaky leg split off from the other, her heel clicking against the concrete.

I shoved a knee between her thighs, locking them in place. Lips parted and pupils blown, she looked up at me as I slipped my fingers behind the lacy fabric and down, down...

She was *soaked*.

"Oh, fuck," I swallowed, nudging the side of her face with the bridge of my nose. She smelled of lavender, like falling asleep, but I wanted to do anything *but* that with her. Her hand wrapped around the back of my neck, her fingers playing with my hair, and the moment I dived between her lips and found her clit, the sound she made nearly drove me to do far worse things.

"Oh my god," she whimpered, her nails digging into my skin. "We're in public—"

"You want me to stop, princess?" I offered her, breathing in her scent with every word spoken. My fingers slipped easily between her thighs, circling her clit, keeping my touch light enough that she wasn't getting enough. I watched as her chest rose and fell erratically. Her back arched against the railing, her gaze flicking between my eyes and somewhere over my shoulder.

"No," she rasped. "Please don't stop."

I slipped a single digit just a little bit further back. It slid inside of her with ease.

Her warmth enveloped me, tight and hot and damp, and it was like a switch flipped. I fucking lost myself in her, pumping her, curling the end of my finger until she gasped against the side of my face, her panting turning to music. My cock throbbed, aching behind the prison wall that was my zipper, and I had to tell myself that I could handle not taking her right that instant. I could handle doing less than everything if I needed to.

Effortlessly, I slipped another finger in, using the base of my palm against her clit as my digits stretched her walls. "Damien," she moaned, her head turning toward mine, each gasp coming quicker.

I kissed her again, quieting her. But it wasn't impulsive this time — no, it was precise, hungry, and almost gluttonous as I devoured her, and she gave it right back. My fingers worked her, pumping in and out like I wanted to do with my hips, her body coming so easily undone beneath me. She was heaven and she was goddamn sin, and by the end of the evening, I was certain we'd be entirely consumed by the latter.

But I wanted more *now*. I wanted the entirety of her fucking body to myself, so much it felt like a roaring fire at my back pushing me ever forward.

Her walls tightened around my fingers, her frantic breathing only elevating. Replacing the base of my palm with my thumb, I swirled it like I had with my fingertips, giving her just an ounce of extra pressure on the bundle of nerves that drove her mad. The moment I felt her body stiffening beneath me, I held my pace and broke my lips from hers.

"Just imagine how much fucking better this would feel

if it were my cock," I rasped, my mind getting the better of me.

Those wild eyes met mine again, too many horrible thoughts floating behind them. I wanted to make more of those, wanted to plant the seeds and let them bloom over the time we had tonight. I wanted her. God, I wanted her, wanted what we couldn't—no, *shouldn't*—have.

"You want that, don't you?" I smirked down at her, watching as her gaze flicked between my eyes and my lips, her mouth popping open as if she wanted to speak but quickly closing. "You want to be filled. Claimed. Dripping my fucking cum."

Every word out of my mouth only made my resistance weaker and my desperation stronger, but with the way she was clenching around me, I could tell it made it so much better for her.

"Damien," she gasped, one hand wrapping around my wrist and holding it in place. A silent request — *don't stop.* "Please, I..."

"Come," I ordered. "Show me just how much you want me to fuck you."

Her mouth parted and her walls closed in as her body released, and before she could make a sound, I pressed my lips to hers. The kiss was sloppy and messy, but I didn't fucking care, not when she was pooling her juices in the palm of my hand, not when her nails were digging so hard into me I thought they might break the skin.

I pulled her through her orgasm, dulling my movements, only stopping once I was positive she'd reached the point of sensitivity instead of pleasure. Her little sounds against my lips slowed, turning back into wanting moans instead of gasping breaths, but I wasn't about to give her more than she needed. At least not yet.

40

Slipping my hand from her underwear, I broke my mouth from hers. I gave myself the chance to inspect the mess she'd made despite knowing what it would do to me. Strings of her dampness connected my fingers, crystal clear and viscous, and the blush that spread across her cheeks almost dragged my attention back to her.

She shimmied her hips and her dress fell back into place, her footing almost being lost. I held her up, and she hummed her approval of it.

"I'm going to ruin you," I rasped, pressing a kiss against her cheek. I splayed my damp fingers across her jaw, holding her in place as I nipped at the skin of her neck, kissed it, sucked at it. I wanted to do the same between her legs. "Come back to my suite with me."

"I think I need another drink," she laughed.

———

Drunk and stumbling, we found ourselves at the top of the Mandalay Bay inside their scenic bar. We drank more, *consumed* more, keeping the buzz going and slipping a little bit further into drunken debauchery.

There was nowhere for us to hide. My only solution was renting a private balcony that was secluded enough to be fit for purpose in our haze, and as we slipped out the doors and pulled the blustering curtains closed, I didn't have the patience to wait to touch her again.

But she was on me before I could even get the chance to pounce.

Her mouth met mine, flooding my senses with lavender

and the lingering taste of the limoncello shot she'd downed moments ago. She kissed me as if she needed it, and I met her fervor, lifting her dress with one hand and gripping her by the back of her neck with the other.

Hooking one finger on the string of her underwear, I slipped them down her thighs, breaking from her lips momentarily to tug them off from her heeled feet. I tossed them off the ledge of the balcony, and to my utter surprise, she didn't even notice.

I pushed her down onto the couch, the lower half of her dress gathering around her hips.

I sank to my fucking knees in front of her.

The taste I'd had back at the Delano wasn't enough. But I was content to torture myself just a little bit longer as long as I was staying between her thighs.

"Have you had someone's mouth on you before?" I asked her, pressing a kiss to the inside of her thigh.

"No. But I think I like you down there." The smile that crept across her cheeks did little to hide the growing blush that coated almost the entirety of her face. Any hints of hesitation had been abandoned back at the Delano, and she was being *bold* now. "What do you think my desk mate would say if you were like this beneath—"

"Touch yourself," I demanded, sinking my teeth into the soft, fleshy bit of her inner thigh to shut her up before she could say something ridiculous.

She blinked down at me, her mouth open in a perfect little O. "What?"

Grasping her hand with mine, I placed it on top of her mound. "Show me how much better I am at touching you than you are, and maybe I'll give you what you want."

She hesitated. I wasn't sure if it was the alcohol that impaired her, making her processing time slower, or if she didn't want to. But a second later, her red-painted nails were touching her clit, her head dipping back into the cushions as if no one was watching.

But I was. God, I was.

I kissed up her thigh, salivating as her fingers moved. One knee hooked over my shoulder, she dipped two fingers inside of herself. My cock strained painfully against my slacks in response. Every passing second that I wasn't burying myself in her was torture, and my reluctance to go beyond what was allowed for us was *waning*.

Frustrated, drunk, and so horny I was losing my mind, I shoved her hand away and replaced it with my mouth.

Olivia gasped, her hand diving into my hair and grasping at the strands. I devoured her, claimed her with my tongue, abusing my straining erection further. Sliding three fingers inside without a single bit of resistance, I knew damn well she'd pleasured herself with things larger than my digits before. There wasn't a hymen in sight. *Fucking hell.* I drank every drop she leaked, savoring the decadent taste of her as if she were water and I was dying of thirst.

"Damien," she mewled. Neither of us cared anymore about the sounds she made, and although the balcony we'd rented was fairly secluded, nothing was stopping her moans from carrying to others above and below us. "Fuck, oh my god—"

Her release came quicker this time, flooding my mouth, clenching around my fingers before relinquishing them. I took every fucking bit she gave me, dragged it out, overstimulated her with my tongue just to hear her cries a little longer.

When the intensity had calmed and my lips and chin were drenched in a mixture of saliva and *her*, I rested my head on her thigh, my fingers still buried inside of her. "I can't lie, Liv," I laughed. "Marriage is sounding better and better by the minute."

I didn't care how desperate I sounded anymore, couldn't give a shit if she thought less of me for it. Not when I wanted her this badly, not when I was this drunk that I would stoop to any level for some wicked angel from my dreams.

She giggled as I slipped my fingers from her. "You'd hate being married to me," she grinned. "I'd want this all the time."

I sighed dramatically, pulling another laugh from her. "That would be the opposite of a problem."

I pulled myself up off the cement balcony, leaning down over her to kiss her, to let her taste herself on my tongue. Her hand drifted over the front of my slacks, stopping as she felt the rigidity beneath them, and slowly but surely, her fingers closed in around the straining stitches. She gripped me with a vice.

"Fuck, Liv, I need you," I groaned, the squeezing only amplifying my problem.

She grinned against my lips. "I need another drink."

———

We were well past the point of no return when my watch read what I could barely make out as half past two in the morning. I was teetering on drunken blackout territory, and from the slurring of her speech and the difficulty she had keeping herself upright, so was Olivia.

Nothing and no one mattered anymore apart from her

and the ways I could touch her. I had no idea how we got to this point — we'd gone from playful banter to desperation in the span of hours.

The flickering light of the surprisingly clean bathroom lit her fully bare body stunningly as she leaned against the wall for support. Even through the bleariness of my eyes, she still looked unreal, like I could split her in two and she would thank me for it. I was only halfway sure we were at a bar in the Bellagio, but if someone had told me we'd flown to Paris and I'd lost my memory of the hours it would take to get there, I probably would have believed them.

Her short frame barely reached my shoulders as I stumbled closer. My jacket abandoned on the floor, my shirt unbuttoned and hanging off my shoulders — for the life of me, I couldn't remember how we'd gotten to this point. Everything was blurring together.

I took her breast into my mouth, lashed against her nipple with my tongue. Her perfect fucking moans filled the small room, and I didn't care how loud she was anymore, not when my rings and fingers were burying inside of her and her entire body was *mine*. The idea of someone intruding didn't even phase me — I'd let them watch if I could have her.

A moment later and my belt was unbuckled, my slacks unzipped, and my cock was wrapped in her painted fingers. It was as if I'd lost the time in between.

"Shit," I groaned, burying my face in the hair at the top of her head. *When had I left her breast?* She rode my fingers as I thrust into her hand, her release coming too quick, too easy, too messy. I couldn't think, couldn't do anything but want her. "I need to fuck you, princess."

"You *need* to fuck me?" she giggled, her fingers tightening around my cock. Her hand looked so small wrapped around it, her digits not even meeting. Her words were slurred and slow, lilting as if she were humming them. "Is this... not... enough?"

"Not with you." Gliding my fingers up the back of her neck, I wrapped my hand in her hair, pulling it taut until her head dropped far enough back against the wall that she was forced to look directly up at me. She winced from the pain, her hips moving against my still hand to counteract it. "This can't be enough with you. Neither of us are fucking satisfied, are we?"

"I'm not..." She hiccuped, interrupting herself. Her laughter filled the room for a fleeting second. "I'm not having sex until I'm—"

"Marry me." The words didn't phase me. The idea didn't, either, not this time. I'd regretted it the first time, but what I'd spoken earlier should have been taken at face value. I'd go this low to take her. I'd do it to make HR happy, to make her happy. It sounded like a brilliant idea now. "Marry me, please. *Please*, Olivia. Fucking marry me."

"Don't say that," she drawled, her head lolling before I tightened my grip again. "You don't mean it."

"I do," I snarled, my hips stuttering as I teetered on the edge. "There's a chapel on every fucking street corner."

Her lips parted as she studied me, her eyes almost going cross-eyed as I brought my lips to hers briefly. "If you come, will you still want that?" she asked, a shit-eating grin lashing out across her lips.

"Yes." My voice hoarse and my body sweating, I knew it wouldn't be enough to stop the need.

She met my thrusts with every stroke of her hand, gripping me, dragging me up and over the edge. I leaked across her stomach, cum dripping between us and onto the tile, and it didn't even cross my mind to back down.

I still wanted more.

"Marry me," I rasped, once more for good measure. "Let me show you how much better this can be."

Heavy lidded eyes met mine and I released my grasp on her hair, letting her mull the words over. Reality *should* have crashed into me the moment she spoke. "Okay."

But dear fucking god, I was making the best decision of my life.

———

The neon lights and the very slight come down from blackout territory to just maddeningly drunk weren't enough to wake either of us up. We were in this fully, cackling as we stumbled down the street at three in the morning, convinced that this was the best thing we had ever thought to do. She practiced her "I do" over and over in silly voices, and I parroted them back at her, committing the one she liked most to memory. It was gone within seconds, though.

Her heels clutched in her hand, I carried her into the late-night chapel.

We signed the paperwork.

We handed over our IDs.

We shared a toast of a champagne flute filled with beer, and I shoved a short veil into her messed-up hair. I stood beside a man in a full-white Elvis costume as she clumsily walked barefoot down the aisle.

I slid my platinum pinky ring onto her left ring finger. I let her do the same for me with mine.

We said *I do*.

"You may now kiss the little mama," Elvis said, and I fucking did.

I kissed her the way I had the first time back at the restaurant, raw and desperate, and clung to her as I tipped her the way a groom is meant to tip his bride.

We posed for photographs for all of two minutes.

We took the gifted Prosecco that Elvis handed us.

"We'll need this for our wedding night," I told her, and the biggest, brightest smile flashed across her cheeks.

Fuck her room at the Flamingo. She was coming back with me to the Bellagio, and I would have the best goddamn night of my life with my wife.

Chapter 5

Olivia

I wasn't sure if it was the horrible, blinding headache or the drying thirst that woke me. Blinking away the bleariness in my eyes, I looked toward the foot of the bed where most of the offending light was pouring in from.

It took me far too long to remember I was in Vegas and not Paris with the giant replica of the Eiffel Tower staring me down.

Vegas.

Vegas.

Bile crept up my throat as my pulse thundered. I was still in my dress from last night, but the bottom of it had ridden up, gathering around my rear and only barely covering my upper thighs and what lay between them. *Oh my god.* The sheets barely even covered me, and from what I could tell, my underwear was missing.

I knew what I'd find if I looked to my right. I knew it with every little fiber of my being. But still, as if to twist the knife just an inch further, I did it anyway.

My hands flew to my mouth, covering the little squeak

that left me before it became loud enough that he'd hear and wake up.

Sprawled across the right side of the king-size mattress, Damien slept soundly on his back. Completely bare from the waist up, I studied his chest and the ripples of muscles. Vague memories from the night before flooded my mind — dragging my fingers along each ab in a bathroom, kissing them, sinking my teeth into his pectoral. A wave of nausea hit me in a flash and I wasn't sure if it was entirely the hangover's fault.

Lower, the sheets covered his knees and feet, his belt unbuckled but his slacks zipped and buttoned. But the fabric was stretched taut over his... bulge.

My cheeks heated as I realized that must be morning wood.

Steadying my breathing to match his measured, sleeping ones, I tried to recall everything that had happened last night. The dull ache between my thighs worried me more than I cared to admit.

The dinner. Scandalous, and he'd joked about marrying me, he'd kissed me. I'd gotten a little too drunk, but nothing wild stuck out to me.

The drinks on the rooftop of the Delano. There was... shit, we were alone then. I'd let him touch me in ways I'd never been touched by another person. I'd come around his fingers in a quiet corner.

The balcony at the Mandalay Bay. Oh, god. That was hazier, like wading through thick fog, but tendrils of memories flashed behind my eyes. Spreading my legs for him as he kneeled on the concrete, his fingers inside of me, his mouth on my—

"Fuck, my *head.*"

Damien shifted, rolling onto his side to face me, his eyes

still closed but a little crease indenting between them. One arm reached out, his hand tucking itself between the left side of my waist and the bed, and a second later he was yanking me toward him, pulling me flush against his bare chest. Hands shaking, I placed my left against his chest to push myself away, pausing the moment I saw it.

His ring. A single platinum band, loosely hanging onto my left ring finger.

It all came smashing down. Him wanting more, me holding out. The way I'd grasped him through his slacks on the balcony. Sitting on his lap in a bar in the Bellagio, feeling his erection beneath my rear, grinding on it. Dragging him to the bathroom. Clumsily undressing him, undressing *myself*, salivating at the idea of him sliding inside of me. Giving him a handjob until he came on my stomach.

The full-circle moment when he begged me to marry him again.

My agreement.

Elvis.

"Oh my fucking god," I gulped, and his eyes fluttered open. "Oh my god, oh my god, *oh my god*."

He blinked at me, confusion rippling across his face. "What's—" Cutting himself off, he looked from me to my hand on his chest, his gaze catching on the ring. He groaned as he turned his head, burying it in the pillow. "Fuck's sake."

"Damien," I gulped.

His hand tightened around my waist. "I know."

Every hammer of my heart against my ribs echoed in my ears. We'd gotten *married*, and that little ache between my thighs seemed so much bolder now, like I could imagine what had gone inside of me. I could barely remember what his cock looked like and I'd somehow managed to marry a man almost twice my age and lose my virginity without even having the memory of it.

"Is it all coming back to you, too?" he asked, his hand dragging up my covered spine until it reached the bare skin at the back of my neck. His fingers splayed out, drawing little calming circles on my flesh, and it was almost distracting enough to calm me down a little.

"We got *married*?" I breathed.

He hesitated, his fingers stopping for just a second, but then he was laughing, full-bellied and genuine, his crows' feet deepening as a smile spread across his cheeks. "Yeah. By Elvis."

I covered my face with my hands as I tucked my head into his bare chest, trying to hide from his line of sight. "Oh my god."

His laugh continued, shaking his body. "We didn't even have sex."

I paused.

We didn't even have sex.

Holy shit, he was fucking right.

"Happy, princess?" he asked, his nose and chin pressing into the top of my head as he chuckled. "You tortured me all night and still won."

I didn't know what to say — the shame and horror still bubbled at the surface, but more importantly, there was *relief*. Relief and cosmic irony that we'd gone through that much trouble, that much temptation, and *caved*, but passed out ten minutes after we'd found ourselves in bed was hilarious in theory. I'd agreed to marry him just to feel good about sleeping with him and even then, I couldn't do it right.

What an absolute joke.

I laughed and he joined in. I gave myself that ounce of grace to find the humor in it because if I didn't, I knew damn well I'd sink into that regret and let it eat me alive. Since I was a kid, I'd been picturing my wedding and my wedding night, and somehow all of that had gone up in fucking flames because a man twice my age had tempted me so wholly that I was willing to be married by Elvis just to have sex with him.

Once we'd calmed down and settled into a somewhat comfortable silence, his fingers resumed their circles once more and his breathing steadied. I tucked myself right up into his chest, pressing my forehead to him, taking in the scent of his cologne and the lingering smell of alcohol. Little tufts of black hair tickled my nose from where they sprouted between his pecs, and for a moment, I was able to calm down, to just... relax with him.

But then he spoke.

"You know," he rasped, his voice hoarse as his fingers traced over the top of my zipper, "there's still time to consummate it."

Oh, god. I wasn't out of the water yet.

His knee pressed at the space between my legs, forcing them to separate enough that he could slip his clothed thigh between my bare ones. He lifted it higher, higher, until he couldn't go any further and my pussy was bearing down on it.

The pleasure hit me before the regret. Little sparks of it took off like wildfire just as I remembered them doing last night. A breathy moan passed my lips as I shifted my hips forward, giving myself just a hint of friction, and his deep, answering hum of approval made my lower stomach twist.

"That's it," he mumbled. Cool air hit my back as he slid

the zipper of my dress down, inch by maddening inch. "Grind on my thigh, princess."

Another pitch forward and my pounding head swam, the hint of satisfaction from it almost canceling out the pain. His hand fisted the front of my dress, pulling the loosened fabric down over my arms and exposing my breasts. Taking one in his grasp, he kneaded at the soft flesh, his thumb grazing my nipple and pulling another moan from me.

"Such a good girl for me," he groaned, his voice like fucking silk. "Or should I say, *wife?*"

Reality slammed back in instantly.

I scrambled, weaseling out of his loose hold and nearly falling off the bed in the process. Catching my footing on shaky legs, I stood, the little mess I'd made on his knee sticking out like a sore thumb. "I'm sorry," he said, shoving himself up onto one elbow.

I pulled my dress up over my chest, my hands shaking, that stupid ring glinting off the blinding tendrils of sunlight that littered the bedroom. The dark red walls, the plush carpet, and the open door that led into a much larger, much grander space told me I was in his suite at the Bellagio. I needed to get out of here, needed to go to my room at the Flamingo.

"Olivia—"

"Oh my god, this was a mistake," I said, my voice quivering. Behind him, on the nightstand, sat the half-drank bottle of cheap Prosecco and the two plastic cups we'd been drinking out of. I barely remembered it. "Fuck, *fuck.*"

He slipped from the bed, his belt chiming as he got himself to his feet. In an instant, he stood in front of me, taking my face in his too-large hands, forcing me to look all the way up at him. "Calm down, calm down," he cooed, his chest rising and falling almost as quickly as mine. It didn't do a damn thing to help. "We can fix it."

The backs of my eyes burned. "How, a *divorce*? Jesus, Damien, I'm twenty-four, I don't want to be a fucking divorcee—"

"An annulment," he clarified. His thumb rubbed my cheek, back and forth, over and over. I focused on it, tried to calm myself with it even though it was coming from a man that I barely knew, who was almost twice my age. "It'll be like it never happened. Like we're erasing a mistake."

"Before we make any more of them," I added, glancing at the bed. I didn't know much about annulments other than the vague references in movies and television shows, but if Damien was right and it would wipe it from our records like erasing a mistake, then that's what we needed to do. Immediately.

"I'll call my lawyer and have him start the paperwork." He flashed me a tight-lipped smile as he let go of me, taking a step back to give me some space. I almost wished he hadn't. "Why don't you take a shower?"

I shook my head and pushed the hair from my face, smoothing it down with my hands. "I think... I think I'll go to the Flamingo for that."

Searching my eyes for something he didn't quite find, he mumbled something under his breath as he slipped his phone from his pocket. One little spinning motion with his finger had me following his instruction and turning around, presenting my bare back to him. Gently, he zipped my dress up, his fingers just barely brushing against the back of my neck where he'd touched me moments ago.

I grabbed my phone, my purse, my shoes, and started the search for my underwear before remembering he'd thrown them off the balcony at the Mandalay Bay. He tapped quickly at his phone, his eyes flicking up to trail my movements, and by the time I was ready to leave, he'd finished whatever he was doing and walked me to the door of the suite.

"The rest of us are going out for drinks tonight at the Wynn," he offered. A single strand of messy peppered hair fell across his cheek, and despite the part of me that was screaming to leave the room, the smaller part that he'd woken last night wanted to tuck it behind his ear. "Come with us."

"I don't think that's a good idea." Wrapping my hand around the door handle, I pulled. "But thank you. For... almost everything."

He said nothing as I left, nothing as the door creaked shut when I was halfway down the hall.

Chapter 6

Damien

The platinum ring on my pinky finger felt like a lead weight.

I stared at it, watching as it reflected off the shifting sunlight that poured in through the car's window. Olivia had given it back in the five seconds of solitude we'd had on the flight back to San Francisco, insisting that it wasn't something she felt right about keeping.

That was fair. If this was real, if we were in a relationship and had gotten married the proper way, I would have bought her something far more flashy.

It was probably for the best that she hadn't come to the bar that night. I'd texted her twice in the hopes that maybe she'd come through the doors of the Parasol Down in the Wynn and I'd get another night with her, but no. Giving myself extra time to try to crack that safe wouldn't have gone down well for either of us.

I still found myself dreaming, night and day, of her — replaying every moment that wasn't too clouded in fog from the whiskey and rum I'd filled myself with all night. It must have just been because I'd failed in my conquest. My interest in every other woman I'd found myself fawning over, throwing myself in front of at my discretion, had faded the moment after I'd got what I wanted from them. But with her, even though I'd come close, even though I'd spent the entire night devouring her in every way she let me, I hadn't felt a single bit relieved from my want of her.

The car door opened to my left and Ethan slid into the back seat next to me, pushing his glasses up his nose as he clicked the seatbelt into place. "You do realize I have a car and I'm completely capable of driving myself to work."

"I wanted to speak to you personally before we get to the office," I said, leaning forward to lift the divider between my driver, Paul, and us in the back.

He eyed me warily as he shut the door. "About your marriage?"

"About my *annulment*," I clarified. I crossed my hands in my lap, hiding the ring from my line of sight as the car started heading toward the office.

"I don't really dabble in family law." He placed his briefcase in the empty space between us, flicking open the clasps. "I suppose I'll need to do some research, though, since I've got another reason to look into it."

"Another reason—?"

A stack of papers slammed down onto my lap. "Before we even begin to discuss the annulment, you need to know what else is going on."

Looking down at the top sheet of the stapled-together bunch, ***Chapter 11 Bankruptcy*** was written in bold at the top. "The fuck is this?" I asked. "We're doing fine."

"Not *you*," Ethan hissed, reaching over me to point to the line just beneath the title. "Three of the companies you absorbed last week and another that Blackwood already held. They sold to you knowing this would happen."

Fuck.

"You've just spent millions acquiring thin air."

"Yeah, I fucking understand," I snapped. "What does this mean for me?"

"They've restructured entirely, naming Blackwood as the portion of their company that will be paying the debt," Ethan sighed, flipping another couple of pages in my lap. My stomach sank, and although I wasn't one for motion sickness, I worried I might paint the back of Paul's seat with my breakfast. "So far, with all of them together, we're looking at... two hundred million dollars of debt to be repaid, if the courts agree to their restructuring plan."

"So we're taking four companies to court is what you're saying," I sighed. I pinched the bridge of my nose and tried to internalize the problem, thinking through each possibility. We could afford the hit, of course, but it would stall numerous projects and shift our wind farm setup to next year. I didn't even want to consider how much I'd offered to the research team at the Korea Institute of Science and Technology for the rights to the water purification system that Olivia had brought to me.

"Yes, and potentially others. I worry that there may be a few more hiding in the background that haven't filed just yet. They seem to have been in... cahoots," Ethan explained. "It's going to take some time to figure this out. And this isn't even the most pressing thing."

Raising one eyebrow at him, a lash of pain whipped through my skull from the stress. "What does that mean?"

He slid the top stack of papers off my lap and set it back into the briefcase before motioning toward the remaining thick bundle left in my possession. "You wanted to know my other reason for looking into family law."

Sighing, I looked down at the papers, my stomach still churning from what he'd already told me.

Custody Modification stood out in big, bold letters at the very top, followed by legal jargon about the State of California and Mr. Damien Blackwood.

What the *fuck* was this?

My mind began racing. Someone I'd slept with, maybe, wanted a stab at the money I harbored. Someone I'd dated, maybe, wanted to tear me down a peg with a ludicrous claim. Or worse, someone so bored and full of themselves, wanted to claim I owned a goldfish with them and cash in on goldfish support payments.

Carefully lifting the first page with shaking fingers, I looked to the second, finding a litany of words I wasn't even sure I could wrap my mind around. I swallowed, my throat suddenly going dry when a single name stood out to me — *Marissa Thompson.*

Stomach acid filled the back of my throat. I covered my mouth with my hand and dropped the paper, focusing my attention instead on the passing world outside as we neared the campus. "What is this?" I croaked.

"You have a son," Ethan said, his words slipping out as if they were so common, so casual. I glanced at him, hoping I'd find a smirk on his face and a laugh bit back behind his teeth, but all I found was a cold, hard stare. "Marissa passed away. She named you as her preferred legal guardian for Noah in her will."

Marissa passed away.

Noah. Noah Thompson-Blackwood. Noah. Noah. Noah.

What the fuck was happening?

Marissa, my ex, hadn't spoken to me in five years. Surely, she would have told me if I had a son. Surely, I'd have been notified, been there for the birth, co-parented with her, or worse, stayed with her. There wasn't a world, in my mind, where she would have kept this from me. We didn't end well, but it wasn't so bad that she'd cut me out entirely — right?

"I need to call her," I breathed.

"Well, you can't, 'cause she's dead."

I blinked at him. Somehow that little nugget of information had gone in one ear, swirled around, and right back out my other. "She's dead?"

"I *just* said that. Twice, actually," Ethan said, slipping the stack from my lap and flicking through the paperwork. "Cancer, apparently. Happened last week. She had time to get all of this set up."

Marissa... was dead.

"*Dead* dead?"

"Christ, Damien, *yes*. Cold as ice. Six feet underground —... no, wait, she was cremated. Scattered over the Pacific by her sister, then, probably," he deadpanned.

I couldn't wrap my mind around this. I'd spent two years with her, considered *marriage* with her, spent god knows how much on an engagement ring — she was the first and only person I'd ever thought I could settle down with.

Stuffing down the suffocating thought that I'd never felt as drawn to Marissa as I did to my actual wife, I swallowed. We'd broken up due to her brief infidelity, and I needed to *focus* on that. "We can't be sure the kid is mine," I challenged. "There was someone else involved at the end."

"I'm aware. I've ordered a paternity test in the meantime, but supposedly, Noah looks like a copy of you. Just... smaller, obviously," Ethan said.

"What do I need to do?"

"You'll attend the appointment I've arranged for tomorrow to submit your DNA. It's just a simple mouth swab. And you'll need to prepare for his arrival in two weeks." He shoved the stack of papers back into his brief-case and locked it as we pulled into the parking lot of Black-wood Energy Solutions. "Marissa's sister will be taking care of him in the interim, so for now, focus your attention on figuring out how to be a father to a five-year-old while I sort out the annulment."

Chapter 7

Olivia

Sophie sipped at her latte as we sat in the back corner of the bookstore, the plush sofas and little table giving us a decent amount of privacy. It was located on the ground floor of the Blackwood building, and during working hours, it was the perfect place to sneak away for a quick break and a conversation about what the actual fuck I was doing with my life.

"My parents are going to kill me."

She pressed her lips together as she leaned forward on the sofa beside me. "You honestly think they'd have a problem with it?"

My eyes nearly bugged out of my skull. "You have no idea what they're like," I insisted. "You think I'm backwards? My brother and I weren't allowed friends of the opposite sex at home. My parents didn't *kiss* until their wedding day. They had chaperones for every date they went on and were barely allowed to hold hands. Damien and I did... a lot more than that."

"Damn," she breathed. "Surely they're not like that with you, though, or they'd have moved out here with you."

63

I nodded. "They left the church when I was a kid, but a lot of those ideals stuck with them. They're still incredibly conservative. And if they find out I married my fucking *boss* in Vegas..."

She offered me a tight-lipped, sympathetic smile and placed a single hand on my knee. I tried not to imagine it was Damien's like when he'd touched me at two thirty in the morning before I dragged him into a bathroom, but failed miserably, and found myself wishing her bare hand was covered in platinum rings and an antique watch. "They won't find out."

I picked up my flat white from the table, wanting the warmth of it between my hands to calm me down. "They will if it goes on a little longer. He's not some nobody, Sophie. It could end up in the news or something."

"The marriage or information about what you two did?"

"Either," I groaned. "We weren't exactly discreet."

Her blonde braid fell to one side as she tilted her head, the sneakiest grin tugging at her lips. "Don't tell me you two were doing whatever you got up to in *public*."

My cheeks heated uncomfortably as I cast a quick, cursory glance over my shoulder to check we were alone. "Yeah," I said quietly, just in case. "Most of it was in public."

"Oh my *god*." The words were too loud, and she noticed immediately, covering her mouth with her hand as her eyes went wide. She checked behind her, too, as if I hadn't already. "Sorry. What the hell? You can't just give me tidbits of information and keep the rest hidden away."

I sipped at my coffee, perfectly content to do just that. "I absolutely can."

"Liv. No. Please. I need to know," she laughed. "How

bad is it? How terrible would it be if it came out? I can help you with damage control if I know what to expect."

I narrowed my gaze at her, knowing damn well that wasn't why she wanted to know. She was morbidly curious, and if I were honest, I would be too if it wasn't happening to me. "Almost everything but sex."

"Oh my god," she breathed. "In *public*."

"Kind of."

"What does that mean?"

"He... I don't know. We were discreet, but we were wildly fucking drunk, so I don't know how effective that was," I sighed. To my left, an older woman stepped into the aisle closest to us, nonchalantly browsing book after book. Should've known it was a bad idea to hide near the romance section. I lowered my voice. "He, uh... touched me, at a bar. But then he rented a private balcony at another bar, and the curtains over the windows kept shifting, and... more things happened."

"Oh my *god*."

"I sat in his lap somewhere else and I'm about fifty percent sure my ass was on display. That was... that was far too public. But the worst of it was behind closed doors."

"In the hotel room?" she asked, her cheeks blushing as she tried to contain her smile. It wasn't working.

"In a bathroom," I clarified.

"Liv. How bad was that?"

"So bad that we were almost having sex," I croaked.

"You realize people will put hidden cameras—"

"*Please* don't finish that sentence. Please."

She nodded as she downed the last of her drink, shaking off whatever heat the topic had given her. "Okay. Right. Yeah, I can see why you're worried." She stared at the carpeted floor for a moment, the cogs in her mind visibly turning, and I wasn't sure what plan she was concocting but I was desperate to hear it. "How big was it?"

Well, that was a disappointment. "Seriously?"

"I'm just curious!"

I shook my head. "I barely remember. I was practically blacking out when I saw it."

"But from what you remember...?"

Covering my heated face with my hands, I audibly groaned into them, wanting to hide from the world and her and my parents and Damien. "I don't think my fingers touched when I wrapped them around it."

"Oh. My. *God*."

"Please stop imagining yourself in my shoes and enjoying it," I huffed.

"I'm not—"

"You *are*."

"Okay. Fine. I am a little bit," she laughed, letting her grin take over. "I just don't understand why you want the annulment so quickly. You could, like, enjoy it a little more. You're married, after all. You could just lose your virginity and be done with it. He's hot as fuck, Liv."

I shook my head, nausea churning my gut at the idea. That wasn't a possibility — not when I barely knew him, not when I'd been saving myself for something special like my parents had drilled into me, even if he was incredibly attractive. "I can't. I don't want to. I need to keep my distance from him."

"But you're tempted."

"Shut up."

"Okay, okay, I'm sorry," she sighed. "Have you spoken to him at all?"

"Nope. Like I said, keeping my distance."

Placing her hand back on my knee, she gave it a little

squeeze. "Maybe you should message him and check how the annulment is going. I know his lawyer's good, but as far as I'm aware, they aren't the quickest things to handle. Maybe just make sure he's started the paperwork. At least then you can have a little peace of mind."

She wasn't wrong. That wasn't the worst idea she'd come up with, and I desperately needed that peace of mind. I just hated the idea of messaging him to get it — it would open that door again, and I'd shut it when I left his room back at the Bellagio. I hadn't even responded to his requests to meet them out for drinks the following night. I'd just holed myself up in my suite, trying not to think about how he'd only just booked my room that morning and how much I'd thoroughly enjoyed myself the night before.

I dug through my purse and slipped my phone out of it. "Fine."

Chapter 8

Damien

"*A child?*"

The incandescent glow of the last of the summer's sunsets blistered the sky as the sun tucked beneath one of the larger hills behind my sister's house, lighting her in thick oranges and pinks as we sat on the balcony. She'd never been one for the city, but never wanted to move far from home, either. Woodacre, a small unincorporated town just outside of San Francisco, was perfect for her.

"Apparently," I sighed. "I don't understand why Marissa never told me. And if she knew she was... dying, why didn't she reach out? Why didn't she prepare me for this?"

Caroline sipped at her glass of red wine as she relaxed back into her lounge chair, her patterned skirt blowing in the breeze. "I don't know, Dame. Didn't it end amicably?"

"It wasn't *great* but honestly, I didn't think it was bad enough to warrant not telling me about a fucking son," I said. Scrubbing at my stubble with the tips of my fingers, I watched as a bird flew above us, far too high for me to tell what kind it was. "I'm waiting on the results of a paternity test."

She nearly spat out her mouthful of red wine. "A paternity test? Do you not believe her? I would have killed Anthony if he'd asked for a paternity test over Lucas."

I shrugged. Her husband, fleeting as he was before his death, wasn't exactly the nicest person around. I wouldn't have been shocked if he *had* asked for that — but I wouldn't have been happy with him, either. "She wasn't faithful at the end. That's why we split. Noah might not even be mine and she could have just hoped that saying he was would mean the kid got a pretty cushy life with me."

"I liked Marissa," she said, her lips pursing as she turned her head to face me. Long strands of auburn hair blew across her cheeks in the breeze, and I could have sworn that looking into her eyes sometimes felt like looking into the mirror. "I don't think that's something she would have done."

"I'd rather know for certain."

"I get that. But you can't just pretend that she is—was—some monster that wanted to ruin your life." She sipped at her wine again, and again, nearly draining half of the too-full glass. Caroline had never been one to play by the rules of society, whether that meant loudly attending protests or beating down archaic rules like how much wine is acceptable to pour into a glass. "You wanted to marry her, for god's sake."

"And that was a mistake."

"I mean... yes, in the long run," she said, her stare beginning to look through me instead of at me, as if she was recalling my entire relationship with Marissa. "But you were in love with her. For two years, you were the happiest

I'd ever seen you. I think you forget just how much you trusted her."

I steeled my jaw. "I haven't forgotten that. That's why I don't trust as freely anymore — I *can't* forget that."

"Then why question her motives?"

I loved my sister. Truly. But speaking with her, easy as it was, sometimes felt like slamming my head against a brick wall. "Because she hid a child from me for five years," I seethed, knocking back the rest of my glass and setting it slightly too harshly on the little wicker table between us. "You'd question everything, too."

She hummed her agreement as she turned back to the view over the hills and forests. Behind her, the hot tub boiled loudly, its cover snugly in place over the top of it. We dropped into a comfortable quiet between us, listening to the steady boil, the chirping birds, and the rustle of the trees. I understood why she liked it out here — it was a far nicer atmosphere than the veranda of my home back in San Francisco.

I spun the ring on my pinky finger absentmindedly, and my thoughts descended back to Olivia. I hadn't responded to her text from yesterday quite yet — I wasn't sure how I wanted to go about it. On one hand, I wanted the annulment, wanted to free myself of the tie to her so I could go back to my normal life and she could have what she wanted. But on the other, the one with the devil on its shoulder, I wanted to claim the prize I'd won. I still hadn't been able to stop thinking about her, and I worried that if I didn't use our *marriage* to its full advantage because of her views, I'd end up obsessed with her for the rest of my fucking life.

"There's something else," I muttered, so quiet I worried Caroline couldn't hear me.

"Something more pressing than a son?" she said, letting out a breathy chuckle before downing the rest of her glass.

"You'll want to refill that before I say it."

She turned to me, her brows knitting as she blinked at me, and picked up the bottle from where it rested on the wooden deck beside her chair. She filled hers and held it out to me — I gladly took it.

I downed two gulps straight from the bottle.

"Fucker," she hissed.

Tucking the bottle between my thighs, I took a deep breath. "I don't know how to say this, so I'm just going to be frank, Carrie."

She clutched her glass of wine in her hand, preparing for the worst. "I already hate this—"

"I'm married."

Silence.

Utter horrible silence. Even the hot tub ceased its noise, seeming to have decided that now was the best time for it to get up to temperature.

"Say something," I begged.

But she didn't. She just stared at me, waiting, wanting more of an explanation. Even her expression didn't change — just a blank, unending gaze.

"Vegas," I offered, trying to give her a playful smile but falling severely short.

"Damien."

"We're getting an annulment."

"Who is it?" she pressed, but from the disappointment coating her features, I could tell she was already hazarding a somewhat correct guess.

"Does it matter if I'm getting an annulment?"

"Yes. Obviously."

I cursed under my breath and took another swig of wine

from the bottle, and then another. "She's an intern at Blackwood."

"Of fucking course she is."

"Actually, technically, as of next week, she'll be a full-time employee."

"How old is she?" she deadpanned, her bright red lips pursing.

"I think she's twenty-four."

"Christ, Dame. She could be your kid," she groaned, setting down her glass of wine so she could have both hands free to rub at her temples. "You're lucky she's agreed to the annulment. Assuming you didn't do a prenup 'cause you were probably drunk out of your fucking skull, she could have tried to stick with you and force you into a divorce."

The thought of that hadn't even crossed my mind. "She freaked out when she realized what had happened. She *wanted* the annulment."

"You're extra fucking lucky, then."

But it didn't feel like it. Not when I was plagued with thoughts of her every goddamn second of the day, not when she infiltrated my dreams at night, not when she was the only thing I could think of when I tugged myself to completion three times a fucking day because just the idea of her made me so horny I could barely function. That didn't feel like luck — it felt like a curse.

"Try to keep your distance from her," she sighed. "You don't want her to change her mind and try to wring you for all you're worth, especially now that you've got... what did you say his name was? Nigel?"

I cringed at the idea that my son could be named *Nigel*. "Noah," I corrected. But she was right — if Olivia, for some reason, pushed for a divorce instead, custody would be a consideration. The money... I couldn't care less about it.

Having half of what I had now wouldn't make a single difference in my life.

"Noah," she hummed. "It's a cute name. Especially if he looks like you."

"Supposedly, he does."

"Do I get to meet him?" she asked, her little grin creeping back into her features as she softened at the idea. "Noah and Lucas could be best friends."

"No, I'm going to keep him from you forever," I laughed. I hadn't even given it all more than a passing thought in the back of the car the other day, but the idea of having a son who was genuinely mine and being able to introduce him to my family made my chest warm just a little bit.

Caroline reached across us, smacking my forearm with the back of her hand. "Asshole. I'll just have to kidnap him."

"Fucking *try*, Carrie."

She laughed as I drank the last drops out of the bottle, the wind carrying her fit of giggles over the treetops. It was nice — calming, even, to see her relax into the idea like I wished I could.

"You'll need to prepare," she said, her laughter dying down and being replaced with a grin. "A bed, some toys, clothes, that kind of stuff. Your house isn't exactly child-friendly, either. And you'll need someone to watch him. I can occasionally, as long as Lucas doesn't kick up a fuss about it."

Fuck. I hadn't thought of any of that, either.

I wasn't used to children. It wasn't that I didn't necessarily want one — I just hadn't even gotten to that point with anyone where I was seriously considering it, except for Marissa. Even then, we had never gone too far into detail, just idealistic imaginings of what our life would look like if

73

we had gotten married. She wanted to be a stay-at-home mom, and that covered everything as far as I was concerned.

But I didn't have that.

Briefly, so quickly that I caught the thought and shoved it back into its locked little box, I wondered if my *wife* would be willing to watch him. But Olivia was only my wife on paper, and putting that responsibility on someone so eager to further herself professionally felt like an insult when she desperately wanted out of our situation.

I couldn't consider it. Wouldn't. Shouldn't.

————

The lobby of Blackwood Energy Solutions was clearing out as the workday came to a close. It was nearing six in the evening, and those who had stayed late were the last to leave, including myself.

Coming down the elevator, I couldn't help but notice the small group of interns huddled in the center of the room, their lanyards giving them away. A handful clocked me and dispersed, scurrying toward the exit as if I were a fucking wolf, but four of them stayed — one head of chestnut hair in particular not even caring to look across the room as my feet touched down on the poured cement floor.

Olivia stood beside a man a couple of inches taller than her, her waves flowing over each shoulder as she played with the ends. Despite the black slacks, black heels, and tucked-in, white button-up, it felt like every inch of her was showing, like she was tempting me.

Like she was tempting *him*.

He grinned down at her, his blonde curls hanging around his cheeks. His lips moved but I couldn't quite make out what he was saying. I moved closer, nearly crashing into John from accounting but sidestepping him at the last possible second.

"Maybe dinner, or a movie?"

I paused.

"Oh, uh, yeah, I mean maybe," Olivia said, her voice a little quivery. "I'm really busy lately but—"

"You can make time," he drawled. His tongue glided across his upper teeth as he leaned in a little, one hand pushing a hanging chestnut wave behind her ear. "Pretty girl like you shouldn't have to worry about keeping on top of things. Unless it's me."

I moved before I'd even decided to.

Coming up behind her and grabbing her by the wrist, I tugged her back half a step, nearly sending her careening into my chest. "Ms. Martin," I hissed.

She spun on a dime, her cheeks heating and coating her face in a deep pink. "I was having a conversation."

"One that seemed wholly inappropriate for the office," I snapped, shooting a glare over her shoulder at the man she'd been speaking to. His name tag read *Charles Stipender*, and I nearly cringed at the idea of her going out with a man with that silly of a name.

"Like you care about inappropriate conversations here," she seethed, her voice low enough that only I'd hear it.

She had a point.

"As far as I was aware, the workday ended an hour ago," she added, her brows knitting as she glared up at me. But behind her, Charles was already retreating, heading straight for the revolving door at the entrance. "I can speak to whoever I want."

Her plump, tinted red lips pursed, and instantly, I was back in the restaurant at the Bellagio, those same lips closing over my thumb, her eyes batting up at me as if it was the most innocent thing she could have possibly done.

Fuck, I wanted her.

Screw what Caroline said.

"Fine. Speak to who you want. But there are some things we need to discuss, *privately*," I said, tightening my hold on her wrist. She didn't even fight it.

"Now?" she asked, her eyes widening as she glanced around at the few people still nearby. "Can we go up to your off—"

"No. Come to my house tonight." I let her go, taking a brief step back before we could draw too much suspicion from wandering eyes. "We've got paperwork to go over."

She studied me, her mouth parting, her gaze flicking between my eyes and my lips. "That feels like a trap."

I shrugged and took a single step to her side, leaning in just briefly and catching a wave of her perfume. "Guess you'll have to find out."

Chapter 9

Olivia

From the moment the door of his home swung open and he stood there in his crisp, white button-up and neatly pressed slacks, fingers fiddling precisely with the latch of his antique Rolex as he stared me down, I knew this was the worst possible idea imaginable.

The small amount of land didn't seem to be an issue for him — the home, if I could even call such an insane building a *home*, seemed to be built vertically. It took advantage of its space on the hillside overlooking Presidio Park and the Golden Gate Bridge, with nearly every side consisting of windows or balconies that unmistakably drew my thoughts back to Vegas. But I'd forced myself not to hesitate as I'd climbed the carved stone steps up to the gate, pressed the buttons of the keypad with the code he'd given me, and slinked through the hedgerow up to his front door.

"You changed?" I asked. It was as if I had nothing better to say, as if I hadn't spent the entire drive over here combing through conversation after conversation we could have. In fairness, I'd struggled to keep myself from imagining each of them ending with his hands on me, so none were truly *usable*. But it was an easy enough icebreaker, especially when I hadn't bothered to change out of my work clothes — just a plain black pair of slacks and a light gray button-up.

His gaze lingered on me as he stepped aside, letting me pass over the threshold and enter into the extravagant space. "I'd hardly call removing my jacket and tie for comfort's sake *changing*."

I swallowed over the knot in my throat as I took in the entryway that led into an intensely modern living room. Polished, pristine hardwood lined the large space that took up almost half of the entire ground floor of the house. On the far wall, floor-to-ceiling windows offered a view over the veranda and the idea of privacy in the heart of a bustling city. Dark grey painted walls and heavy artwork lined the space, with a mounted, massive television on one side and a sofa set that looked like it had come out of my fucking dreams.

I knew he was rich. Owning a company like Blackwood's would of course come with its perks, but this was... more than I imagined. And this was only *half* of the ground floor.

"You're quiet."

I followed him through the home, my heels clicking uncomfortably loudly, until we rounded a corner into one of the largest domestic kitchens I'd ever seen. "I just... I don't know. I wasn't expecting this," I breathed.

He stepped behind the island and plucked two small, crystalline glasses out of the black cabinetry before placing them in front of his array of bottles on the shiny black countertop. Black, black, black. The entire kitchen was dark, save for the under-cabinet lighting, light gray backsplash, and metal hanging lights. Even the high-top chairs that lined the breakfast bar were dark, and somehow with the hardwood floors, it didn't look bad. It looked sleek, and my god, it looked *expensive*.

As he placed a circular chunk of ice in each glass, I knew that what he was doing was a bad idea — for both of us.

"What *were* you expecting, Olivia?" he asked, glancing over one shoulder as he poured an amber liquid over the ice. "A hovel?"

I didn't know what to say to him, didn't know how to comprehend how someone lived in a space this lavish. It felt like I was sitting in the back row of the movie theater that was my mind, watching all of this through a screen instead of actively piloting myself. If I had any control here, I wouldn't have come in the first place.

He rounded the counter, each hand holding a glass. His rings glinted off the overhead lights as he held one out for me. "I get that it can be a little overwhelming," he said, his hardened features unchanging despite the softness of his voice. "This should help."

The ice clinked as I stared at it, hesitation eating away at me. I shouldn't drink. I knew what could happen if I did — what had *already* happened between us. But some part of me bent to him so easily, and I found myself reaching for it, taking the sweating glass in my palm, and holding it like a vice.

I couldn't bring myself to sip it, though.

The silence was deafening as we stood there, no more than three or four feet apart, my heart pounding as little droplets of condensation coated my fingers. Somehow, the man in front of me, towering over me, all muscle and money and nearly twice my age, was my legal husband. How the *fuck* had it come to this? How had I let any of this happen? I was better than this, better than drinking myself into oblivion, better than walking down an aisle in a hastily built chapel with Elvis and Damien at one end and a cheap photographer and me at the other, better than standing in his home with just the two of us and tempting fate.

"Paperwork," I choked. "You said you needed to go over some paperwork with me."

He nodded as he sipped at his glass. From the scent alone, I was pretty sure it was whiskey, something far fancier than whatever he'd been buying for us back in Nevada. "I need your signature on a consent form. My lawyer, Ethan, will be filing on our behalf, and you need to sign off for him to do so."

I paused.

My signature.

He just needs my fucking signature.

"Seriously?" I asked, a hint of irritation creeping into my voice. I set the untouched whiskey on the counter beside me. "You just need one signature?"

"Is that a problem?"

"We could have done this in the office," I gulped, stepping back from him. "With other people present. With your *lawyer* present."

"I thought you wanted this done as quickly as possible." The little smirk he gave me as he took a sip of whiskey told me he knew exactly what he was doing here — he knew he was tempting me. Tempting *us*. "Sign it tonight and Ethan can file it first thing in the morning."

The way he looked at me as if he could swallow me whole made my throat close in. "I could have signed it the moment I got to work. I didn't have to come here. This... this could have been handled—"

"What?" The sides of his eyes crinkled as his smirk grew wider. "Don't trust yourself around me, Olivia?"

My mouth went dry. Of course I didn't trust myself around him, not after the catastrophe of the business trip. But I also didn't trust *him* around me. Clearly, the man had no boundaries when it came to getting what he wanted from a woman, and my walls around it were nothing more than a challenge for him.

And god dammit, I hated that I found that exciting.

"We just... we shouldn't..." I started, jutting my chin out, "...be alone together. I can't be alone with—"

"Why?" He swallowed a few more sips before placing his mostly empty glass beside mine. One step and he was closer, sending my pulse racing. "Why can't you be alone with me?"

I stepped back instead. "You know why."

Again, he closed in, and again, I moved back. "Perhaps I do," he grinned. "But I want you to say it."

My back hit the wall as he took another step, crowding me, towering over me, giving me nowhere to go but sideways — but even that was eliminated when his hands pressed into the wall on either side of my head.

Rum, vanilla, and crushed almonds invaded my senses, and god fucking dammit, all I could think about was the way his chest looked beneath the shirt he was wearing and how sexy it had been when it was hanging limply off his shoulders. A knot formed at the back of my throat from just thinking about it.

"Damien, *please*," I croaked. I couldn't do this, couldn't stay here, couldn't be swarmed by him like this and expect myself to make it out the other side intact. There wasn't a chance in hell. I needed to leave, needed to slink out of his hold, but my body had a mind of its own around him and didn't want to react to the cues I was feeding it. My feet stayed planted. My fingers twitched toward him. My mind fucking *warred*.

"What exactly are you asking me for?" he purred, dipping his chin so his eyes were level with mine. "You look like you're halfway between kicking me or touching me between my legs."

Great. So it was obvious.

"If you don't want this, all you have to do is say."

I knew that. In my bones, I knew it. But I couldn't bring myself to form the words, couldn't even lodge them in my mouth in preparation, and even deeper than my bones, I knew I didn't *want* to say them. "I can't trust myself around you," I breathed, trying to dig into myself for the confidence I was lacking.

One hand dipped out of view before coming up under my chin, forcing me to look up at him as he gripped onto it. "Do you need to?" he asked, dragging his thumb across my lower lip and pulling it down. A shiver went down my spine as a heavy twisting took root in my lower stomach, warming the space between my thighs. "I am your *husband*, after all—"

"Not for long." The words came out muffled from the disruption to my lips, but something shone in his eyes nonetheless. *Finally, a drop of confidence.* His pupils expanded and his mouth parted, those fucking crows feet deepening as he grinned.

"You're mouthy when you're feeling bold," he rasped, his thumb pressing against my clenched teeth as a challenge. His ability to make me melt with a single touch made my blood run cold. The temptation to open my teeth was maddening — I wanted to do it for him again, wanted to wrap my lips and tongue around him and feel the scrape of his ring against my incisors. Fuck, I wanted to do everything he'd done to me in Vegas. I wanted to feel as alive as he'd made me feel that night. But I also wanted to bite him, wanted to tell him to fuck off, wanted to *not want him.* "There's more you want to say. I can *see* it in the way you look at me. Do it."

His knee pressed against mine, and for a second, I fought it. I didn't let him through. But without even increasing the pressure, my body shifted for him, letting him invade my space. *Say it. Say what you feel.* "I think you're an asshole," I breathed, the venom I'd intended to lace the words with falling flat. "I think you're desperate to win me over because of what I won't give you, and I can *tell.*"

He leaned in closer, his lips brushing against the curve of my ear. "You think *I'm* desperate?" he whispered. A chill shook me, forcing a little gasp from my mouth, and he took his opportunity. His thumb slid between my teeth, pressing down firmly on my tongue and dragging along it. "Would you not call grinding on my cock in the middle of a bar *desperate?*"

My breath caught. *He remembered that.*

"Would you not say that throwing yourself at me on the balcony of the Mandalay Bay is *desperate?*"

He took my earlobe between his teeth, biting down and sending a little shockwave of pain through my body before releasing it. His leg came in closer, pressing between my upper thighs, and oh my god, why was I letting this happen? *Why can't I stop myself?*

"Do you think marrying me to feel good about wanting to fuck me wasn't *desperate?*"

My pulse pounded in my ears. He wasn't wrong, and I fucking hated it. It was desperate — desperate and stupid, desperate and needy, desperate and debauched. He hadn't been the sole player in that game. We'd danced that foolish dance together that night, and although I'd avoided him, we'd been doing it since.

His thumb retreated and smeared my saliva across the side of my cheek.

"Fuck you," I whispered, not a single bit of bite in the words.

His nose brushed against mine, his lips just a breath from my mouth. "If you're going to call me desperate, princess, then you better be fucking honest with yourself. You wanted it. You *want* it."

"I can't," I croaked.

"You fucking can."

His mouth met mine before I could breathe in, and fuck, it was just like it had been at the bar, just like it had been all night in Vegas. His kiss was messy and hungry, his tongue berating mine and coating it with the taste of his whiskey. I didn't fight him.

Hands grasped my cheeks, his fingers splaying across my skin. "You can," he said again, his words muffled against my lips.

My throat closed in, my chest pounding.

Maybe he was right.

Maybe I could be honest with myself.

Breath stuttering, I let my fingers think for me. They reached for his shirt, up to the split in the fabric where his chest poked through, and fumbled with the buttons. One popped, and then another, and he hummed his approval against my mouth.

Fuck.

This wasn't what I should have been doing.

I should have been signing my name on a piece of paper.

I should have been walking out the door.

84

I should have been halfway home.

I should have been lying to myself.

Something raw and aching blossomed in my chest as I threw an arm around his neck, cementing him to me as I returned the fervor of his kiss. I pulled harder at the line of buttons on his shirt, my extremities shaking as I tried to pop another out of its hole, but his hand came down swiftly on top of mine. He tugged with one quick motion, and the sound of little mother-of-pearl buttons cascading across the tile floor filled the massive space.

I wanted him. God fucking dammit, I wanted him, wanted this, wanted to stop *waiting*.

"There you are," he said, the words almost guttural as they rumbled his chest. His shirt hung open, the ends tucked into his slacks, and I pulled the tails free. "Didn't even need a drink."

My hand flush against his collarbones, I dragged it down along his pecs, over the solid ripples of each ab. I broke from the kiss and looked between us at his exposed flesh. I hadn't had the chance to fully take him in when I was drunk out of my skull, and looking at him now, all muscle and tanned skin and the slightest tuft of peppered chest hair, was enough to make my head swim more than it already was.

His lips trailed to my neck, and I found myself reluctantly tearing my gaze from his chest and tilting my head back, giving him further access. Nimble, steady hands worked carefully at the buttons of my blouse, his lips trailing in their wake and moving down across my collarbones. He popped each one open, his ringed fingers brushing against the bare skin of my chest and stomach.

"Look at me," he ordered, lifting himself to his full height. Bright blue eyes met mine, but his pupils were wide enough that I could barely see a sliver of the intoxicating color. "The moment you say stop, we stop. Do you understand?"

The knot in my throat tightened as his free hand traced the edges of my lips and trailed down, down over my chin, down the slope of my neck. His fingers curled around my throat, caging me — he didn't apply an ounce of pressure, but the presence alone was enough to send my pulse to new levels. He could squeeze. He could cut off my oxygen. He was big enough to fucking kill me if he wanted. From the look in his eyes, I could tell it wasn't a threat. It was an *offer*.

"Do you *understand*?" he asked again, his fingers tightening just the smallest bit, not enough to hurt me in the slightest.

"Yes," I breathed.

"Good girl." His free hand loosened my shirt from where it was still tucked in around my waist, freeing the thin material. My breath caught as his fingers dragged across my stomach, wrapped around the buckle of my belt, and began their removal. "You like this, don't you?"

I blinked up at him in confusion, the warring in my mind beginning to calm. He squeezed his fingers a little more before relaxing them, giving me the context of his question, and it was as if every other thought in my mind that didn't surround what I wanted him to do to me ceased. The part of me that had been screaming to run and keep myself away from him just... disappeared. I should have been frightened, but instead, the space between my thighs was *aching*. There was a comfort, a corrupted hunger, in letting myself be vulnerable here. "Yeah," I croaked.

"Thank fuck," he rasped. He held me to the wall, and with one quick motion at the back of my slacks, he pulled down sharply, tugging them and my underwear over the swell of my ass and partway down my thighs. "Because you look so fucking pretty with my hand around your throat."

My cheeks heated as I kicked off my heels, dropping myself a couple of inches and giving up just that little bit of leverage. A moment later and my slacks and underwear were abandoned on the floor, and he was hoisting me up, up, up — forcing my legs around his waist and my pussy against his bare lower stomach. He took the weight of me, releasing my neck to hold me instead.

He kissed me, and I let myself sink into it, let myself close my eyes and turn off the outside world. I could feel his steps beneath me, felt it as we climbed up the stairs, his hands too focused on my skin and the latch of my bra to care about the handrail. I could barely focus on my surroundings — the dark gray walls of the staircase faded into dark gray walls of a hallway that faded into a wider space with more and more windows, the low light of twilight filling the room.

I only realized we were in a bedroom when my back met an intensely comfortable mattress and the softest sheets I'd ever felt.

I wasn't sure where my shirt had gone. I wasn't sure where my *bra* had gone. I was entirely bare beneath him, the two sides of his shirt hanging limply as he towered over me at the edge of the bed, his suit trousers still in place.

Until he fisted the buckle of his belt.

I could barely remember what his cock looked like. I'd seen it back in Vegas, held it, stroked it the same way I'd seen it done in porn, but I'd been so close to blacking out that the memory was blurry. I'd imagined it since, tried to piece together the memories to form an idea of it while I touched myself in the shower, but the moment his slacks unzipped and he pulled them down, I knew that my mind hadn't done justice to whatever hid beneath the raging bulge in his boxers.

"You're fucking *dripping*," he rasped, his eyes locked between my thighs. "I haven't even touched you yet and you're ruining my sheets."

His button-up fell over his shoulders and he abandoned it beneath him. My mouth went dry as my cheeks heated, and I tried to lift my rear. "I-I'm sorry—"

Large, ring-covered hands grabbed at my hips and shoved me back down into the plush sheets, making me lose my breath. "I wasn't complaining, princess."

He leaned over me, holding me in place with his hands, the soft light of twilight glinting off his watch as his lips pressed against the inner side of my knee. The fabric of his boxers shifted, his cock twitching, and with every kiss he planted against my skin growing closer and closer to the dripping space between my thighs, I could help but want to reach out to him. I wanted to touch it again, wanted to see it without the warped haze of alcohol tainting my memory.

Who the *fuck* was I around him?

The second his tongue slid across my clit and his contented grunt filled the air, my mind went blank. Autopilot took over, and it didn't care about who I was, my morals, or pleasing my parents.

He feasted on me, every glide of his tongue feeling like goddamn heaven, and I couldn't help myself. I fisted the sheets, writhed, moved my body in ways that felt *right* against his lips. Using my toes, I crept my foot up to the hem of his boxers, desperately trying to push it down. I wanted more. Fuck, I wanted it all.

One hand came to rest on the waistline of them just beside my foot, and the other snaked its way across my skin until his fingers pressed against my opening.

I shifted my hips forward.

His answering chuckle vibrated against my clit, and that in combination with what I could only assume were two fingers sliding inside of me, made me lose it.

My head tipped back, and through squinted eyes, I could barely make out the shape of an ornate headboard at the top of the bed, and—

Oh, god.

Oh, *fuck*.

It was a fucking *mirror*.

Outlined in dark stained wood, it reflected *everything*. Even over the mound of pillows, I could see myself laid out like a damn starfish, completely bare, one foot on his hip and one knee up, my hands fisting the sheets. I could see his face between my legs, could see his fingers start to tug on the waistband of his boxers. I could see them slip down his legs.

His eyes met mine in the reflection, and I swear, his lips tipped up into a smirk.

"Oh my *god*," I breathed, letting myself look down my body at him instead of the mirror. I could feel my release already beginning to build, and the moment another two fingers slipped inside of me and the burn of the stretch mixed with the pleasure of his tongue, I was damn sure he'd throw me over the cliff far too soon. "Damien."

His head obscured what the mirror didn't. I couldn't see his cock, couldn't see what his hand was doing, and I found myself caught between what I wanted to watch — his mouth on me or his hand in the mirror. But before I could commit to either, his lips broke from me, his fingers curling inside as he licked his damp lips.

And I could see him.

Even in the low light, it was enough to send me spiraling.

It wasn't the length that had me catching my breath. No, it was the width, the girth of him, that shook me a little more than I'd imagined. I'd seen similar sizes to him before online, but right now, in this fucking room where his fingers were buried inside of me and both of us knew damn well where this could lead, I hadn't imagined something that looked like it could tear me in two.

But the memory from the bathroom in the bar became clearer now. This was what I couldn't wrap my fingers all the way around. His free hand wrapped around the base of it, making the veins bulge even more than they already did. The swollen, deep red tip leaked and dripped onto the edge of the bed as he lifted himself to his full height.

I salivated. Any hesitation I still harbored reared its head briefly before fizzling away.

"*Please.*"

His thumb grazed against my clit briefly, making my spine twitch. "Well, that's a welcome change," he chuckled. "I'm not the one begging this time."

I didn't care if it brought me back down to the level he'd been on that night. I wanted him. God fucking dammit, I wanted him, and he wasn't *giving* it to me, and I could barely think through the pleasure that wasn't quite enough to get me to that edge anymore. I haphazardly reached for him, brushing the tips of my fingers along the underside of his tip, and the sound he made as he sucked in air through his teeth only made me want it more.

But I wasn't expecting the hesitation from him. "We don't have to."

His fingers began to retreat, and I grabbed for his forearm, keeping him in place. I almost couldn't believe the words that came from my mouth, couldn't believe that *I* could be the one to speak them. "I want to. *Please*."

His answering grunt as he climbed onto the bed was the confirmation I was desperately seeking. He reached across me and I let his fingers retreat, the emptiness that followed feeling wrong on too many levels, and watched as he pulled open the bedside drawer.

"What are you doing?"

"Lube," he said, plucking out a glass bottle with a pump top.

"But I'm... uh, wet."

He situated himself between my raised legs, sitting on his knees, and deposited three pumps worth of the clear liquid into his palm before chucking the glass bottle onto the sheets. "Doesn't matter." He smeared it across his length before coating my entrance. I twitched again as his fingers dipped inside of me once, twice, and a third time for good measure. "Do you have toys this size?"

I gulped as I glanced back down at his cock. "No."

"Then it might hurt a little. And as much as you'd like to believe I'm an asshole," he started, withdrawing his fingers, "I'd rather keep that pain to a minimum."

The tip of him slid across my clit, and oh *god*, he was warm. Every toy I'd ever used was cold, rigid, and lifeless in comparison to the way his cock felt against me.

He slipped it lower.

And lower.

It caught against the bottom of my entrance, his mouth parting on a little grunt, and it was as if reality came screeching back in.

Don't.

Stop.

You'll regret this.

91

You hardly know him.

You're only married on paper.

My chest rose and fell erratically as we both hesitated. He didn't move a muscle, and all I could do was bring my gaze up to his, hoping that maybe, just maybe, I'd find the confidence in him that I was suddenly lacking.

Every hard line that made up his facial features had softened.

"You can say no," he offered.

I gulped. I didn't want to say no. I didn't want to keep fighting the side of myself that thought I needed to hold myself back. I was twenty-four, for god's sake.

And, technically, he was my husband.

I reached up to him, wrapping my hand around the back of his neck, and pulled him down closer to me. For a moment, we stayed there, breathing the same air, looking for confirmation that evaded us both. He held my gaze, and in the steadiness of the silence, both unmoving and searching for answers in the other, I could feel myself breaking down again, could feel each wall I'd hastily assembled crumbling.

"Please," I breathed.

It was everything we'd been waiting for.

The sharp sensation of my entrance stretching hit me first. My mouth parted with a gasp, but he covered it with his lips, kissing me as he slowly began to slide in inch by aching inch. I tried my best to relax, but oh my *god*, he was girthy, and the sting made it hard to focus, made it hard to *want* this.

He paused, halfway in and halfway out, as if he could tell how it felt. As if he knew his own destruction.

One hand slid across my skin, down the center of my stomach, and dipped between my thighs. A simple touch, just his fingers grazing across my clit, made a world of difference in my level of anxiety. The pleasure made the pain fade enough, and my muscles relaxed.

"That's it," he mumbled against my lips, sliding himself in just a little further. "Good fucking girl."

The sensation as he bottomed out and held himself there was unlike anything I'd felt before. I'd never been so *full*, so *whole*, so innately *satisfied*. We paused again as he gave me time to grow accustomed to it, but I wasn't sure I ever could entirely. I understood, now, why he'd been so drunkenly desperate that night in Vegas.

But I understood even more the second he began to move.

I was convinced I'd lost my mind before, convinced I'd gone blank and had nothing but a deep want left in my head when he'd started touching me. I'd thought it again when he'd removed his boxers, when I'd touched him without being under the influence. But this — *this* wasn't on the same level. There was nothing left. No worries, no concern over who I was or what I wanted, no hesitation or fear or self-consciousness.

I thought it was meant to hurt the entirety of your first time. But dear god, I was so, so wrong.

My fingernails dug into his skin as his mouth broke from mine, a sound I'd never heard myself make dragging from my throat. He took his time, moving slowly, letting me feel every inch of him as he pulled himself nearly all the way out before sinking back in as far as he could. But I needed more.

"More," I begged, the word coming out whimpered, broken, *needy*.

His pupils blew so wide I couldn't see a hint of blue in the darkening room. But he gave me what I asked for.

In an instant, we were moving, his cock slipping out of me as he turned me onto my front. Large hands grabbed at my hips, lifting them up, forcing me onto my knees with my face buried in the sheets, his legs between mine. For a split second, I felt so intensely exposed, but then he was sliding back in, hitting me at entirely new angles I'd never felt before from any toy.

"Oh my *god*."

"Touch yourself," he ordered, and memories flickered in my mind from when he'd said the same thing to me on the private balcony of the Mandalay Bay. I followed his instructions, letting my hand slip between my thighs.

My fingers ghosted against the topside of his cock as I swirled them over my aching clit, and something in him snapped.

His onslaught began.

He fucked me almost punishingly, every strike of his hips setting off little wildfires in my veins. His nails dug into the skin of my ass, little bursts of pain heightening every pleasurable sensation and doubling it, tripling it, coaxing more moans and sobs from my lips.

But it was when he reached forward, grabbing a fistful of my hair and tugging back to lift my head, that I lost my mind, too. "Watch," he rasped.

Straight ahead of me, I could see us both in the mirror.

I could see the look of pure satisfaction and pleasure on his face, the way his muscles contorted with every drive of his hips, the wreck that I was turning into beneath him. Makeup smeared and mouth parted, I could watch *myself*, the way my face looked when I moaned, the way my body molded to him, the way my breasts pressed into the mattress. The way my lips moved as I whined his name.

But more than any of that, I could see the way he saw me, the way he looked at me with a mixture of *pride* and greed, the way that I turned him on by just existing.

My release hit me out of nowhere.

Every part of me broke, my body shaking as wave after crashing wave of ecstasy invaded my system. It was too much of everything at once, and my fingers stilled, his hips stuttering, my muscles contracting and releasing around him. It was better than any orgasm he'd given me in Vegas, and those had been better than any I'd given myself. I could barely focus on our reflection, but I found him, found the way he watched me in awe, found the way he grinned as if he found pleasure in *my* release.

God, everything made so much sense.

Slowly, achingly, he released my hair and let my head fall back down, his movements choppy, his hands grasping my hips instead. I pushed back into him with every thrust, but I could barely control myself anymore, could barely feel a thing beyond his cock inside of me and his hands on me.

And then he stopped, one last groan coming from him.

Warmth flooded me, heating me inside more than he had before. Damien breathed heavily, his fingers twitching as they moved along my sides and my spine.

"You," he said hoarsely, "will be the fucking death of me."

Chapter 10

Damien

Three days.

Three days, and she somehow hadn't left my mind. I'd had my fill of her, and she should have been erased — she shouldn't have lingered in my thoughts the way she had been. But she'd been exhausted after and although I'd offered to let her stay the night, she'd left after signing her name where I needed her to.

The moment she went out my door should have been the moment I felt satisfied.

But it hadn't, and so as I stood in the middle of the room at the vintage watch auction thoroughly unimpressed with the selection this time, I couldn't help but imagine how she'd felt wrapped around my cock. I couldn't help but imagine all the ways I wanted her to do it again.

The man behind the podium read out words at a fairly normal pace this time, giving my mind room to wander. *Fifteen thousand, do I hear fifteen thousand? Fifteen thousand. Going once, going twice. Sold!* It blurred into the background as she filtered in, that fucking look on her face as she watched me in the mirror, her features contorting as her walls collapsed so fucking heavenly.

Three days of this torment, on top of the ones I'd spent pining after her since Vegas.

I'd gotten my work done. I'd given our signatures over to Ethan. But I hadn't done a damn thing about Noah.

I was a week and three days out from his arrival, and yet, I'd bought nothing. I hadn't prepped. I hadn't even Googled how to be a fucking parent. I'd been so caught up in Olivia that I hadn't even focused on my now-confirmed son — I hadn't even given myself space to process the fact that he truly was mine. My schedule had taken control because I couldn't police myself on it, and so I stood at the vintage watch auction, not even bothering to place any bets because none of them truly called out to me, because it was something I'd added to my calendar.

I need to add an hour somewhere for processing a child and another for online shopping.

I left empty-handed, my mind filled with white noise and indifference. The setting sun between the reflective buildings in Mission Bay made me squint, the warm, golden hue almost too much after being cooped up in the auction house for hours. The cool breeze carried the scent of salt from the nearby harbor and the hum of city life, honking cars and shouting voices, but beyond that, wrapping around the buildings as I turned the corner, the laughter of children.

Across the road from me, alight with the buzz of excitement that a Friday evening brings after school, the Mission Bay Kid's Park was full to the brim with exhausted parents and energized kids. As a man, I knew it wasn't ideal for me to stop, to take in what would likely become my life soon —

but I found myself leaning against the fencing anyway, my arms draped over the rail, absolutely *fascinated.*

Parents from every walk of life either held their child's hand as they went down the slide or stood off to the side with their arms crossed, eyes glued on the energetic mini-me's they'd created, watching them like hawks as they climbed and swung and see-sawed. Some looked genuinely happy to be there, their faces lit by the joy they saw in their children.

Others, though, looked as though they just wanted to be in the college years already.

I couldn't help but wonder which one I'd be. I'd never been particularly great with children, but I never disliked the idea of having one myself. Taking in a five-year-old I'd never met could swing me in either direction — hatred for the way it changed my life, or a deep appreciation for something I hadn't asked for but received on a silver platter. But I hoped it was the latter. I hoped that I did not wish he'd grow up as quickly as possible.

My life was messy, though. Full of too much time and yet not enough, with a *wife* I'd married on a whim and a business to run. And as much as I wanted to see Olivia again, as much as I'd been tempted to call or text her the last three days, involving myself with someone who I was actively trying to legally remove myself from felt like a bad decision when I considered a child being a part of that. I needed to make as much space as I could for Noah, and keeping a woman who seemed to take up rent in my mind around didn't exactly allow for that.

· · ·

With the sun entirely below the horizon and the stars out in full glory, I lounged on my veranda, the low hum of cars on the streets around me fading into the background. I knew what I needed to do — I'd known it for a few hours now. I just hadn't worked up to it yet.

It was nearly nine in the evening when I finally decided to call her. She answered on the third ring, and hesitant, non-committal *hello?* creeping down the line of the phone.

"I need to be honest with you," I sighed. I looked up to the night sky as I rubbed at the corners of my jaw, desperately trying to release the pounds of pressure in my muscles from being tensed all day.

"Honest how?" Olivia asked. I could hear the shifting of her phone, and a second later, the background noise amplified as if she'd put me on speaker. The unmistakable sound of the unscrewing of a cheap bottle of wine filtered through.

"My life is about to change. Drastically," I explained. "And although I appreciate that you weren't exactly looking for a relationship with me, I need to... draw that line in the sand. From my end."

Silence. Silence, and the harsh sound of wine being poured into a cup.

"I know we're getting an annulment. I know that's what you want, and don't get me wrong, I want that too. But I need to put all of my focus into handling this, and that means I need to cut this off before it turns into anything else — whether that's a casual thing, something entirely different, or even nothing at all once the annulment goes through."

A beat of quiet passed before she spoke. "And you didn't consider this before having me over the other night?"

99

Shit. "I'm sorry. I shouldn't have asked you to come over. I shouldn't have initiated it. We shouldn't have done what we did, and that was on me."

A click from her tongue was silenced as the sound of her sipping her wine filled the line. *"We shouldn't have done what we did* is a funny way of saying you shouldn't have taken my virginity." I could hear the little clips of anger in her voice, could feel the small stab she made with each word. She was right though — she deserved for me to be upfront.

"I shouldn't have taken that from you," I offered. "Not when I have other things going on. Not when I need to put whatever would happen here on a back burner. It wasn't fair, and I genuinely apologize."

"It's fine," she said, the tone indicating anything but. I'd been with enough women to know that tone anywhere. "I get it. I assumed it would happen, anyway. I mean, that's what they say, right? *He'll lose interest the moment he gets what he wants?* Pretty sure that's in every abstinence campaign I've ever heard."

"Olivia—"

"No, no, it's on me. I should have known better. I *did* know better," she laughed, the sound raw and not at all from any humor in the situation. "I didn't hold out like I should have. You can be my eternal fucking consolation prize."

Ouch. I deserved that. "Can I explain, at least? So you don't fucking hate me forever?"

Another quiet sip, and then another, and then the *tink* of a glass meeting some kind of hard surface. "Is it a *good* explanation, Damien? Or is it just to make you feel better?"

I... hadn't even considered that. Was telling her even a good idea, or was it just for my gain, my own peace of mind?

No. It wasn't for me. She was my wife for the time

being, and if any of this came up, if any of it needed to be assessed in the annulment, she had a right to know in advance.

"I have a son," I said, the words feeling wrong and other-worldly as they left my lips. She was the first person who wasn't immediate family that I'd told — not counting Ethan, of course, because he brought it to me in the first place. It felt clunky in my mouth to try to speak about it. "He's five."

Silence.

"His name is Noah," I offered.

Again, silence.

"He's—"

"Why didn't you tell me this before you married me?" The words felt almost like knives despite the confused tone of her voice.

I hated this. I barely knew the girl, and I'd flung her into chaos unknowingly — and I'd fucking doubled down after I'd found out. "I didn't know," I sighed. "I only found out about him a few days ago. His mother, my... ex, left him to me in her will."

"Her will?" I could almost hear the cogs turning in her mind.

"It's been a lot to take in. And in my desperation to make myself feel somewhat normal, I tried to forget about it for a few days, and that led to... well, you. Here." Even with the light pollution from the city, I could just barely make out a passing satellite in the sky above me, blinking white as it traveled behind a cloud. "He arrives next week. And if I'm being honest with you, Olivia, I'm so fucking unpre-pared for it that I feel like I'm going to be sick."

More sloshing of wine filled the line as she poured another glass. I couldn't help but wonder where she was, if she could see the satellite I was watching, if it had come out the other side of the cloud from her perspective. "Will this affect the annulment?"

I let out a breath. No hope of finding comfort in her, then. "Ethan said it shouldn't. It's not a divorce, so it's not like we're splitting things down the middle here. But you deserve to know in case it comes up."

"Okay."

"I'll have Ethan bring you the papers to sign when they come back," I added.

"Okay."

"And I'll keep my distance from you at the office, but we'll likely still be around each other."

Again, an upsetting, disillusioned, "Okay."

"You sound like you hate me," I sighed.

A beat of silence passed before she exhaled. "I don't hate you, Damien. I'm just upset with myself. Your reasons are valid and I understand, I just wish I hadn't..."

I gave her the space she needed if she wanted to elaborate, but she didn't.

"It doesn't matter, anyway. Neither of us wanted to be where we are now to begin with, so this really shouldn't have hit me out of left field. I'll be fine."

"Okay." *That's all I can say?*

"Good luck with Noah. And I'll sign the papers when I get them."

I opened my mouth to reply, but the three little beeps through the phone cut me off, and the line went quiet. She'd hung up.

Chapter 11

Olivia

Standing smack dap in the center of Damien's office not twenty-four hours after that fucking phone call wasn't exactly what I'd imagined when I'd hung up.

The midday sun invaded the space, pouring in through the massive windows and glinting off every reflective surface in sight. He watched me over the top of his computer screen with his eyes narrowed, his brows knitting together, as if I was somehow affronting him by just being in his damn office — but he knew I was coming. I'd scheduled this with him first thing in the morning.

"If this is about—"

"It's not." I took a step toward his desk, the right side of my body warming immediately as it came into contact with the rays of the sun. "I read last night that you acquired the rights to the water filtration I did my presentation on."

His mouth turned to a thin line as he lowered his laptop screen an inch. He leaned back in his chair, his black suit jacket tugging at the sides and opening up just a little further, showing more of his white button-up. "Before or after I called you?"

"After. I just... I know I outlined its usages in my proposal, but I wanted to bring something up that I hadn't marked down." Another step forward and I ended up just behind the wingback chairs opposite his desk. I leaned forward on the back of one, desperate to feel casual. *Who's the one tempting fate now, Olivia?*

His eyes met mine, crystal clear blue nearly making me pause. But he said nothing, and I took that as my signal to keep going.

"You know just as well as I do that there are places here, in the US, that could use this technology to combat water problems," I said, swallowing around the lump in my throat when his eyes flicked back to his screen for a fleeting second. "You also know that it could be useful around the *world*. And with it being able to generate electricity, I was thinking — if Blackwood could produce enough of it and absorb the cost, you could give it to those places for free as a means for filtration and purification, and sell the energy produced. That could be where you make money from it, instead of selling the product as a whole. They get the benefit of clean water at no cost to themselves, and you get the benefit of energy production that you can charge companies to use."

The ray of sunlight reflecting off his Rolex nearly blinded me as he scrubbed his face.

He looked unimpressed.

Shit.

"Olivia," he sighed, pushing his perfectly styled peppered hair back away from his face. He looked out the window, his eyes locking on to *something*, and my stomach sank. He wouldn't look at me. "I appreciate your enthusiasm and your passion regarding this, and frankly, your passion for everything in this space. But we simply can't afford that right now."

What? Blackwood Energy Solutions was one of the largest sustainable businesses in the country. I'd seen his house. I'd seen this *building*. How could he not afford that? "What do you mean?"

His tongue dragged along the edge of his top teeth, his jaw ticking. "I mean, although I understand where you're coming from, Blackwood cannot afford to eat the cost of that right now. We need positive cash flow."

"It would be positive cash flow. You'd just have to wait for it to pay for itself," I offered.

"We can't wait for that. Not at the moment."

I blinked at him. Since when was Blackwood not able to wait for their returns? Plenty of our projects operated in similar ways, whether that was setting up a project just for a return from the government or flat-out donating our resources. That didn't make *sense*. "Are you punishing me?"

His gaze snapped back to me, his eyes blowing wide. "What on earth would I be punishing you for?"

I let the silence fall, let him sit in that for a moment in case he wanted to come to the conclusion himself, but from the perplexed look coating his features, he wasn't getting there on his own. "For how I spoke to you last night," I explained.

"Absolutely fucking not."

"You sure about that?"

"Liv." My spine stiffened. *Has he called me that before?* "Look, I wasn't going to say anything because I don't want any of the staff panicking, but the company is dealing with some monetary problems, okay? No one's job is at risk, but it means we're a little... tight. It's nothing to do with you or how you spoke to me. *That* was entirely justified."

He leaned forward onto his desk, his eyes darting to the analog clock beside him. I didn't know what to say to him — I didn't think it was unfair of me to assume that it had to do with us, but I guess I was wrong.

"I understand you're passionate about it," he continued, his voice softening, *deepening*. As much as I wanted to forget what had happened between us at his house, that voice, that angering voice, brought me right back to it and had me crossing my legs. "I will take your idea on board and see what we can do. Genuinely. But I can't promise anything, princess, not just yet—"

He cut himself off. Wide eyes met mine once more, and my cheeks heated, my lips pursing. "Please, don't—"

"I'm sorry. I shouldn't have said that." His Adam's apple bobbed as he swallowed. He flicked the screen of his laptop back upright, diverting his attention to that instead. "My head's in so many places. It's probably best if you go."

The longer I studied him, the more I noticed the lines above his brows were deepening, and the space beneath his eyes had darkened. He looked exhausted, and the way that he carried himself usually—tall, proud, sure of himself—was almost nowhere to be found. He was hunched over, fumbling his words, not quite right.

Despite what had happened between us and the anger I harbored toward myself because of it, I couldn't help but feel a little bit sorry for him.

"Can I help?" The words came out before I'd thought them through. His eyes met mine again, unreadable. "You've got a lot going on. Is there anything I can do to take some of the load off?"

His mouth opened as if he had words prepared, but quickly shut.

"What are you working on?" I asked, plucking up the

courage to step further than the wingbacks. I set my bag down in the chair and came up beside him behind his desk, leaning down to get a good look at the screen.

Children's beds.

That's what filled his screen — bed after bed, exorbitantly priced, some shaped like race cars and others with frames and princess-style netting.

"I have no idea what I'm doing," he breathed. The sentence was so fucking raw, so exhausted. It made my chest ache for him. "I don't know what he likes. I don't know what he's used to. I don't know *anything*."

"If it's any consolation, I don't know much about kids either," I offered, and he shot a small smile at me in return. "But I *was* a kid more recently than you, so..."

He snorted, ringed fingers coming up to cover his mouth. He turned the laptop so it was facing me fully. "Yeah, fine. You've got a point."

I scrolled to the next page, and then the one after. We studied them in silence, bed after bed, each one of us liking some more than others or straight up disagreeing on one shaped absurdly like a dinosaur. I tried to keep in mind the basics — when I was kid, what did I want? Of course I wanted something cool, but I would have regretted that two years down the line when I was no longer into the big red dog. And considering Damien had no idea what Noah was interested in...

"This one," I said, clicking into the listing and pointing my finger at the screen. A simple black bed frame, double sized, big enough for him to grow into and basic enough that it could change with him. "You can find out what he likes when he arrives and get him some bedsheets that go along with that."

His brows knitted as he looked up at me from his office chair, and I groaned my frustration.

Flicking into another tab, I pulled up the most basic graphic sheets I could find to get my point across. An all-over print of the original Alice In Wonderland illustrations on basic, polyester fabric. "Something like this, for whatever he likes."

He shook his head in disbelief as he turned the computer back to him. "I didn't even know you could get sheets like that. I always had basic ones growing up."

"That's because you're old," I grinned.

"No, it's because my parents were overly convinced that every part of their house needed to fit *their* design," he griped, rolling his eyes.

"Whatever you say, Grandpa."

"Oh my god, Liv, I'm forty-five," he laughed. "I *just* became a dad. Please don't make me think about grandkids yet."

I shot him a grin and he returned it, the winkle above his brows beginning to smooth. "Okay, okay, sorry. Just a middle-aged *dad*."

"How *dare* you call me middle-aged. I'm not even fifty yet."

I chuckled and shrugged. "If we're going off of male life expectancy..."

He scoffed playfully as he focused in on the laptop again, adding the bed frame and mattress to his cart. I didn't want to look at the price of it, and from where I stood, it seemed like he didn't even bother to check. He added two sets of sheets, and at my suggestion, added a third and a fourth. Just in case.

We picked out some basic toys. We picked out some wallpaper with glow-in-the-dark planets on them. We picked out one of the newest game consoles, boxes upon boxes of Legos, clothes in varying sizes, and a bundle of books.

He checked out on every website with me standing beside him, his credit card face up on the desk where I could easily see it. I wasn't sure if it was a sign of trust in me that I wouldn't steal his details or just the flippant nature of being that wealthy that it wouldn't matter — but either way, it was oddly... comforting.

Even if I shouldn't have stayed to help him with it.

"Thank you," he said, closing the laptop in front of him. I shifted, allowing him space to stand, and when he didn't bother to back up an inch from my personal space, I did it for him. "Genuinely. I wouldn't have thought of all of that on my own."

I shook my head. "You would have figured it out eventually."

"I don't know," he shrugged. "Maybe. Maybe not. For all I know, I could have ended up empty-handed until he arrived, then frantically asked a five-year-old what he *needed* as if he could reliably tell me."

I studied him for a moment, the way he kept his gaze from me, the way his fingers tapped against the solid frame of his desk. The way his chest rose and fell. The way the crease above his brow deepened again. "Are you prepared?" I asked, the words coming out a little weaker than I wanted. "For everything to change, I mean."

He took a deep breath, letting it out slowly through his nostrils. The steady stream of air wafted the scent of his cologne all over me, and I couldn't help but remember how it invaded me when I'd had my head in the crook of his neck. "If I'm honest, will you think less of me?"

I shook my head.

"No. I'm not prepared. Not by a long shot, Liv. But I have to be, and I'll find a way to be."

He tugged the sleeve of his coat back, checking the leather and silver antique watch on his wrist. I wasn't sure whether it was the way he'd said that as if he was defeated in a war he hadn't even waged yet, or if it was just the left-over emotions I'd somehow let blossom for him — but I found myself moving closer to him, slipping between him and his desk, his cologne painting the inside of my nostrils.

I found my arms wrapping around his neck.

I found my head against his shoulder.

Just... a hug. Easy, normal, with only the wildest temptation to lift my lips to his instead of just the simple embrace. But he wrapped a single arm around my waist, holding me there, chest to rigid chest.

"Thank you," he said again.

But he shouldn't have thanked me. Every second the embrace continued, I realized more and more that this wasn't selfless. It was an act that let me be close to him, however he would allow it now that he'd placed up boundaries.

I held him for myself.

Chapter 12

Damien

The buzzing of my phone roused me from sleep. Constant, over and over, *buzz, buzz, buzz. Buzz, buzz, buzz.*

The sun had only barely begun to rear its head, painting the sky in light blues and pinks and brightening my bedroom just enough that I could find my phone face down in the low light. I grabbed for it.

Buzzer pressed on west gate.

Buzzer pressed on west gate.

Buzzer pressed on west gate...

I swiped on the notifications that were piling up by the second. The live video feed flickered to life on my phone, and standing outside my gate, frantically and angrily pressing my buzzer over and over, was a woman I only vaguely recognized.

I pressed the button to speak through it. "Hello?"

I watched as the woman glanced around before realizing the sound was coming from the speaker. She leaned closer to the camera. "Hi, Damien. Can you let me in, please?"

Scrubbing my eyes, I focused on her again, trying to work out why her face rang bells in my mind. But it was far too early — six in the morning, if my phone was to be trusted — and I couldn't bring myself to wake up enough to place her. "I'm sorry, the camera is broken," I lied. "Who is this?"

"Christ, you'd think someone as rich as him would have a working camera," she grumbled.

"I can hear you."

"Sorry, yeah, it's Grace. Grace Thompson."

Grace Thompson...

Shit.

I sprung from the sheets, stumbling to my dresser as I pressed the *unlock* button on my app. Grace Thompson. Marissa's sister. The one who was handling all of the handover details about Noah. Why she was here at six o'clock in the goddamn morning was beyond me, but if I needed to sign something or she needed to drop something off, I was more than willing to let her onto my property.

The sound of the doorbell rang through the empty house. I pulled on the first pair of joggers I could find and slipped a plain white t-shirt over my head as I trudged down the stairs. This would be the first time I would be speaking to her directly since Marissa and I split over five years ago — almost everything so far had been handled by Ethan.

On some level, I was nervous. But my stomach sank into a black abyss the moment I opened the door.

Grace stood in her pastel green scrubs, name tag dangling from her neck, her auburn hair chopped short and blunt at her shoulders. And beside her, a quarter of her height, clutching a tiny toy car, a head of dark brown curls and staggeringly bright blue eyes stared up at me.

Nope. No. I was going to pass out.

"Damien, this is Noah. Noah, this is your father, Damien Blackwood."

I took a step back from the door.

"This is your new home from today," she continued, lowering herself to a squat.

She was a week early. Why the *fuck* was she a week *fucking* early? "Grace," I croaked, half expecting her to explain herself and half expecting this to be a goddamn fucking nightmare. I couldn't think. I couldn't *breathe*.

"What?" she snapped, the bite of that single word telling me everything I needed to know about the situation at hand.

"You..." Fuck, I couldn't find words. *Breathe. Fucking breathe.* "Next week. You're supposed to drop him off *next week*." I stared her down, my gaze unwavering, partly because I hadn't mentally prepared myself yet to even be able to look at the kid I'd made and been unaware of for five whole years. I should have said hello to him. I should have been ready.

"There was a mix-up in the schedule. He's yours from today," she said. "I told your lawyer last night."

"When?" I pressed. "When last night?"

"I don't know, nine or so?"

I pulled my phone from my pajama bottoms and looked at the notifications that had piled up overnight, scrolling past each separate one from the buzzer. And sure *fucking* enough, at nine-thirty last night, three missed calls from Ethan.

I'd been in the shower. I'd been thinking about Olivia. I'd been doing all fucking manner of things to myself.

Oh my *god*. "I'm sorry," I breathed. "I'm not... I'm not *ready* yet, Grace. None of his things have come in yet."

"What?" she snapped, but quickly took a deep breath

and looked back down at Noah. "Noah, buddy, how about we go inside and you can have a look around your new house while Damien—sorry, your dad—and I speak?"

Noah looked between us, his too-big eyes lingering on me. *Say something, you idiot. Say something to your fucking kid.* "Okay."

He slipped past me before I could work up the nerve.

"Auntie Grace, look! Stairs!"

She chuckled as she stepped in behind him. "Exciting!"

He raced up them, and already my mind started to race, thinking about everything I'd left out upstairs that he could get into. Everything he could question. Everything that absolutely should have been put away before a child rummaged around.

"What the fuck do you mean none of his stuff has arrived?" she hissed.

I turned back to her as I closed the front door. "You weren't supposed to bring him until next Saturday. Everything I bought is arriving this week. I have *nothing*, Grace."

"You didn't think to purchase things the moment you found out about him?" She crossed her arms over her chest, her name tag squishing against her breast.

"I didn't know what to fucking buy," I spat. "It's not like you supplied me with a list."

"Google exists, Damien."

"Right, sorry, next time I'll just search up *what to buy to prepare for a five-year-old son you've never met coming to live with you for the rest of his adolescence.* I'm sure there are loads of articles about that specific scenario." I reached for the bottle of whiskey I'd left on the couch and the unlit pack of cigars beside it, instinct kicking in and telling me to clean up the things that were definitely not kid-friendly.

"Jesus, you couldn't even clean up?"

She trailed behind me as I brought the alcohol and cigars into the kitchen. "I didn't *know* he was coming today."

"So you just live like this—"

"Why did you change the days, Grace?" I snapped, spinning on my heel to face her. She was significantly shorter than me, her round face and dark brown eyes reminding me far too much of her sister. If only she'd gotten the curly hair gene. "You knew damn well that I wouldn't be ready. Two weeks isn't a lot of time to prep, and cutting it short by an entire *week*... Did you want him to arrive like this? With me unready and a house that doesn't feel welcoming to him?"

"I need to work this week." She shrugged as if it was the most nonchalant thing she could say.

"So do I! I run a fucking company—"

"Why are you yelling at my auntie?"

My blood ran cold as I turned to the second stairway that deposited into the kitchen. Noah stood there, toy car still in hand and a blanket from my upstairs guest room in the other, his big eyes watering. I barely knew the kid, had barely had a second to even comprehend what was happening, but my chest blossomed so goddamn painfully for him that it nearly had my knees buckling. "I'm sorry."

Grace glanced back at him. "It's okay, bud. We're just having a discussion. Why don't you go play with your car in the living room?"

"Where's that?"

I cleared my throat. "That big room by the front door," I said.

Noah nodded once and took off.

"Let me make one thing clear, Damien," Grace said, her voice dropping in volume as she turned back to me. "I'm not happy about this. Any of it. I don't understand why my sister left him to *you* and not me. Bet your bottom dollar that I'll be filing for custody the instant I can get the paperwork done."

Well. There it was.

She had done this on purpose. She'd flustered me, manipulated the situation, and got herself a solid case.

"You... you haven't even given me a chance with him," I sputtered, disbelief wracking my brain as I tried to wrap my mind around what was happening here. "You can't just base my abilities as a father around ten fucking minutes at six in the morning, unprepared and out of my depth."

"No, I can't. But you're one of the richest men in this country and you couldn't even prep for a kid in a week. You have no experience with children. You've never met him. I'm a pediatrician, Damien, and I've been in his life since the moment he was *born*." She turned away from me, angry footsteps heading toward the living room and, I imagined, the door.

"How am I supposed to get the upper leg here when I didn't even know he existed?" I followed her, keeping my words as quiet as I could with Noah listening in from his spot on the couch. He *vroomed* the toy car across the cushions.

Grace stopped before Noah, pressing a kiss into the top of his curly hair. "I've got to go, Noah. I'll come check on you soon, okay? You can call me whenever you want, just ask Dam—your dad."

"Stay," he pouted, his eyes glossing over again as if they were endless puddles. "I don't want you to go." *Oh my god, he doesn't understand. She can't just leave him like this.*

"I know. I'm sorry."

I opened my mouth as I stepped toward them. "Grace—"

"Don't," she snapped. "You'll make it harder than it needs to be."

———

A sniffly, crying preschooler trailing me around my house as I desperately tried to work out what to do with him wasn't how I imagined my Friday morning going.

I had a meeting with the board at ten o'clock, one that I could not miss. We needed to go over what was happening with the lawsuits we were filing against the businesses we'd obtained that had gone bankrupt, and pushing that back at all would look like I was floundering. I needed to come across as strong — but I had a five-year-old with a toy car and nothing else asking me questions I didn't know the answer to every three seconds, and no one to watch him.

"Please, Caroline," I begged, my cell tucked between my shoulder and my ear as I tried to scramble some eggs for Noah. Grace hadn't even given him breakfast. He'd asked for cheese, but when I offered the only kind I had on hand — Stilton — he'd turned his nose up at the mold and asked for the *thin, square kind*. "I don't have anyone else to watch him. I can't miss this meeting."

"I'm so sorry, I can't," my sister said, the loud sound of something whirring in the background. "I'm not even in California. I thought he wasn't coming until next week?"

"So did I," I sighed.

"I've got to go. Maybe try Mom? I heard she flew back recently, she might still be in town."

"I spoke to Dad yesterday and he said she was flying back out to Hawaii today." I took the pan off the gas burner and set it to the side. "Where are you?"

"Philly. Just about to helicopter out to New York, though. I've got to go."

"All right. Love you."

"Love you."

The line ended and I turned to Noah, his small body just barely peeking up over the breakfast bar from the high-top seat. "Who was that?" he asked, his eyes fixated on his blazing red car as he made it squeak across the black marble countertop.

"Your aunt. Not the one who dropped you off today, but one you haven't met yet," I explained. Every sentence to him felt clunky in my mouth, and I hoped that this would get easier, that this would come more naturally.

His eyes widened as he looked up at me. "I have another aunt?"

Forcing the most convincing grin I could, I grabbed a plate that seemed far too breakable for him from my cabinet. "You sure do. She's great. You'll love her."

I scraped the eggs out onto the plate and slid them across the bar to him, pulling a single fork from the drawer and plopping it into his waiting, too-small hand. "Do you have any smaller ones?" he asked, waving it about like a weapon.

I leaned onto the counter and put my face into my fucking hands. *Another thing to add to the list.* "No."

He shrugged and dove into his food.

"How... how good are you at entertaining yourself?"

"What's that?" he asked through a mouthful of eggs.

118

I took a deep breath in. *You'll get used to this. You will.* "I need to bring you with me to work today," I explained slowly. "I have a very important meeting. If I leave you with... I don't know, a tablet and a phone in my office, can you stay out of trouble?"

His little brows shot up his forehead. "You're going to leave me *alone?*"

Okay. Yep. Horrible idea. "Nope, forget I said that."

He shrugged. "Mom used to take me to work all the time before she died."

The abrupt bluntness caught me off guard, and I almost found myself laughing at it before catching the chuckle in my mouth. He said as if it was yesterday's news — as if it didn't phase him. I knew it had to, knew that he likely went through cycles of being okay with it and being drastically *not* okay with it. But that... that was another thing I needed to get used to.

He got about halfway through his eggs before letting a glob of them fall out of his mouth and back onto the plate. "This is yucky."

"Yeah, I don't like them without cheese either," I chuckled.

"*Yucky* cheese," he clarified. "It smelled wrong."

"You'd like it if you tried it, though," I said.

"Okay." He perked up immediately, dropping his fork and his car. His eyes met mine, expectant, and I couldn't for the life of me figure out what he was doing.

"What?"

"I'll try it."

I eyed him suspiciously as I righted myself to my full height. "You'll try it?"

He nodded. "Mom said *better to try than deny.*"

"Do you even know what that means?" I laughed, grabbing the Stilton from the fridge. I rummaged through the pantry at the side of the kitchen for a box of crackers — better to try it cold on that than make a whole fresh batch of eggs.

"No. But I know it means I need to just try it."

I plucked a cheese knife from the cutlery drawer and cut off a small sliver of the blue cheese, smearing it along the topside of a cracker. I kept it light for him — better to not invade his senses. "Your mom was right about a lot of things," I grinned, passing him the cracker.

He eyed it as if the blue spots would kill him, but one nod from me and he stuffed it in his mouth.

He chewed.

And chewed.

And chewed.

His eyes lit up the moment he swallowed. "You're right," he chirped.

"I'm right?"

"I like it. Another, please?"

For the first time in two hours, I felt slightly okay about the situation. I gave him another.

Chapter 13

Olivia

"Liv, I'm so sorry, I need to ask you for a favor."

I spun in my office chair, coming face to face with a stressed-looking, poorly-dressed Damien and a smaller, curlier-haired version of himself carrying a little toy car. The smaller one waved at me.

Well, that's certainly one way to start the morning.

"What... the fu—"

"Come with me and I'll explain," he said, anxiously checking his watch before grabbing for my hand.

I let him take it, let him lead me out of the cubicles and down the hall toward the elevators. *Those fucking elevators.* I'd only just got to work less than thirty minutes ago, had barely had time to down a coffee from the cafe downstairs, and now instead of being able to get on with my work, I was being thrown into... something.

The elevator doors closed behind us, and a panicked Damien started rambling. "I'm so sorry. I'll pay you extra. Overtime or something. I have a board meeting in twenty and his aunt dropped him off a week early," he explained, motioning toward the wholly unbothered child beside him.

121

"My sister's away and Ethan's a part of the meeting. I have no one else to watch him. It'll be an hour, maybe two at the most. I didn't know what else to do—"

"Calm down," I sighed. "It's fine. I can watch him."

"Thank you. *Thank* you. Just... hang out with him in my office, or take him somewhere, I don't know." He pushed his barely styled hair back as he tried to breathe. "I'd reschedule, but it's about the financials—"

"Take a deep breath. It's okay."

The elevator dinged for his floor and we stepped out, rounding the long corridor. The smaller version of Damien ran ahead, his footsteps heavy on the tile floor, his eyes scanning the names on each private office. He stopped immediately in front of his dad's, looking up at the plastered letters that spelled *Damien M. Blackwood, Owner and CEO* with wide, wondrous eyes.

Damien opened the door for him and the little one bolted in.

I grabbed his wrist before he could follow, checking down the hall for any prying eyes. It was completely empty this early — no one who had a private office up here worked on any specific schedule.

"I'm sorry," he offered again.

"Stop apologizing. It's okay." I took a deep breath and gave myself a moment to catch up — the kid was dropped off early. Damien was panicking. This was fine, I could help, I could do the right thing. I could be his saving grace for now. "You look like a mess, Damien."

He looked down at himself, and before he could start fidgeting with the mismatched buttons, I let myself reach out to him. I didn't think about it, didn't question it, just *helped*. My fingers brushed against the bare skin of his chest as I unbuttoned and rebutted the ones that were slotted in the wrong holes. I unfastened and retied his tie. I fixed his stupid little pocket square. "It's been a long morning," he offered, and I shook my head.

"It's fine. You said he was dropped off early?"

"She showed up at six," he said quietly, low enough that his son couldn't hear from where he climbed across the wingback chairs inside the office. "She wasn't supposed to come until next Saturday, Liv. I have nothing. *Nothing.*"

"Why did she do that?" I asked. Auto-pilot was taking over, and instinctually, I reached up, fiddling with his hair. He didn't even blink at it.

"I don't know. I think she's upset that her sister didn't give her custody of him. She called my lawyer to change the date last night, and Ethan called me, but I missed it." He took a deep breath, in through his nose and out through his mouth. "I nearly had a fucking heart attack when I opened the door. I wasn't ready. I'm not ready."

"You're doing great," I said, and surprisingly even to myself, I meant it. "I'm sorry she caught you off guard like that."

"She wants custody," he breathed. "She's going to file for it."

"Okay, Damien, you've got to calm down," I urged, placing my hands on either side of his suit jacket. "I don't mean to belittle that because that is horrifying and I'm so sorry, but you've got a meeting. Have you reviewed anything for it?"

"No," he croaked. "I'm screwed."

I looked up at him. He looked better than he did before I'd fixed him — a lot better. But not nearly his normal, well-groomed, calm self. It was harrowing seeing him like this, seeing him panicked and stressed and overwhelmed to the point of almost breaking.

It made my chest ache for him, made me want to do what I could to fix it.

"You're not screwed," I said. "I've got him, okay? I'll watch him for however long you need, just make sure my manager knows that you've asked me to do, uh, something, I guess. I'll handle this so you can handle that. You've got, what, fifteen minutes? Ten? Use that to go over what you need to go over."

He nodded. "Thank you."

"Is there anything I need to know?"

He glanced into his office nervously, checking up on the little guy. "He's five. His name is Noah, if you forgot. He's pretty calm as far as I can tell, but I've only known him for... fuck, three hours? He might talk about his mom being dead but he seems very unperturbed by the whole thing, but the internet says that can flip-flop, so be careful with that. Otherwise... you know about as much as I do."

I nodded. "Five. Noah. Calm. Dead mom. Got it."

He cracked a grin, and finally, he looked a little more normal. "I owe you, princess."

"You do."

In a fleeting second of what was likely the leftover adrenaline fueling him, he took my face in his hands, pressing his lips to the center of my forehead. I froze. "Thank you," he said.

Leaving me there, stuck in position with far too many thoughts racing through my mind, he stuck his head into his office and called out a quick *goodbye* to Noah before disappearing down the hall.

. . .

Most of my experience with children came from my brief stint of babysitting when I turned twelve, and my experience being a child, so I didn't have much to go on. But going for ice cream seemed like the best idea, and meant I wouldn't need to worry about someone coming into Damien's office unannounced and asking questions.

I hadn't been expecting *Noah's* never-ending stream of questions, though.

"How old are you?" he asked, his fist gripping the bottom of his ice cream cone, liquid sugar dripping over his fingers.

"Twenty-four."

"That's *old*. How old is Damien?"

It shouldn't have weirded me out that he was calling him by his first name, but in fairness, the kid barely knew him. "Forty-five, I'm pretty sure."

His mouth popped open into a circle. "That's like, really, *really* old," he said. His free, not-sticky hand gripped mine as we crossed the road, the high-rise office in sight. His fingers twitched as I held them, his eyes focusing in on our joined hands. "That's... nine."

"Nine?" I glanced down at him, making sure his ice cream wasn't leaning too far to fall off onto the busy sidewalk.

"Yeah. My age nine times."

Damien said he was five, right? Five times nine... Math wasn't my strongest subject by any means, but my god, the kid was right. Was that normal? "You know multiplication?"

He nodded. "Mmhmm. Mom taught me my times tables before she died."

125

Well, there was the dead-mom-thing Damien said to look out for.

"Where's Damien?"

"In a meeting," I said, scanning my keycard at the side staff entrance. I hoped that if we came in through there and not the main entrance, we'd avoid some of the looks we'd gotten on our way out. "He should be out soon."

"What kind of meeting?"

"A board meeting. They're really important."

"Have you ever been to a meeting?"

I shook my head as I ushered him toward the elevator. "Not one like that."

"I wonder if I'll ever go to a meeting." His head cocked as he watched himself in the reflective surface of the elevator, his ice cream still dripping, splattering his shoe. He'd barely touched it.

In my head, I'd imagined this going a lot worse than it did. But the kid was insanely calm about everything, and although he'd been ever so slightly rambunctious when we'd stopped off at the park briefly and he chased a pigeon, I couldn't help but wonder if dealing with the death of his mother and the overwhelming shift of gaining a new parent and leaving behind everything else had matured him prematurely.

My brother had gone through something similar when one of his friends broke his neck falling off a bike in front of him. It was as though he was someone new, someone intensely mature and reliable, overnight.

"You know, for being thrust into a whole new life and a weird situation, you're handling it really well for a five-year-old," I said.

"Thanks." He full-on *bit* the top of his ice cream, stuffing so much into his mouth that his cheeks blew up like a chipmunk. *Okay. Maybe not wildly mature.* "Is Damien nice?"

"What do you mean?"

"He was nice to me this morning, but he wasn't very nice to Auntie Grace. I don't want him to not be nice to me."

I took a deep breath and dropped down to his level, watching in the corner of my eye as the number on the elevator rose. "Your dad is..." *He doesn't need to know about my situation with Damien.* "He'll be so nice to you, Noah. He just didn't know you were coming this morning, that's all. It caught him off guard, you know? Surprised him. He was only upset with your aunt because he didn't have enough time to get the house all ready for you. He wanted it to be perfect when you came."

The elevator dinged one floor below the one I'd pressed. The doors opened, and there was Damien, his eyes fixed on something far to his right as he called out an overtly poised goodbye to someone I couldn't see. But then he looked at me, squatting on the ground in front of his child, and everything about him softened.

"Speak of the devil," I chuckled.

Noah's eyes flicked between me and Damien. "Huh? What does that mean?"

I shook my head as I stood up. "Nothing. Just a turn of phrase for when someone you were just speaking about shows up."

"Are you saying that he's the devil?"

"She better not be," Damien said, stepping across the threshold and letting the doors close behind him. "Mint chocolate chip, huh? Good choice."

Noah held up the half-eaten scoop on the disintegrating cone with pride.

. . .

———

"Did you know he can do multiplication?" I asked, keeping my voice down as I leaned against the edge of Damien's desk. Noah sat on the leather sofa on the other side of the office, a tablet in front of his face as he tapped aimlessly at the screen.

Damien's brows knit as he looked down at me. "Is that normal?"

"No clue. I wasn't expecting it, though. I told him you were forty-five and after a few seconds, he said that was nine times more than him." I looked across the office at Noah, studying him. Part of me wondered if Damien even needed to worry about him adjusting — but I figured the breakdown would come at some point, along with the inevitable questions of why his life was changing so drastically.

"Add that to the list of things I need to google," Damien chuckled. "Listen, I know I've said it a million times already, but—"

"You don't need to thank me again."

"I know. But I'm going to. So, thank you," he said. "I wouldn't have been able to make it through that without your help."

"It's fine," I insisted, pushing off the desk. "Anytime."

"That's, uh…" He swallowed, his eyes shifting nervously from his son to me. "That's something I wanted to speak to you about, actually."

"What?"

128

"*Anytime.*"

A sound played from Noah's tablet and an excited *yes!* stole our attention for half of a second.

"I don't know what you mean," I said, turning back to him.

He sucked his teeth, the gears in his head visibly turning. "Is there any chance you'd be able to help me out with this until I can figure out what I'm doing in terms of childcare?"

I narrowed my gaze at him. "I mean... I can help where I can, but I do have a *job*, Damien."

"I'll clear it with your manager," he offered. "I'll pay you double your salary for every second you're at work or helping with him. More than that, if you want."

That was... excessive. A lot. More than I'd expected when I'd agreed to watch him for a couple of hours. It wasn't like I had kids of my own or was exceptionally good with them — it didn't make *sense*. "Why me?"

He chewed his lip as he watched me. "I don't have that many people in my life, Liv. My sister works more than the average person, but she can help out occasionally. Ethan can too, but he's not exactly the most reliable person in the world, and he's working day and night on the annulment and the four lawsuits the business is having to file. And my parents live in Hawaii," he sighed. The more he spoke, the more that stress from this morning filtered back in. "It wouldn't be for long. Just until I can find a good school for him."

I didn't know what to say. I wanted to help, truly, but this felt messy, felt like I was stepping back into a situation I didn't belong in *again*, a situation he'd made it clear already that he didn't want me involved with. "But you wanted me out of the picture."

He winced. Genuinely, physically winced. "I know. And I know it's not fair of me to ask this of you after that."

I took a deep breath. I wasn't exactly against the idea, but more time around him wasn't ideal for either of us, not after what seemed to *keep* happening when we were around each other. "What kind of help are you expecting?"

"Watching him during the day when I can't," he said. "I can get you set up to work remotely. We can tag team it when we both need to be here. I sometimes work in the evenings, as well, so I'll need some help there, too."

Jesus. "Damien, as much as I want to help, my apartment isn't exactly set up to have a kid in it, even if he's well-behaved. It's cramped and I wouldn't be able to focus if I was working from home—"

"Watch him at my place," he said. His eyes met mine, and there was a vulnerability to them, a plea that was hard to back down from. "You can work there, too. I can set it all up there so you wouldn't need to haul your stuff back and forth."

"That's—"

"I know you don't have a car," he added, and a burst of shame bubbled up in my chest. I didn't technically need one here, not with public transport, but it felt like a dig even if he didn't mean it as one. "I'll have my driver pick you up and take you home. I'll make sure someone's on standby if there's an emergency. I can hire whatever you need."

"But not a nanny?"

His mouth formed a hard line. "I'd rather not hire someone hastily to watch him. Background checks and all that."

I took a deep breath, in through my nose, out through my mouth like he had been doing this morning.

"Please, Liv. *Please.*"

"That's a lot of back and forth—"

"Then move in."

I locked eyes with him, expecting to find a hint of humor in them, a nudge that told me he was joking. But I found nothing but steady sincerity. "You saying that feels a lot like the first time you asked me to marry you in Vegas."

His lips formed a hard line for a moment as my quiet statement hung heavy in the air between us. "I know."

"And you wanted me out of your life as much as possible days ago."

"I know that, too."

"This is a massive one-eighty," I added.

"I'll make it worth your while as I possibly can," he offered. "You want more than double pay? Fine. Triple. Quadruple. Name your price. I'll pay for your rent while you stay with me. I'll buy you a fucking car. I'll... I don't know, Liv, I'll pay off your student loans or something. Just, *please*, help me with this. As my employee, as my wife, as my *friend*, just... please?"

That crease along his forehead came back tenfold, and even without the extravagant offers that tempted me, my chest ached for him. He was desperate, that much was clear, and he had far too much on his plate — and my people-pleasing tendencies were rearing their fucking head.

Maybe I could keep to myself in his house. It was big enough for that.

"You'd genuinely pay off my student loans?"

"*Yes.*"

"You can't be serious," I breathed.

He took a step toward me. "I'll pay them *today*."

"I owe, like, fifty-eight grand." I blinked up at him. The idea sounded impossible, improbable, far too good to be true. Especially when I was considering taking his offer *without* that. "You said Blackwood's having financial troubles."

"That's the company. Not me personally," he explained. "I'll pay it."

I shook my head, searching for the right words, the ones that evaded my tongue. They swelled in the back of my throat, catching behind my teeth, that angry part of me that hated myself for what we'd done nights ago telling me to keep this to myself. *Don't do it. You know what will happen. You know how this will end.* "I'll do it, Damien, but you don't need to do that."

Chapter 14

Damien

I took the rest of the afternoon off. Everything else was able to be put on the back burner, and the moment after Olivia had left my office, I'd written out a check for sixty grand, placed it into an envelope with her name on it for Ethan to deliver, and left out the front doors with Noah by my side.

"Where are we going?" Noah asked, slipping into the backseat of my driver's car with the work tablet I'd given him and his toy car clutched in his hands.

"Shopping," I grinned, ducking in behind him and shutting the car door behind me. He pouted as he shimmied up into the car seat I'd strapped him into this morning — the same one that caused me to be ten minutes later than I was expecting because I had to arrange for it last minute.

"I don't like shopping," he groaned, his head falling back against the little cushion as I fumbled with the straps. *Have they changed since this morning? Surely they didn't. Where the fuck does this one go?*

"This will be *fun* shopping."

He eyed me, his excitement lingering just beneath the surface. "Toy shopping?"

"You can absolutely get some toys," I chuckled. I finally secured the last strap, not giving two shits about the honking car behind ours. "And anything else you want."

His eyes went wide as saucers as I sat back in my seat and gave the go-ahead to Harry. Within seconds, we were moving. "Can I get a stuffed animal?"

I raised a single brow. "Of course."

"What about a Lego set?"

"Yep."

He made it so easy to tell when he was thinking hard about something. His face scrunched up, his little finger tapping against his chin as if he'd learned it from television. "What about... one of those little robots that you can play with?"

I had no idea what he was talking about. "If they have it at the store, yes."

He squealed as he kicked his legs out, the tablet dropping onto the seat between us. "You are *so cool*. Can I get a horse?"

I snorted. "Like a real-life horse?"

He nodded ferociously.

"Uh, I don't think they'll have that at the store and I don't really have the space for a horse at my house. But if you want a horse, Noah, we can look into getting you a horse. We'd just have to stable it outside the city," I explained, but somewhere in my words he started losing his mind, the excitement riling him up.

"Oh my *GOSH*. A horse. A horse!" He giggled, flopping back dramatically as if the idea alone was enough to destroy him. "You're the *best*. Mom never would have got me a horse."

134

Oh.

That wasn't what I wanted him thinking about at *all*.

"Noah," I gulped. I wrapped my hand around his little arm, getting his attention fully from his racing mind thinking about everything I'd buy him. "Listen to me real quick, okay?"

Wide blue eyes met mine, still poised for the next exciting thing I would say. *First real parenting moment. Shit.*

"I don't want you to compare me to your mother," I said slowly, and the excitement drained from him. "Yes, I can buy you the things you want. And I'm sure your mom would have done the same for you if she could have."

His head tilted to the side. "Why couldn't she? You can."

I should have considered that this conversation was a possibility if I started openly buying him things. I wanted to chalk it up to not having the time to play every potential situation in my head before his arrival — but I knew damn well that this was just my blind spots coming back to bite me in the ass. "Your mom didn't have as much money as I do," I said, hating the words. "And that isn't because she didn't want to. It's not a bad thing to not be able to spend as much on you as I can."

"I don't get it," he pouted. "If she needed more money and you *have* more money, why didn't you give her some?"

We pulled into the parking lot of the first store I'd marked down for Harry — a children's furniture store. I still needed to cancel the orders I'd placed online, but I'd get to it after this. "Because I didn't know she needed it," I sighed. "I didn't know you *existed*. If I had, I would have given her anything she needed. For both of you."

His little fingers went to work on the straps, unbuckling

each one. *Is he supposed to know how to do that?* "Why didn't you know?" he asked.

I pursed my lips. If I had an answer to that question, I probably wouldn't have told him regardless. But I didn't. I had no idea why Marissa never told me about him, especially when she knew he was mine. She knew what I would have done for them despite what she'd done to me.

She knew I would have helped them however I could. She must have known.

"I wish I knew, Noah."

———

Noah sat curled up next to me on the sofa, his tablet on silent as he played some kind of game where you had to flip burgers and assemble them for customers. The front door and back double doors were wide open for the people who carried item after item through them, hauling giant boxes up the stairs and depositing them in the room Noah had chosen for himself. Last-minute-movers disassembled the plain guest bed that had once occupied the space, while others assembled the new bits of furniture we'd picked out together.

It was barely six in the evening, and I was *exhausted*.

My phone buzzed in my pocket, the one he was leaning against, and on instinct he moved to let me reach for it, his eyes still locked and loaded on his game.

Olivia: I can't accept the money.

Olivia: I'm not cashing the check.

"Who's that?" Noah asked, not breaking eye contact

with the screen for a split second. The burger he made was at least twelve layers high.

"Olivia," I sighed. "The one who took you for ice cream earlier."

I typed out a reply. *You don't have to. Just keep it in case you need it.*

"I like her," he chirped.

"That's great news," I chuckled. "She's moving in tomorrow."

His mouth opened in a circle as he finally broke eye contact from the game, wide eyes meeting mine. "She's moving in *here?* With us?"

I nodded. Another buzz from my phone.

Olivia: I can't do that. It's not mine. It's too much money.

"She'll be watching after you when I'm at work," I explained, trying to keep my mind in two places while I replied to her. *Call it a bonus, then. For the proposal you wrote and the fantastic ideas you have.*

"Wait," Noah said. His burger toppled in the game and he set the tablet down between us, shuffling his little body to face me. "Is she going to be my new mom?"

My phone buzzed, but I couldn't bring myself to look at it. I was far too taken aback by the insane question my *son* had just asked me. Yes, Olivia was technically my wife. Yes, I was attracted to her — of course I was. But that... now wasn't the time, the place, the scenario to consider it. I couldn't even let that thought wander around my head for fear that it would seat itself somewhere. "What?"

"What?" he parroted.

"She's... she'll be... uh, like a nanny. Do you know what a nanny is?"

He shook his head.

"Okay, she'll be like a babysitter that lives with us," I faltered, words escaping me from the sheer bluntness of his line of questioning.

Noah's eyes narrowed. "So, a mom."

"You have a mom," I countered.

"My mom is dead. Olivia is alive. Plus! Plus, I have a friend, his name's Olly. He's really cool and he has this awesome scooter. It's, like, bright blue. But he has *two* moms." He held out two fingers as if it proved much of a point. "I could have two moms, maybe."

"We really need to discuss how blasé you are about your mother passing away," I mumbled, sinking into the sofa a little more as I unlocked my phone again.

"What does that word mean?"

"Blasé? It means... it means that your mother's passing is a serious thing, and it's not something to be so... relaxed about," I sighed. "But I understand that you don't fully understand that yet."

His head tilted again, as if he were a puppy and I'd said something that he didn't quite catch.

"Noah," I said, placing my hand gently on his shoulder. "If you ever want to speak about your mom, you're more than welcome to come to me. I want you to know that."

He shrugged. "Okay."

I let myself drift back to the texts with Olivia as he reached for the tablet again.

Olivia: :(but that means I'll have to pay taxes on it.

I chuckled as I wrote out my reply. *Then cash the damn check, princess.*

Chapter 15

Olivia

I stood on the front steps of Damien's house, the cold evening air biting through my thin coat. I tucked my fingers into the sleeves and wrapped them around the handle of my suitcase, the soft glow from the downstairs windows just enough to see in the low light of the evening. Each second felt like an eternity as I waited for him to open the door, my heart pounding with a mix of anticipation and nervousness.

I didn't even realize I'd been holding my breath until the door swung open and I lost the air in my lungs.

He stood there in a thin white t-shirt that clung to him like a second skin, a pair of flannel pajama bottoms hanging low on his hips. I just could barely make out the V of muscle that acted like a stupid fucking arrow. My saving grace came only in the looseness of his pants.

"Did you have to wear that?" I asked.

He snorted. "Are you planning to comment on my attire by way of greeting *every* time you come to my house?"

He took my suitcase from my grasp and opened the

door further, motioning me through. "I mean, I wasn't planning to," I grumbled.

I shut the door behind me, taking the moment to study the amount of high-tech locks that were in place on it. I'd probably need to learn how each one worked if I stood any chance of getting out one of the doors here at some point.

But I had tomorrow to learn the ropes of the house before Damien went back to work on Monday, and I'd be here, with Noah, working from... working remotely.

"Noah's asleep," he said, tilting his chin up the stairs as he carried my bag to the foot of them. "I'll bring your bag up to your room. I think I've mastered the whole *not waking him up* thing."

"After one night?" I laughed.

He grinned at me and nodded. I watched as he carefully trudged up the stairs, my intensely heavy bag almost nothing to him, and slid my coat from my shoulders. Might as well make myself at home.

I kicked off my shoes, grateful that I'd chosen to wear joggers instead of tight slacks this evening, and wandered through the massive living room to where I knew the kitchen was. I knew better than to get myself a glass of wine — even though I wanted one. Even though it would help with the nerves of just being here after what happened last time.

So, instead, I poured myself a glass of orange juice.

"You know you're welcome to have *anything* from my kitchen, right?"

He stood in the division of the kitchen and the living room, one brow raised as he watched me sip my orange juice. "I figured," I said. "But... you know."

"I get it." He looked toward the double glass doors, the light from the kitchen's wall of windows painting the veranda in warmth despite the chill of the city atmosphere. "We should go over a few things while he's sleeping. Do you want to go outside?"

"It's cold."

"I've got blankets." He stepped past me and padded across the floor to the doors, unlatching one lock at a time with a mixture of his hands and his phone. "I can turn on the fire pit, too."

He swung the doors open and the low hum of the city flooded in, filling the quiet space with life and the sounds of night. The sun was far below the horizon, not a single speck of its warmth in sight — just the faint flicker of stars through the light pollution and the view over the Golden Gate Bridge.

I followed him out, shutting the doors just enough that only a crack remained open. Just in case.

To the right, just on the other side of the living room window and the bottom of the staircase, was a plush, rounded outdoor sofa, and a wide electric fire pit in front of it. One flick of a switch from Damien and it roared to life, warming the air around it that was encased by a pristinely trimmed hedgerow on the backside.

Despite my better judgment, I sat down beside him.

He passed me a blanket — thick and soft, a plaid green and blue pattern weaved into it. I pulled it over myself and brought my knees to my chest. He didn't bother with one for himself, though, and I couldn't help but let my eyes wander across his chest and the fabric that clung to it.

"I want you to know that I'm well aware this will be awkward as shit," he said.

I loosed a breath as I let my head fall back onto the cushions. "Good. I can't pretend like it isn't."

"I don't expect you to. Even around Noah, you don't need to hide it if you're feeling uncomfortable."

"Thank you," I chuckled. "How was the rest of yesterday with him?"

He stared at the flickering ethanol flame in front of him, one foot on the edge of the pit and the other planted on the ground. "It was good, I think. I'm learning. I took him shopping, mainly so I could get the shit he needed as quickly as possible, but... I kind of offered him whatever he wanted. I thought it was a good idea at the time, you know? Thought that he'd get excited and warm up a little more to me if I bought him things. And he did, but—"

"Don't tell me you tried to buy his love," I deadpanned.

"Not necessarily buy his *love*. I wanted to buy his comfort around me. But you'll be happy to know that it backfired," he said, a little laugh seeping out of him as he mindlessly stole my glass of orange juice and took a sip. "He was excited. Too excited. Started saying that I was the best and that his mom never would have bought him that much stuff."

His finger scrubbed along the lip of the glass, and the more I watched him do it, the more I realized it was an anxious tick. "Was his mom not as well off as you?"

He shook his head as he took another sip. *I should have grabbed another glass.* "No. Last I heard she was working as a manager at the airport. She wasn't broke, but... she probably wouldn't have been able to buy him anything he wanted. He picked up on that."

I pulled the blanket higher up around my chest. It was warmer in front of the fire pit than it had been outside his front door, but there was still an edge of discomfort. "How'd you handle that?"

Sharp blue eyes, reflecting the orange and yellow hues

of the fire, clashed with mine for a fragment of a second. "I told him that just because I was able to purchase things for him, that didn't default me as the better parent, especially when she'd been there with him from the day he was born and I hadn't. I don't think he quite understood."

I pursed my lips as I watched him study the fire, wondering if he'd find answers there that I couldn't provide. "He's only five," I countered. "It's okay if he doesn't understand."

"I just don't want him to convince himself that I'm the better parent when he's only known me for a day," he sighed. "Because I'm not. I'm not the better parent, Liv, and his mom doesn't deserve for him to see me that way. I'm doing this blindly and erratically, but that's not what he sees."

I reached out to him, just barely touching his shoulder with the back of my fingers. "I think it's better that he doesn't see how hard this is for you," I said. "Imagine how he'd feel if he knew that it was this stressful for you. Would you want that?"

His jaw hardened as he slowly turned his gaze toward me. "No. I wouldn't want him to know."

"Then you're doing the right thing."

We fell into silence for a moment, just the crack of the fire and the distant sound of cars over the hedgerows. He leaned back into the sofa, close enough to touch if I wanted to, but far enough that it wasn't the most uncomfortable thing in the world. I watched him, watched as the light from the fire pit flickered across his face, watched as he anxiously checked through the window every thirty or so seconds to make sure that Noah hadn't come down the stairs. If he didn't already have flecks of grays through his hair, he'd absolutely have sprouted some in the last few days.

"I told him you'd be staying with us for a little bit," he said, the words so quiet I almost didn't catch them. "He's excited. He likes you."

"He barely knows me," I laughed.

Damien shrugged. "He barely knows me, too. You know what he asked me when I told him?"

I shook my head.

"He asked if you were going to be his new mom," he chuckled, passing me back the now half-empty glass of orange juice. Somehow, the sentence didn't phase me — it seemed like a pretty average thing for a five-year-old to question. "And then when I brought up the fact that he *has* a mom, he played the dead-mom card again."

That look came back over him again, the worried one, the stressed one. "If it makes you feel any better, I wouldn't know how to deal with that, either."

"That does. Thank you." His hand wrapped around the base of my knee, squeezing for just a moment, and then as quickly as the embrace had appeared, it was gone. "I spoke to a child psychologist earlier. She said that any reaction to a parent's death is okay. They all process things differently. She said to keep an eye on him and to be prepared for it to potentially all hit at once, so I guess you should be on the lookout for that too."

I swallowed. I wouldn't have any idea how to handle a situation like that if it happened when we were alone — it caught me off guard enough when he'd just casually mentioned it to me.

"If that happens," Damien continued, "I don't expect you to deal with it. I want to make that abundantly clear, Liv. Call me, and I'll drop whatever I'm doing. I'll handle it."

I let out a breath. *Thank fuck.* "Okay. Thank you."

144

He turned to me then, his eyes finally meeting mine fully, even if they did flick over my shoulder to check the window occasionally. "There's something else, too," he sighed. "I know this blurs a lot of lines. And I know that's confusing. I don't want you to think that I'm trying to play mind games, or trying to get you to do things you wouldn't otherwise feel comfortable with. If you want to keep your distance from me here, that's fine. I understand. I've set up an entire office for you on the top floor, and your room is at the opposite end from mine on the second. We can avoid each other if that's what you want."

That's not what I want.

Fuck, it should be what I want.

The sound of a car honking its horn made him jump, and he checked behind me again, watching the base of the stairs. But they stayed clear.

"That's not what I want," I said, letting my thoughts ring clear. Half of them, at least. "But we can't... do what we did. No sex. That would muddy things too much, and like you said, you've got a lot going on. That's my rule. That, and we both sign the papers the moment Ethan has them. I can't stay married to you for longer than necessary. My family will freak out, Damien."

"No sex, sign the papers. I can do that. Promise," he said, nodding to himself. He relaxed again on the sofa, his body turning to face me, his eyes holding focus on mine. Despite the air of uncertainty and the biting awkwardness of our situation, there was still a part of me that felt comfortable under his gaze, even with him so close. So close I could reach out and touch him with minimal effort. So close I could bring myself into him if I wanted. "If it's any consolation, princess, it's all confusing for me, too."

Princess. He'd apologized the first time he'd used it after

145

that phone call — but somehow it had weaseled its way back into his vernacular. I didn't hate it, though. And that was probably a problem. "I'm glad I'm not the only one," I said, letting out a breathy chuckle.

My breath caught the moment his fingers brushed against the skin of my cheek, pushing a single strand of wavy hair behind my ear. "I have to hold myself back," he breathed, the words so quiet they nearly disappeared in the air between us. "But I find myself not wanting to."

I swallowed around the knot in my throat. I didn't know what to say to that — didn't know if I should agree, if I should let him know he wasn't alone in that, or if I should run for the fucking hills.

His fingers cupped my cheek, the touch so soft, so fucking gentle, that I wouldn't know it was there without the warmth and little crackles of cold from his rings. Blue eyes flicked down to my parted lips before meeting my gaze again, then over my shoulder, then back.

I didn't pull away when he leaned closer.

I didn't pull away when his lips brushed against mine.

An open invitation, begging, tempting, waiting on me.

I placed a single hand against his chest, my fingers twisting in the fabric, and let myself push forward into him.

"Dad?"

Reality slammed back in.

I scrambled from Damien as he did the same, his head twisting toward the door as he put space between us. Noah stood in the open doorway, his blanket fisted in one small hand, clad in his matching pajama set. He scrubbed at his eyes with his free hand.

Damien was up before I could even process what had happened.

"What's up, bud?" he asked, crossing the veranda with

his bare feet before squatting in front of Noah, placing both hands on his shoulders. "Why are you awake?"

"I had a bad dream," Noah said, the little squeak in his voice breaking my heart. I pushed the blanket from my body in case Damien wanted me to do anything.

"Oh, no. Do you... do you want to talk about it?" he asked. I couldn't tell if the small shake in Damien's body was from the cold or the unexpectedness of the situation, but as he took Noah's blanket from his palm and wrapped it around his son's shoulders, I assumed it was the cold.

Noah shook his head.

"Okay. Why don't you get yourself a snack and calm down a bit, and then I can come up with you and read you a story?"

"Yeah," Noah squeaked, wrapping his arms around Damien's neck briefly before he released him and padded back into the kitchen.

Damien stood back to his full height as he grabbed the handle of the door, shutting it behind Noah and giving us a moment without the intrusion. But he didn't turn to look at me — he stared at his hand, his body still shaking, his mind frozen.

"Are you okay?" I asked, pushing myself up from the sofa.

Slowly, he turned to me, his lips parted, his breath catching. "Yeah," he said. "It's just... that's the first time he's called me *dad*."

Chapter 16

Damien

Lucas, eight years old and nearly twice the size of my son, bounced a basketball so hard against the ground that it shot up probably ten or so feet in the air — and somehow expected Noah to catch it.

Noah missed by a long shot.

"I can't believe you moved her in," my sister *tsked*, her head shaking as she passed me a glass of red wine from our spot on the railing of her balcony. The boys played below, two heads of curly hair moving at the speed of lighting. "Actually, scratch that, I can totally believe it."

"I didn't move her in to fuck her," I clarified, rolling my eyes as I knocked back half the glass. "You were in Philly, remember? I needed help watching over Noah. And she agreed to help."

"Does she have *any* childcare experience?"

"No."

The look on Caroline's face as she glared at me told me that I was being an idiot. The joke was on her, though — I was well aware of that. "Dame."

"He likes her," I added. "And she's doing an amazing

148

job. She took him to The Exploratorium the other day while I was at work and he spent the whole night talking about it."

She took a sip of her wine and rested her chin on the palm of her hand, watching with a deadpan expression as Lucas tripped over his foot and slammed into the grass. He picked himself right back up and kept running. *Is that tag they're playing now? Where the hell did the basketball go?* "That's good, I guess. Has he seen his aunt? Marissa's sister?"

I shook my head. "Not since she dropped him off. She hasn't gotten in contact, but I imagine she's knee-deep in paperwork," I sighed. "Did I mention she's decided to try to file for custody of him?"

Caroline's brows shot up her forehead behind the thick red rims of her hyper-modern glasses. "No. You didn't. How do you feel about that?"

"Like I'd rather throw myself off the Golden Gate Bridge than let that happen," I deadpanned. It wasn't even a question in my mind at this point — I fully fucking meant that. "She's horrible, Carrie. I'm sure she's probably nice enough to him, and I get why she's upset, but if she had it her way, I would have never known about him. And I know it's only been... fuck, six days that I've had him, but I can't imagine him not being in my life now. Is that insane?"

She shook her head. "No, that's not insane," she grinned, giving my arm a quick squeeze before going back to her wine. "He's your son. It hits pretty hard and pretty fast."

"Dad!" Noah shouted, his arms waving wildly from the ground below the balcony, a smear of mud on his face. "I caught the ball!"

Every time. Every goddamn time he called me that, it felt like a blow to the chest, a combination of the best possible feeling imaginable mixed with an ache of pain I couldn't quite place. "Good job!" I called back, and he squealed his excitement before focusing back on Lucas. "I'm still not used to that," I said quietly.

"What?"

"Him calling me *dad*."

She grinned. "You don't really get used to it," she explained, refilling her glass and topping mine off. "You just get used to the feeling of it."

I wasn't sure if that was reassuring to my psyche or reaffirming that I'd just keep feeling that stab in my chest for the rest of my life. Somehow it felt like a mixture of both.

"How's the annulment going?"

I shrugged. "Ethan's working on it. I've got enough on my plate to even consider worrying about it."

Caroline's teeth slid across her top teeth, her glasses wiggling on her face as her nose scrunched up. "I'm not sure if you've considered this," she started, inching a little closer to me so she could drop her voice. "But if Grace is going to try to file for custody, it might look better on paper to be married."

I stilled. I hadn't even considered that.

"Is Grace single?"

"According to Ethan, yes. Recently divorced, unsurprisingly."

She nodded, almost to herself, but her eyes flitted up to mine. "Maybe hold off if you can swing it. Just until the custody thing isn't up in the air anymore. You've got the money, the home, the necessities for him, but she's known him his entire life. She's a pediatrician, right? That's got to have some sway. You should use every bit of ammo you can."

Shit. She wasn't wrong — that would absolutely work out better for me if it came to that, and from what Ethan had said about the mound of paperwork he'd already received, it looked like that was the direction we were heading. But Olivia had made it clear that she wanted our marriage annulled the moment it could be...

I wondered if she'd agree to it if it was for Noah's sake. Wondered if she'd give up just a little more for me.

"Hey!" Caroline snapped, her voice switching from calm sister to angry mother. Across the lawn, Lucas was poised with a fist full of mud, his hand cocked and ready to throw at Noah. "Absolutely not! Put it down!"

Noah bolted toward the house as Lucas dropped the mud, and Caroline sighed exasperatedly.

"Being a parent is so much fun," she said, her voice thick with sarcasm.

But I was too engrossed in the message I was writing to Ethan, too caught up in the idea she'd presented me with.

Me: Hold off on filing the papers for the annulment.

Chapter 17

Olivia

A knock on my door just barely pulled me from sleep. The blackout curtains that covered the floor-to-ceiling window of my ridiculously large bedroom blocked out most of the sun, but little flickers of light broke through the edges, warning me that it was only just past sunrise.

Another knock. And then another.

"It's too early!" I called back, shoving my face into the plush, soft pillows I was absolutely never going to live without. I'd steal them when I moved back into my apartment.

The door cracked open and more light filled the room before abruptly darkening again as the door shut. "Liv."

For fuck's sake. *Is this a nightmare?*

"Liv, wake up," Damien said, his voice soft as butter as he came closer.

I pulled the blankets down enough that I could squint through the darkness, his face just barely visible in the low light. "Why are you in my room?"

"Because I'm desperate for my son's approval and you play a pivotal role in that," he chuckled.

I stared at him.

"Too honest?"

"Too honest," I agreed.

"Fine. Because you deserve a vacation, and so do I, and I want to surprise Noah. So get up." He tapped the button on my bedside table that gently brought the lamp to life, filling the room with soft, warm light. He was in pajamas — joggers and... christ, a fucking tank top. *Why do I not deserve relief from him?*

His hand fisted the sheet, and all at once, I was far more awake.

"Please don't," I breathed, gripping as much fabric as I could in my hands, my cheeks heating. I wasn't wearing a single bit of clothing beneath the sheets, and up until this moment, I hadn't considered that I might need to.

The line between his brows deepened for a moment before he realized. "Oh. Oh, shit, sorry," he fumbled, taking a step back from the bed and raising his hands. "You should, uh, get dressed. And pack a bag."

I shook my head and pulled a single arm out of the sheets. "Pass me my shirt," I said, pointing aimlessly in the direction of my abandoned, gigantic sleeping shirt that I'd left somewhere off the side of the bed.

Within a second it was in my hand.

I ducked beneath the covers and pulled the shirt over my head, wiggling until it was situated well enough over my body. He waited silently, his presence almost forgettable, but when I pulled back the sheets and forced myself to sit up, he was still there, still waiting, still expectant.

"Right. Okay," I said to myself, pushing back my mop of hair from my face and feeling far too vulnerable with nothing on my lower half but the bottom of my shirt. "Explain to me exactly what you mean by a *vacation*."

. . .

———

"DISNEYLAND?"

Noah's screeching voice splintered straight through my eardrums, momentarily deafening me and filling my ears with a high-pitched ringing.

I couldn't help but laugh at how cute it was.

"Does that sound like a good idea?" Damien asked, eyes widened at his shrieking son. When he'd pitched it to me, he seemed excited himself, but I could see the worry in his eyes that maybe this wasn't the right choice — that perhaps he was doing what he'd done before when he'd taken Noah shopping, when he'd spoiled the kid rotten in the hopes that it would win his favor.

But this didn't come from a need to make him feel at home, it didn't come from a need to bond with him in unhealthy ways.

It came from a *want* — a want to take a vacation to somewhere he'd never been, and have a new experience with his son. And me, for some reason. But I wasn't about to say no to a trip to Disney.

"*YES!*"

Noah's chest rose and fell rapidly as he gripped the sheets on his far too large bed, his curly brown hair sticking up in all directions, his toy car abandoned beside him, his pajama top slouched at an angle. Damien sat at his feet, halfway up the bed, and from where I stood in the doorway, it was almost like a private moment. Both of their attention focused wholly on each other.

It was hard to believe it had only been two weeks.

"And if you're okay with it," Damien started, shifting a little on the comforter so he could glance back over his shoulder, right at me, "Olivia's coming too."

Noah's bloodcurdling scream ripped through the walls of the house and he freed himself from the sheets, crawled across the short distance, and threw his arms around his dad's neck, practically hanging from him like a baby gorilla. Damien's arm curled around him as he tucked him into his chest, his gaze flicking between me and the boy in his arms.

He looked so... *soft.*

There wasn't a better way to describe it — it was as if every fine wrinkle smoothed, as if the pressure of the world that normally showed in the way his jaw ticked or the way he stood with his shoulders high, had just... settled. As if none of it mattered.

I wasn't sure if the swelling in my chest was from Noah's eccentric excitement or the calm that stemmed from watching the two of them interact. But it made me feel good, for once, to be wanted in whatever form by both of them.

"We'll take my boat down to Long Beach," Damien said, his eyes locking on mine as he spoke to his practically vibrating son. "We should get there by morning and can spend the entire day tomorrow in the park. And as long as Olivia's up for it, we can stay the night and go back again the next day."

I shot Damien a soft smile and nodded once. "I might need to do some work in between, but yeah, we can do that."

He shook his head. "You're not working. I already contacted your manager."

You just hired me as a full-time employee and I've

already taken about half of that time off because of you. I wanted to say it, but I knew what he was doing — he was giving me this time as paid time off. He was giving me far more than the contract had said when I signed it.

I was appreciative, but I couldn't help but feel it was a little unfair to everyone else who worked there who *wasn't* looking after his son, and who *hadn't* slept with him.

When Damien said *boat*, I'd been imagining what any normal, sane human would — an average-sized boat, maybe a speedboat if he was expecting to arrive in time for us to get a hotel and sleep before going to Disney.

I had not imagined the monstrosity in front of me on the dock.

The white and black *boat* had to have been at least ten times my height, towering over us and casting a shadow as my steps grew smaller, slower, until I stopped in stunned silence. I should have assumed — should have known that when he'd *boat*, he'd meant *mega yacht.*

People flitted about the two levels of the ship in stark white uniforms, some with clipboards out and others carrying coolers or cushions. One of them, disappearing into the interior, carried a set of sheets over one shoulder that looked suspiciously like they were covered in the characters from Cars.

Noah rocketed past me at the speed of fucking light, and that coupled with Damien's frantic shouts from somewhere behind me pulled me back to reality instead of standing there speechless.

"Don't run on the dock! Shit, Liv, can you—"

I took off toward him, his short sleeve, white button-up blowing behind him in the breeze, but before I could even reach him, one of the staff who was disembarking locked eyes with me and swooped him up in her arms.

Noah spun, his grin massive as he turned to face us in the stranger's arms. He wasn't even a foot from the ledge, and my fucking heart pounded in my chest, but somewhere behind me Damien was laughing, catching up more and more.

"Thank you, Sarah," he chuckled. He stepped around me, one hand brushing across the small of my back and the other carrying both my bag and his. My breath caught in my throat.

"No problem, Mr. Blackwood. You got him?" she asked, her light brown eyes practically twinkling up at him as Noah playfully tried to escape her arms. Her white staff shirt and short black shorts clung to her body, her blonde hair up in a ponytail and flowing over her back in perfectly manicured curls. She looked about my age.

Something about her angered a piece of me that I was desperately trying to keep quiet.

"I got him," Damien confirmed, reaching out and taking Noah's hand in his. Sarah released him and stepped back onto the ship, disappearing around the corner. "I *told* you not to run on the dock."

"Sorry, Dad. I got excited."

"It's okay. Just be careful."

A man in similar clothing to Sarah collected our bags from Damien's hand. I wasn't sure if the ship being full of staff was a positive or a negative — at least we wouldn't be completely secluded together, but the idea of having people wait on us hand and foot like a miniature cruise was... weird.

The yacht, reflecting the morning sun off its shiny surfaces as it floated easily in the water, must have been at least as long as Damien's house. There was a lower deck at the back, one that was easily accessible from all sides and seemed to be the main point for boarding. The front, slick and black, had one singular balcony along the top edge, coming to a point in the middle like the front of the Titanic.

Don't fucking think about the Titanic, Olivia.

Along the back and sides of the ship, a third balcony wrapped around it, with a large opening at one side and the other closed off. I didn't know a thing about boating besides my short experience on a little engine-powered dinghy my friend had back in high school, and this was so entirely different.

"Do you like it?" Damien asked me, a small life jacket in his hand as he motioned for Noah to hold out his arms.

"The yacht? It's... massive," I breathed.

"Is that a bad thing?"

Noah did a little spin before Damien grabbed him again and started fastening the clips.

"No, I just wasn't expecting it. You said *boat*," I explained.

"I mean I've got a smaller one, but we can't sleep on that, and we probably wouldn't get there in time," he said. He picked up Noah under his armpits, the kid's legs dangling wildly, and plonked him onto the back lowest deck of the yacht. "Noah, go that way and follow Adam through those doors, okay? Don't want you hanging out down here without the railing."

Noah nodded before taking off into the interior cabins.

Damien offered a single hand to me. He wore a white button-up hung loosely over his frame, unbuttoned down to almost the center of his chest, and his slacks, the same color and made of some of the finest, nicest linen I'd seen. Both billowed effortlessly in the ocean breeze, and I almost felt silly wearing the elastic waistband black shorts and slightly too big, white t-shirt he'd loaned me. I hadn't packed anything to bring to his house that was remotely geared for this.

But I took his hand.

"As a heads up," he started, motioning for me to step across the small gap between the dock and the boat, the water sloshing beneath my feet, "there are only two bedrooms on board."

I stepped easily onto the yacht and froze. "Damien—"

"You can have my room," he said calmly. "I'll share the smaller one with Noah. I just didn't want you to panic when you realized."

I blinked at him. "What? I don't need the bigger room."

"Trust me," he grinned. "It's much nicer than the spare."

That doesn't make sense. "Then let me have the spare and share the bigger one with Noah."

He shook his head. "There's plenty of space for me and Noah in the smaller room. Plus, yours has more privacy in case you just want to be on your own for a bit. Take it, Liv. It's yours."

I stepped backward on the lowest deck, the lack of a railing stressing me out with the rocking of the boat, and watched as Damien stepped across the divide easily. I wanted to fight back on it, wanted to ensure that he and Noah would have the best time they possibly could, but he didn't seem like the kind to budge on something like this.

. . .

———

It was odd how little the unmatched speed of the boat affected my stability on it.

I couldn't remember exactly how fast Damien said we were going, but the goal was to travel quickly throughout the day so we could keep the speed lower while we slept. The wind and the quickness of the water passing below us were the only real giveaway. It didn't feel like I was being rocked around, or like I couldn't walk from point A to point B easily.

Noah spent most of the day playing in the pool — the one I hadn't noticed from the ground, situated at the very back of the middle deck. Damien had watched him like a hawk, nervous that he'd fling himself over the glass edge of it and inevitably fall onto the lower deck without the railing, and then into the waters below. I'd been nervous about it, too, and had found it increasingly difficult to keep my attention on the book in my lap.

Around six in the evening, one of the staff delivered a plate of chicken nuggets and a side of raw carrots for Noah's dinner. Damien asked me to watch him, that same usual pleading look on his face despite that literally being a part of my job now, before stifling himself indoors to make some calls.

An hour later Damien returned, the crease between his brows deeper and his shoulders stiff. He picked up an exhausted, sleeping Noah from the lounger beside me. "Dinner is in thirty," he said quietly, his eyes meeting mine.

"You're welcome to eat wherever you'd like. But I'd prefer it if you joined me."

I closed my book. I'd *finally* had the chance to get to the most interesting part with Noah zonked out beside me, but when it was Damien interrupting me, when he looked the way he did in his stupid fucking linens and the breeze whipping his hair, I didn't care. "Where are you eating?"

———

Pulling my legs up cross-legged onto the plush white cushion, I sat at the pristinely polished table at the back of the top deck, trying not to pay too much attention to the wine in the ice bucket or the setting sun beside me as I waited for Damien to get back.

Sarah, the woman who had caught Noah on the dock this morning, dropped off a plate of cocktail shrimp and various dipping sauces. I nervously picked at them, my eyes lingering on the only entrance to the secluded little space. This wouldn't be the first time we'd eaten together since I temporarily moved in, but it was exactly a *normal* thing, either.

I didn't know what to expect from him. He'd looked stressed when he'd come back after his phone calls, but now that Noah was asleep and less of a danger to himself, there had to be a bit of calm. I almost craved it — a small sense of normalcy despite the intensely abnormal thing we were doing.

Damien's eyes were glued to the watch around his wrist

as he stepped through the entryway, but quicker than he'd appeared, he looked at me instead. And he froze.

"Hey," he said, the word so quiet it almost didn't reach me over the sound of the wind and the engine. Glass walls connected the sides of the deck to the roof around us, and only the very back where I sat now had open walls looking over the back of the boat. My hair, tied up in a bun with little waves falling around my cheeks, blew gently in the small breeze, but he was unaffected that far in.

"Hi."

He swallowed as he came back to life, stepping across the sleek wooden floor and stopping at the edge of the table. "You look lovely."

I snorted as I glanced down at myself. The too-big shirt, the elastic shorts, the rattiest pair of flip-flops I owned... I did not look like I belonged on a mega yacht. I'd barely had time to put on mascara before we'd left this morning. "I look exactly the same as I did twenty minutes ago."

"You don't," he said, shaking his head as he slid onto the cushions that wrapped the length of the table. He shimmied down until he was beside me, close enough to reach out and touch, but far enough that it wouldn't feel like an imposition. He'd seemed to have mastered that. "I don't know what it is. Maybe it's because Noah's down, maybe it's because you got to the good part in your book."

I narrowed my gaze at him.

"You think it wasn't obvious?" he laughed. "Your legs were crossing when I came back out. Your lip was between your teeth. What's in that thing, anyway?"

My cheeks heated as I tore my gaze from him. There was *no* way I was that obvious. Surely.

"I'm not judging you, for what it's worth," he chuckled. "It's good to give your mind a break occasionally."

I leaned back and pulled my knees up to my chest as I popped another cocktail shrimp into my mouth. "You say that like I'm always turned on."

Wide blue eyes met mine so quickly that it made me pause.

Oh fuck. Oh no. Wrong word. "I—I meant switched on. *Switched* on. Like with work." Even the passing breeze wasn't enough to cool the intensity of the heat in my face.

He brushed it off as if it hadn't even happened, clearing his throat and proceeding. "Well, you are, really. When you've not been focusing on Noah, you've been burying yourself in work. I think you needed this just as much as I did."

I swallowed the shrimp around the lump in my throat. "Yeah. Maybe."

Damien leaned forward and plucked the bottle of wine from the ice bucket. He fiddled with the wiring around the cork, expertly releasing each one, and I couldn't stop myself from watching, couldn't stop myself from taking in the way his tendons in the back of his hand flexed with each little movement, couldn't stop myself from imagining them doing what I'd read about minutes ago.

"Are you, uh, not worried about Noah getting up?" I asked, the words far breathier than I'd intended.

His gaze flicked to mine, and god fucking dammit, I could tell by the way he looked at me that he knew exactly what was running through my head. "Not now," he said calmly. "I've stationed one of the staff outside his door so he can't just get out and fling himself off the deck. And I'll be there to watch him overnight."

"You seemed stressed watching him earlier."

"So did you, Liv."

The muscles beside my lips twitched as a smile tugged

at them. "Well, yeah. I didn't want him to get himself killed."

Damien's breathy chuckle filled the air between us just as the *pop* from the cork freed the wine — oh, that wasn't wine. That was champagne. I stood no chance. "You'd think five year old's were suicidal or something," he grinned, pouring out two chutes worth for both of us. "Didn't think I'd be as worried as I've been. And then the fucking phone call."

"Do you want to talk about it?" I asked, plucking another shrimp from the tray and shoving it in my mouth. "You looked more stressed after that than I've seen you in days."

His lips pressed into a thin line as he reached for a shrimp himself, picking up the glass of champagne with his free hand. "It was Ethan," he said. "There are some issues with the lawsuits we're filing. That's all."

"You say that like it isn't something you should be allowed to stress about. You're allowed to be stressed, Damien. Anyone would be in your shoes," I told him, my eyes catching on Sarah as she stepped through the entryway with two hands expertly balancing trays of food.

He was quiet as she placed the food down. Whole lobster, scallops, seared rounds of steak, baked potatoes, thinly sliced sashimi, cooked broccoli, asparagus, medley after medley of grilled vegetables... It was far too much food for the two of us. But it looked *fantastic*. Far better than Noah's chicken nuggets.

Sarah slid a loaf of sliced soft bread into the center of the table, a mound of seasoned butter beside it, and despite the grin she flashed us both, she lingered on Damien. Her eyes held his for longer than I expected, and when she spun, her ponytail flicked and bobbed as she walked to the door, shutting it behind her.

"I—"

"Have you had sex with her?"

Wild blue eyes collided with mine faster than lightning as he set his glass on the table. It took a moment for my brain to catch up with my mouth, and the moment it did, I wished I could go back to that blissful ignorance where I hadn't registered what I'd said, where I hadn't even *asked* it, where I hadn't made it abundantly clear how I'd feel about that scenario.

"No," he said curtly. "I haven't."

"I'm sorry," I breathed. "I didn't mean—"

"You did."

"I..." I swallowed, my mouth going as dry as the Sonora Desert. He was right. I did mean what I said. "I'm sorry. I shouldn't have said that. I shouldn't have *asked* that."

"It's fine," he said. But it wasn't.

"I should, uh, I should eat in my room. Maybe this wasn't a good idea." I put my knees down, unable to even look him in the eyes, and shifted myself along the soft leather toward the exit of the curved, wrap-around seat.

Something warm and large wrapped around the smallest part of my wrist, stopping me in my tracks. "Don't," Damien said, the word just a little guttural. "I wanted you to have dinner with me. I still do."

"You don't," I gulped, looking over my shoulder toward him. I expected a stern expression, something that showed his irritation and his maturity, but that's not what I found. Instead, his gaze lingered on me softly, dragging down over my too-large shirt and back up to the messy bun atop my head, all hard lines smoothed out except the one between his brows.

"Please," he rasped. "I don't care about what you asked or what you *think* I want. I want you to stay. I want to... fuck, Liv, I just want to spend some time with you. Is that too much? Is that crossing a line?"

His fingers tightened around my wrist. The knot in my throat only grew wider. I didn't know what to say to him, didn't know whether to trust my gut or the screaming woman inside my head that I tried to keep locked away, the one that wanted me to stay, wanted me to seat myself on his lap, wanted me to fling myself at him like a lost puppy. I'd chained her up, but my god, she was putting up a fight.

"Liv," he pleaded.

"Okay," I sighed, sitting on the soft cushion again and shifting back toward him. I left a little more space than he had, but he let go of me nonetheless.

We picked at the food in silence, nothing but the scraping of knives and forks against porcelain, the rattling engine, and the whipping wind to fill the quiet, dead space. Everything tasted incredible, far better than any restaurant I'd been to, far better than what I'd cooked at his home for myself in the dead of night when I moment for myself. It was nicer than the spaghetti he'd made for us four nights ago at ten in the evening, but the lighthearted conversation we'd had then was everything in comparison to the sticky silence we had now.

"You asked about Marissa," he said, cutting through the emptiness as I pushed a forkful of lobster between my teeth.

Marissa? I thought her name was Sarah.

"The other night. You said something like, *I wish I knew what his mom was like so I knew what Noah was missing.* I didn't answer you." He sipped at his champagne as he leaned back against the padded rear of the seat, one arm outstretched along the edge, his hand just an inch from my back. My mind spun — Marissa was Noah's mom. "Do you still want to know?"

I swallowed the lump of lobster meat and turned toward him. "Only if you want to speak about her. All I know is she's, uh, passed."

He nodded. "Yeah, early last month. I hadn't spoken to her in over five years," Damien said, plucking my glass of champagne from the table and passing it to me. I hadn't touched it yet — I'd been too worried about what it would do to me around him. But if he was going to speak about her...

I took it, gratefully.

"But before that, before we stopped speaking and before Noah existed, we were together. For two and a half years, we were serious." His head tilted back toward the harsh oranges and pinks that littered the sky, the sun just barely visible over the horizon. He looked almost other-worldly as the colors painted him, and all I could do was watch — watch, and wait. "I wanted to marry her. Bought a ring and everything. I was convinced she was the person I'd been waiting my entire life to meet."

I took a sip of my champagne, craving something to do, something to distract myself from the heaviness of his words. I couldn't admit to myself that I didn't like hearing about this — not when that was an admission to other things. I couldn't even admit that it was a relief to hear that he was capable of an actual relationship.

"I was wrong," he rasped, tilting his head back up, his eyes meeting mine in a flash of blue amongst the pinks and oranges. "For a lot of reasons, I was wrong, but overwhelmingly because she wasn't... faithful. There was someone else in the picture, someone she'd met fairly recently toward the end of our relationship, and she didn't tell me until I proposed. I'd gone through the motions of it all. I'd dropped to one knee. I'd expected an enthusiastic yes, I'd told my friends, my family. I couldn't... I couldn't keep it in. But I'd received a look of genuine fucking horror and a blubbered apology."

Oh, *god*.

"I had a speech ready. I had everything planned. But it went to shit," he sighed. "And I've had almost six years to come to terms with it and get over it, and I have, but with Noah coming into the picture and everything hitting me in the face once again, it's felt like I've been reliving it. Like she deceived me again, because she *did*. I don't for one second that she was a good mom to Noah. I know exactly how she would have been with him — how she was with any child we met, how she planned to be for the kids we would have. She loved him. She wanted him to have the best possible opportunities in life, even if it meant the shit with Grace, even if it meant thrusting him upon me and owning up to her secrets."

He downed the last of his glass of champagne before pouring himself another. I didn't know if there was something I could say that would make it better — wasn't even sure if there was a reason he was telling me all of this. But if he needed to speak it, I was willing to let him, even if it made my stomach churn.

"I still don't understand why she never told me," he breathed, the words so quiet I almost didn't hear them. "That's the one thing I can't wrap my head around. Maybe she knew back then that she was sick. Maybe she wanted as much time with him as she possibly could have, alone, before she had to leave. Either way, I'll never know, and that fucking *haunts* me."

His hand slid down the cushions, coming to rest gently on the top of my knee. I stilled.

"I'm sorry. I don't know where I was going with this," he mumbled, pushing himself upright and leaning onto the table, one elbow carrying the weight of his face in his hand. He squeezed my knee gently, and all I could think to do was put my hand over it, hold it, and show him in the only way I could that it was *okay*. "You asked about Sarah. And all I could think was, *shit, does she think I'd fuck anything that moves? Does she think I don't have a single bone in my body capable of caring for anyone other than myself and Noah? And I...* I don't know. I don't want you to think that about me. I don't want you to think that I'm some monster that fucked you purely out of a need to perform a conquest—"

"I don't." *I do. I don't. I don't fucking know anymore.* "I don't think that, Damien."

He offered me a half-hearted smile as he released my leg, his hand coming up instead to cup the side of my face. Warmth blossomed from his touch, and I found myself heating, both in my cheeks and elsewhere. "You do, princess. And it's okay that you do. I would too if the tables were turned."

He tucked a stray wave behind my ear and that woman I'd chained in my mind reared her head, screaming, desperately tugging at her restraints.

"For what it's worth," he added, his fingers trailing along the edge of my jaw, the backs of them bushing back over it, "I care about you. In whatever weird form this is where we're married and taking care of my child and tearing it down for good reason, I care about you."

Oh, fuck. The snap of metal, and a single restraint broke in my mind.

"I never wanted to hurt you," he breathed.

I was moving before I could bear to stop myself.

The second and final restraint cracked and broke and I was on him, crawling into his lap, my chest against his, my hands encasing his face in them as I pushed him back against the cushions. His champagne flute shattered against the wood floor as he grasped me in his arms, and all I could do was hold him there, watch him, our lips an inch apart and our eyes locked.

He took it that step further for me.

His mouth met mine, a flurry of sensations wracking my body from nausea to heat, and I could taste the salt air on his lips, could taste the lingering bit of champagne on his tongue. His hand fisted the too-loose fabric of my shirt, twisting it, burying his fingers against my flesh and holding me tightly.

"Fuck," he rasped, and I took that minuscule break between our lips to kiss his jaw, his neck, the curve of his Adam's apple. The scent of roasted almonds, vanilla, and rum invaded my nostrils, and for some reason I couldn't comprehend, it smelled more like *home* than my apartment. "Liv."

The way he said it was like a warning, and I knew what would come after. "Don't," I begged. "Please."

"But you don't want—"

"I do." I popped open button after button on his shirt, dragging my lips along his collarbones, along the top of the muscle that ran beside them. His hand grasped the back of my neck, holding me to him, acting in opposition to his words. "If you do, I do."

"Of course I do," he swallowed. The strain beneath my parted thighs, pressing up against the soft linen of his slacks, confirmed that well before he'd said it. "But we put up boundaries."

Freeing the last button, I pushed his shirt open, revealing the entirety of his heaving chest.

"You were conflicted the last time we crossed your lines," he reminded me. But he didn't stop me as I continued, as my hand reached between us for the button of his pants, as my other trailed along the expanse of his chest, across ribbons of muscle and the tips of his nipples. "We're barely married, Olivia. We're getting an annulment. Yes, things are... different, on my end. And you're with me more than I expected. But I don't know if I can give you what you want out of this."

I don't care. I did. *I don't.*

I swallowed my pride. I pulled my lips from him.

I looked him dead in the eye.

"Until it's over, then," I breathed. "Give me that."

The hand that held my neck rounded to the front, cupping my cheek, holding me in place as he stared directly into me. "What are you saying?"

"Until the annulment is done, you're still my husband, and I'm still your wife."

His thumb swiped across my cheek, his lips parted, his breathing just a little heavy. "Like an expiration date."

I nodded as I freed the button of his pants, my fingers trailing along the top of his boxers. "Yeah."

"Fuck," he grunted. He pulled me to him, pressing his forehead against mine, the swelling beneath my core and between his thighs growing harder. "*Yes.*"

Chapter 18

Damien

The feeling of her sinking onto my cock was something I would never, ever get tired of.

Right fucking there at the table, her shorts lost in the pile of glass on the floor, my shirt that was far too large for her hanging limply around her body. She clutched my shoulders like a vice as she sank, impaling herself, stretching herself far more than she was ready for. I didn't even have lube on me — but she didn't seem to need it. Not with how much she had been leaking across the front of my pants, not with how fucking slick she was as she'd dragged the head of my cock against her slit.

Her face scrunched in pain as she paused, her breathing shaky, half of me inside of her and the other half exposed to the wind chill. Twilight was in full swing behind me, lighting her in soft pinks and blues, and my god, she looked stunning. Anything she did, she looked otherworldly, but tonight, with her lips parted and her hair up, barely a smidgeon of makeup and wearing *my* clothes, she had the power to destroy me.

It felt like she might.

Dragging a hand up her thigh, I slipped it between us, lifting the fabric of the shirt and dipping my fingers into her dampness. I could feel her pulse hammering on her swollen, molten hot clit, and I swirled my digits against it, fighting that sting of pain she was feeling and dampening it.

"Fuck," she whimpered, her forehead falling to mine, her lips just a breath from me. Slowly, gently, her legs met mine, and her warmth enveloped me completely.

I kissed her as she stilled, accommodating me, her walls twitching around my cock. She took every movement of my lips greedily, hastily, needy — god, I wanted nothing more than to stay like this for as long as possible. As long as she'd let me.

"I've only seen this in porn," she mumbled against my lips. "So I'm not entirely sure what I'm doing."

As much as it pained me to release my hold on the back of her neck, I relented, dragging it down along her fabric-covered back before cupping her rear. "I'll show you," I rasped.

She followed the push of my hand, dragging her hips forward against me and the slip of my fingers in a grinding motion, a steady little moan slipping past her lips. I guided her back, angling myself just a little better, feeling the slide of her walls release me little by little before bringing her straight back toward me. The temptation to drop my head onto the cushions, to *feel* her, to give myself a moment to drink her in like the embodiment of perfection that she was, almost got the better of me. But I stayed upright. I watched her.

"Christ," I groaned. "You feel so fucking good, princess."

Her shallow breaths stuttered, her fingers weaving into my hair and tightening around the short strands. The moment I knew she was confident with her movements and didn't need my guidance, I let my hand that wasn't preoccupied with driving her closer to the edge wander.

Slipping beneath the fabric of her shirt, my fingers dragged across the bare skin of her back, following the divot of her spine up, up, up—

No bra. No fucking bra. *All day*.

Fuck.

The temptation to lift her off my cock, flip her around, and force her face down across the table atop the dishes and food so that I could take her, claim her, fuck myself into her over and over until she was shrieking my goddamn name, was nearly overpowering. I dug my nails into her flesh instead, right where her bra *would* have been. I bared my teeth to her.

"Fucking temptress—"

Glass shattered again somewhere behind her.

She stilled in my lap, her ragged breaths filling the space between us with warm air. I stilled the movement of my fingers between her thighs and with one little shift, I looked over her shoulder.

Sarah stood in the doorway, her face pink and her hand clutching a bottle of champagne. Across the floor, broken glass reflected the last little rays of light, along with a discarded black tray and cracked macarons littering the polished wood floor. Liv's heart thundered in her chest, loud enough that I could hear it, hard enough that I could *feel* it against my hand.

"I'm sorry," Sarah fumbled, her eyes frantically darting between me, Olivia, and the mess across the floor. She squatted down, her shorts tightening and tugging at her skin, her hand reaching out toward the broken glass.

"Stop," I barked, the echo of my voice bouncing off the glass walls and windows.

Sarah froze. Liv's body trembled, her walls clenching around me. I dropped my hand from her back, letting the shirt fall back into place, completely covering her rear and where we joined. I didn't dare remove the fingers between her thighs, though.

"Leave it," I said, my voice coming out too rough, too gravelly. "Just leave it, please. Go."

I could see the shift in Sarah's throat as she swallowed even from where I sat. She stood.

"*Go*," I repeated.

She retreated, her eyes lingering every step of the way, each footstep almost louder than the wind and the engines behind us. But the door closed behind her, and she was gone, and all I was left with was a shuddering Olivia in my lap, her pussy still wrapped around my aching cock.

"I'm so sorry—"

Liv's creeping laughter cut me off, her body still shaking, her walls clenching with every breathy chuckle. "Don't," she grinned. "Don't apologize."

Brows furrowing, I took her face in my free hand, caressing the curvature of her jaw. "Why?"

Beaming lips parted on a hasty little breath, her pupils blown wide as fucking saucers. Her hips moved forward, my cock burying inside of her *so* fucking easily, my fingers slipping against her clit. She was *dripping*.

Dear fucking god. I should have known from the way she'd responded to our public indecency back in Vegas that she was only excited by this. I was a goddamn idiot to have forgotten.

I pushed my hand back, slipping between the tied-up

strands of her messy bun, and latched on. She hissed her approval as I tightened my grip, pulling her head back, forcing her chin to jut out at me as she looked me dead in the eyes.

"Little fucking exhibitionist, aren't you?" I laughed, nipping at the tip of her chin.

Her cheeks heated, little flushes of pink blistering out across her face. "Maybe."

I slipped my fingers from between us and sank my teeth into her pouting lower lip. "*Maybe*," I mocked, raising my hand, inspecting the threads of her arousal that dripped in perfect little beads down the sides of my fingers. "Look how fucking wet that got you."

Her hips shifted again, slowly restarting their movement. I used my grip on her scalp to turn her head, to force her to look at the mess she'd created.

I could barely see a hint of green irises around her pupils as she locked her gaze on it. "Open," I ordered, and her lips parted immediately. "Clean it up, princess."

My fingers slipped across her tongue, the silken hot feeling of it only making me harder inside of her. I couldn't help but imagine her mouth wrapped around me instead, the heat of it, the softness of the back of her throat, the little muffled sounds she'd make. The way her hands would wrap around my thighs, the way she'd drip onto the fucking floor, the way I'd practically edge myself by watching her clean it up with her mouth.

I wanted to do so many things with her, *to* her. I wanted to reach new lows of depravity.

Her mouth popped as she released my fingers, damp and coated in a thin layer of saliva but pristinely cleaned of her. One hand pressed against my chest and her other buried between her thighs and taking care of *my* job, she moaned, her walls clenching around me.

"Did I say you could touch yourself?"

She stilled.

"I don't think I did," I growled, tightening my grip on her hair. I wrapped my fingers around her wrist, pulling her hand away from her clit. Almost instinctively, she began grinding on my cock again, seeking friction, seeking *more*. "Fucking greedy little thing."

"Touch me, then," she whined. Her nails into the bare flesh of my chest, leaving little half-moon indents. "Please."

"You're so lucky I'm generous, princess." Releasing her wrist, I slipped my fingers back into position between her parted lower lips, giving her *too* much pressure. She shuddered in my lap, her body trying to retreat from the intensity, but I kept her locked in position as she fucked herself on me. "Say thank you. I could just as easily ignore your clit altogether and keep you desperate and on the edge all fucking night."

Her breathing quickened and her walls clenched my cock so hard I thought she might expel me. "You wouldn't let me come?" she whimpered, her voice echoing an air of betrayal, but her *eyes*, fuck, they looked so goddamn intrigued. Her movements were choppy, messy, desperate, and I lessened the pressure just a hair on her clit, giving her a little bit more of what she wanted.

"Fuck, you like that idea, don't you?" I laughed. She nodded weakly, her little sounds telling me she was close. I was getting there myself. "Don't tempt me, Olivia. I am more than willing to tease you all fucking night, touch you in all the wrong ways, never let you find that release, have you *begging* me. I—fuck, *fuck*, I'd kill for that. You look so goddamn pretty when you beg, princess. *Shit,* oh my *god.*"

I could barely find the words I wanted to say, could barely fucking think with her moving the way she was. I wanted to stop touching her, wanted to do what I was saying, but she moaned so prettily, she felt so goddamn *good* that I couldn't bring myself to do it. My composure was breaking, and so was hers, and neither of us stood a chance for much longer.

But I didn't want it to end. And right then, emotions firing on all fucking cylinders and the only head I was thinking with was that of my cock, I stopped. I stopped *everything*.

"What—"

I pushed her body back from me, forcing my length from her, hating the harshness of the cool breeze against it instead of her warmth. "Bedroom," I rasped. "I need to *fuck* you, Olivia. *Properly*."

———

That oversized shirt was the first thing to go.

I'd let her wear it on the walk back to the cabin, even though the temptation to remove it first and force her to walk completely fucking naked through the internal halls was maddening. But despite it falling just beneath her ass, I could still see the glistening dampness leaking down her inner thighs as she'd walked in front of me.

I didn't give her a chance to take in the room or the views it boasted out of the front end of the boat. I shut the door behind us, and before she could break the charged silence, I forced the fabric up and over her head, leaving every part of her exposed.

God, everything about her was sinful.

Her breasts, small but full, with little pink nipples that I wanted nothing more than to have between my teeth. The soft curves of her abdomen, the roundness of her hips and her ass, the barely-there tan she'd begun to acquire from her hours on the main deck today. I could have eaten her alive.

I *would* eat her alive.

Shucking the unbuttoned shirt off my shoulders, I let my desire fuel me, let it make every fucking decision. I grabbed her by the throat, my fingers ever so gently pressing in on the arteries on either side, and crashed my lips into hers. I could taste the lingering flavor of *her* from she'd licked it clean off me, could feel the desperate little whimper she made that I absorbed.

I led her backward, creeping toward the bed, while undoing the button on my pants that I'd hastily refastened. I needed my clothes off. I needed to be inside of her.

"Damien," she breathed, her chin tipping up again to look at me as I stopped at the foot of the mattress. Her eyes focused and unfocused, looking through and looking *at* me, and I lessened the pressure of my fingers. Blood rushed through her veins and she faltered on her feet, the head-rush making her lips part.

"On the bed," I ordered, pushing her back just enough that she'd fall out of my grasp onto the cushy mattress. She swallowed, crawling backward, a string of dampness connecting her thighs. "Face down, princess."

Her eyes blew wide as I pulled off my slacks, my gaze fixed wholly on her. But she rotated her body, flipped herself over on the soft, dark green sheets, her legs just barely spread, her ass beckoning me like a goddamn light in the dark. I wanted to sink my teeth into it, wanted to grip her so hard she'd be left with bruises, wanted to bury myself into her so harshly she'd barely be able to walk tomorrow.

And I *could*.

Climbing onto the bed, I grabbed her by the hips, forcing them up, up, up, until her face was buried in the sheets and her hips were high in the air, the softest parts of her presented to me like a fucking meal. If I had any ounce of patience left, I would have eaten her, would have drank every drop from her leaking pussy, but I didn't. I couldn't wait. Not when she looked like this.

I knocked her knees further apart until she lined up exactly where I needed her to. I pressed the head of my cock flush against her entrance, the slip of it so easily guiding me into place, and with one hissed *please* from her, I buried myself inside of her, so deep it was nearly dizzying.

"Oh my *god*," Olivia whined. "Please, *please* tell me you're going to let me come like this."

I laughed as I dragged my hands along her spine, my thumbs dipping into the divot that ran up the center of her back and parting at the top, my fingers wrapping around her arms. I pulled them back, joining them at the forearms and folding them over each other. "You'll have to wait and find out, princess."

Her walls squeezed the living daylights out of me. There wasn't a chance in hell of me lasting very long after all of this.

I dragged every inch of myself out of her, leaving just the tip as I gripped onto her restrained arms, and a second later, I was plunging back in, giving her everything, *taking* everything. The harsh moan that vibrated through her made me thankful that Noah was sleeping soundly on the other side of the boat, with far too many rooms between us and him to even need to worry about her noises cutting through.

Over and over, I fucked her thoroughly, burying myself and retreating, feeling every bit of her tug along my length. I dug my nails into the softness of her ass, my grip unrelenting, breaking blood vessels and flushing her skin in little red spots. Every withdrawal from her left my cock glistening from her seemingly never-ending pool, and every thrust left my head spinning.

This was different. This wasn't lust, this was something deeper, more raw, more degrading. This was a harsh, infinite *need*, a need that pulled at me from every angle, a need that took my fucking breath and refused to give it back.

"Please, Damien," she begged. "Please, please, *please*."

But she sounded so fucking pretty. So *fucking* pretty that I lost myself in her, my hips stuttering, my grunts and groans devolving into gasps and growls, and I found myself spilling into her. I released her arms as I filled her, heat spreading out in her and around me, my body heaving, my breaths too shallow. She rocked back into me, still riding her edge, still desperate, and within a second, I was moving.

"Dame," she whimpered as I slid myself from her. "*Please*, I need you. I need this."

I flipped her onto her back and she was on me in an instant. Her arms around my neck, her mouth against mine, her hips torturously bucking up toward me. I kissed her through the haze of my come down, but I couldn't leave her like this, couldn't leave her wanting when I'd had my fill, as tempting as it was.

"You were so good for me," I rasped, her lower lip catching between my teeth. "*So* fucking good for me."

"Does that mean—"

Slipping a hand between us, three fingers slid into her like slicing through melting butter. She moaned against my mouth, her hips already working, already seeking what she wanted. I met her halfway, my thumb stroking across her heated, throbbing clit. I'd already committed, but a part of me wanted to take that right to her orgasm away again, wanted to give it five minutes in the hopes that we could go another time, and then another, and another, or as many as she had in her before she broke and sobbed and offered me anything I wanted just to have her release.

But I was far too nice when it came to her.

I kissed down the side of her neck, across her collarbones, over the curve of her breast. My teeth latched onto her nipple, biting down just enough to cause a ripple of pain through the pleasure.

"*Fuck*," she whined, her hands pushing through the strands of my hair, holding me in place. Her walls tightened around my fingers and her breathing escalated, so easily brought to that cliff edge. She leaked around my hand, a viscous mixture of both of us oozing out. "*Please*, Damien, oh my *god*—"

"Come, princess," I ordered around a mouthful of her breast. "You earned it. You fucking earned it."

She broke instantly, a shriek ripping from her throat before she instinctively covered her mouth, her body spasming and shifting beneath me. Her nails clawed at my fucking skull, little bursts of pain erupting from plucked hairs, and all I could do was drag her through it and drink it in, wishing I'd left it longer, wishing I'd done this every night since I met her, wishing I had all the time in the world to *keep* this.

I pulled my fingers from her.

I licked them clean, taking in both of us and the concoction we'd made.

I kissed her. I held her. I ached for her long after we'd finished.

And, stupidly, from the rocking of the ship and the goddamn pool of bliss she'd given me, I fell asleep with her, flesh to flesh, beneath the sheets.

Chapter 19

Olivia

Walking through the gates of Disneyland was a struggle after what we'd done, but I kept the part of my mind that was angry at myself for letting my wants get the better of me tamped down, at least for today.

I'd warned Damien that despite the looks, a leash for Noah might have been a good idea to keep him from running off every two seconds when he saw something that interested him, but Damien didn't want to do that. I couldn't blame him — leash kids were... well, leash kids. But that meant one of us had to hold his hand at all times, which wasn't the worst thing in the world, but meant I couldn't get a moment to speak to Damien out of earshot of Noah.

"This is *AMAZING*," Noah shrieked, his eyes locked solely on Sleeping Beauty's Castle at the other end of Main Street. Ahead of us, a man in a mouse costume spun in a circle with a balloon, and further back, his girlfriend signed autographs.

I'd gone to Disney World a handful of times growing up, but never Disneyland — for all of us, this was something new. I could say with certainty that I'd never been to an amusement park while the space between my legs ached in the best possible way.

Damien scooped Noah up the moment he tried to bolt and plopped him up on his shoulders. "This *is* amazing," he said, craning his neck to look up at Noah, "but it would be even better if you stopped trying to get kidnapped."

"Sorry, Dad."

Despite his apology, Noah gripped his father's hair with both hands as if he could pilot Damien by tugging in a certain direction. To my utter surprise, Damien didn't feel the slightest bit ashamed of the crowd of people around us and humored him, dipping in random directions and practically running into people with each tug on his head. Noah shrieked with laughter, and I couldn't help but chuckle along at the absurdity of it.

"Are you laughing at me?" Damien challenged, one brow raised as Noah piloted him back to me. He stopped directly in front of me, towering over me in the middle of Main Street, his lips tugging back into a smile.

Fuck, he looked so... *normal*. In such a good way. "Yes," I grinned. "Is that a problem?"

Noah pulled back and Damien followed suit, slowly walking backward toward the castle. "I guess we'll find out later, *princess*."

———

Twenty rides down, and I was exhausted. I had no idea how Noah found the energy to keep running from spot to spot.

There had only been about five so far that Noah couldn't ride, and although he was disappointed about those in particular, he'd gotten that energy right back to head on to the next one within seconds. It was go, go, go with him, and even though I could tell Damien was exhausted as the morning turned into late afternoon, he didn't show it one bit when Noah was watching him.

I could see it, though. I could see it in the little things, like the way he didn't smile quite as large when Noah lost his mind about meeting Captain Hook, like when he looked to the sky for a second of peace when Noah asked for his fifth churro, like when he squeezed my hand in the small amount of privacy that the Haunted Mansion granted us, his eyes locking with mine for just a second, the tightest grin on his face. He was tired, but he wouldn't ever let Noah know.

"Jungle Cruise next!" Noah said, pointing in a direction that definitely wasn't Adventureland.

Damien plucked the map out of the back pocket of his black jeans and put one hand on the top of his son's head, turning him to point in the correct direction.

"And then we go meet Peter Pan," he added, skipping off in that direction.

Damien and I followed behind him, keeping him in our sights and within reaching distance as we desperately tried to keep up with the never-ending energy of Noah. For a second, Damien's attention caught on something else, his hand dipping into his pocket and pulling out his phone before grumbling something too quiet for me to hear and putting it away.

"You okay?" I asked. I wrapped my fingers around his bicep, just a small touch in a sea of people without Noah paying attention.

"I'm fine. Ethan keeps calling," he said, his eyes flicking between me and Noah. "It's probably nothing."

"That doesn't sound like *nothing*." I gave him a little squeeze as we dipped into the line for Jungle Cruise beneath a sign that read out 35 *Minute Wait*. "I can watch Noah if you need to call him back."

Quickly and discreetly, he pressed his lips against the side of my head, cupping my cheek to hold me in place before letting me go. "I appreciate that, but honestly, it's probably—"

The sound of an incoming text cut him off as he fished in his pocket again.

Damien stopped in his tracks halfway down the empty line, his eyes going wide, the ropes on either side of us keeping us in. I reached out and grabbed Noah by the wrist, pulling him back to us. "Watch him," he said quietly, taking a step back. "Please. I'll be right back."

I nodded once, and he slipped under the rope that divided the exit line from the entry line, heading back toward where we'd come in. Of course I'd watch Noah no matter the circumstance, but I couldn't help but wonder what had made him change his mind that quickly as I pulled Noah to the side of the line where they kept the little drinking fountains.

"Where's Dad going?" he asked as I sat down on the edge of the curb.

"I think he has to make a phone call. Don't worry about it, squirt," I said, faking a wide grin as I pulled him into my lap.

"But the Jungle Cruise," he pouted.

"I know. He'll be right back. I promise." I ruffled the top of his head as I gave him a little squeeze. He was sticky and smelled of sugar and cinnamon, but I'd grown used to his stickiness now. I pulled out my map that I'd stuffed into my bag hours ago and unfurled it for him. "What do you want to do *after* the Jungle Cruise?"

He studied it extensively, going quiet for what felt like minutes and leaving us with the soundtrack of the ride playing and the birds chirping in the trees. It was the first chance I'd had to actually calm down all day, and having him here and focused only seemed to make it easier, somehow.

But then he excitedly pointed to a random ride in Tomorrowland. "This one! And then we can go here, and then here, and then—"

Damien reappeared in the line, wild blue eyes looking frantically in front of him, not quite clocking us on the ground. From the way he walked to the way his mouth parted, I could tell something wasn't quite right.

I pulled myself and Noah to our feet immediately, and Damien's eyes found me, and oh, *god,* he looked like he was either going to throw himself off a bridge or vomit across the cement.

Before I could even ask what was wrong, he was squatting down in front of Noah and taking his son's face in his slightly trembling hands, his gaze flicking up to meet mine only briefly before going all in on him.

"Noah," he said, taking a deep breath and rolling his lips between his teeth. "I'm so sor—"

"Olivia said we can go to Tomorrowland next!" Noah beamed, fully not understanding whatever was happening here. I didn't know what to do, didn't know how to handle whatever was going on, so I took a step back instead and let Damien lead it.

Damien shook his head and grasped Noah by his little

shoulders, something glistening in his eyes. "Listen to me, bud. I'm so sorry, but we need to go *now*."

Noah went far too quiet.

"We can come back," Damien offered. "I promise, as soon as I can swing it, we will come right back here and we will do the Jungle Cruise and we will go to Tomorrowland and ride every ride you want. We can meet every character you want. We can stay for a whole fucking week."

"You said a bad word," Noah said, his voice so small, so goddamn sad.

But it was Damien's cracking one that made me panic. "I know. I-I'm sorry, buddy. I promise, I will make this up to you. Both of you." His eyes flicked to mine briefly as he wiped at his nose. *What the fuck is going on?* "But we have to go now."

Silence fell over both of them, just the crickets and the birds and the music of the Jungle Cruise while a handful of people passed us in the line. But then Noah nodded, and Damien was back on his feet, ushering Noah under the rope that he'd gone under before, and we were heading out of the line for the Jungle Cruise.

———

Damien made one negotiation with the five-year-old — he could hit the souvenir shop at the top of Main Street for ten minutes and buy whatever he wanted.

We stood off to the side in silence, watching as the kid ran frantically around the shop picking up stuffed animals and costumes and anything he could get his hands on. He wasn't even picking things he liked, just whatever he could find, whatever would keep the memory of today alive for him.

Damien checked his watch over and over, flicking between that and his phone.

"How long does he have?" I asked.

"Five minutes."

I squeezed his arm. "Is that long enough for you to tell me what's going on?"

He took another deep breath in, in through his nose and out through his mouth, before turning to look at me. "Grace has filed for custody officially," he said quietly, trying to disguise his shaking lower lip by hiding it between his teeth briefly. "She has an exceptionally strong case."

Oh, *fuck*.

Noah rushed over, his arms completely full, and Damien handed his card to the small child and sent him off to the register.

"How can she—"

"I don't know," he said, cutting me off, that same warble back in his voice. "But she wants sole custody, no visitation. After dropping him in my life and not visiting him for *weeks* despite having every opportunity and nothing stopping her, she wants to take all of that away from me. She wants to take *him* away from me. I... I can't just do that. I can't just give him up. I *won't*."

He let out a shaky breath as I pulled him toward me, my arms wrapping around his neck as I forced him down to my level. For the second time that day, I found myself unhelpful, unknowing of the right thing to do or say to calm him down. And even if it made Noah question things, even if it garnered any sort of attention from the strangers who didn't give a shit about us, I hugged him. I wrapped myself around him.

Damien buried his face in my neck, his hands gripping into my back so differently from how they did last night, and all he could do was breathe. Over and over, just breathed.

I wished I knew what I could say that would make it better, but I just... didn't.

"There's a plane waiting for us at the airport," he said quietly, the sound muffled from where he held himself. "But I've already booked a hotel room for all of us, if you want to stay."

"Not a chance in fucking hell," I breathed.

He held me tighter.

Chapter 20

Damien

It was nearing ten in the evening by the time I'd managed to get everyone home and squared away and could get out the door.

Olivia stayed behind with a sniffly, half-asleep Noah, his heart still broken from having to cut our day at Disney short. I felt fucking horrible about taking him from it early, but I needed to sort this out as quickly as I could, needed to figure out how the fuck I was going to fight this and what I needed to do. If keeping him meant upsetting him this one time, I would sacrifice a good memory for a million more.

With my house completely off limits for this conversation and Ethan's house filled with his roommate's friends, we had two options — a private bar where I could book us a room, or the office downtown where anyone working late could find us.

I chose the former.

"You can't just throw money at this and hope it works," Ethan snapped, downing the last bit of his first glass of whiskey and setting it down on the table in frustration. He seemed just as stumped as I was, just as angry as I was — or maybe he was just as overworked as I was. "I'm sorry but that's not how this works. You're going against a fucking pediatric nurse who has known him his entire life."

"But he's my *son!*"

Ethan reared back at the outburst. In fairness, I'd put way too much emotion into that, but I'd barely been given a moment to process any of this outside those thirty seconds that I'd had with Olivia in the gift shop. I'd hoped Noah would nap on the flight home, but he was too hyped up on a sugar rush from too many churros, and so I'd been left on the verge of breaking for *hours*.

I leaned onto the pool table, two glasses deep and my mind a fucking wreck, and put buried my face in my hands. "I'm sorry," I mumbled. "I'm not doing well."

"I can see that."

"There has to be something we can do," I said. "There *has* to be. I know you said I can't throw money at this, but there must be someone I can pay off, the judge, her lawyer, *someone.*"

"That's bribery, Damien, and it's illegal."

"I fucking know!" I spat. "Help me. Please. What can I do?"

His gaze hung on me as he poured himself another glass from the bottle. He slid off the stool and poured another two fingers worth into my abandoned glass. "You won't like my idea."

"I will like any fucking idea that guarantees me custody of my son."

His tongue slid across his bottom teeth as he pushed his glasses up his nose, taking instead to leaning against the private, empty bar instead of sitting at it. "Fuck the annulment. Stay married, for now. I've filed the papers but it's not too late to cancel. It will strengthen your case. She's not married, she lives alone, so it would be a single-parent household. Two-parent households are preferred, from what I can tell, but again, I don't know nearly as much about family law as I do business—"

"I can't do that," I breathed. I'd given endless hours of thought to it after I'd sent him that text asking him to pause the annulment — Olivia would fucking kill me if I did that. And he'd already sent them at that point, anyway, so I'd given the green light to carry on. But knowing damn well that it would help now, in this situation and not the one I thought I was dealing with, tempted me far too much. "It's not just me I need to worry about. It's Olivia, as well."

"I understand. But you wanted my suggestion," he said, the words feeling far too cold. I reached for my glass, downing it, pouring another, and taking a gulp. "Marissa left you. The court will of course take into consideration her infidelity, but in their eyes, she left a relationship when she found out she was pregnant and left him to you in a state of what Grace is claiming was medical incompetence at the end of her life. You have to understand how they will see this and the best ways you can combat it, and your best bet is to show that you have a loving, stable home with *two parents*."

I shook my head, struggling to fully process his words. All I could think about was her, her reaction to this, how she'd fucking hate me for it. She wanted the annulment, desperately. And I wanted to give her that.

I wanted to give her far more than that.

"I don't want to ruin this," I breathed.

Ethan looked at me, his jaw ticking. "When you say *this*—"

"All of it. Noah. Olivia. The whole thing. I'm being tugged in two different directions."

"Why does she factor into this? She's just a girl that works for you, Damien. How is that on the same level?"

"It's not," I insisted. "But she's drastically taking over parts of myself that I didn't fucking realize I still *had*. Do you understand that? Do you hear what I'm saying to you?"

He downed the rest of his drink in silence, closing the binder laid out on the table. "You can't be seriously telling me that you love her after, what, three weeks? Four weeks?"

The words hit me like a brick, winding me, sobering me just slightly. Of course I wasn't saying that. That would be insane. And I wasn't someone who jumped into things like that so easily and so quickly, especially not now, not with Noah in the equation. *Liar.* "I'm not saying that I do, but I'm saying that I think I *could*. And I haven't opened up like that in almost six fucking years."

"And salvaging that is worth more to you than your son?"

No. It wasn't. But it was still a fucking factor.

He was right, though. I was putting a *maybe* on a pedestal that although didn't come close to the one I'd raised for Noah, was still high enough to be a problem when all of this was on the line. I'd crossed lines I'd set for myself, backed down from what I'd said to her on the phone that night. I'd developed feelings when I knew I was mostly incapable of commitment again, and fucked myself over in the process.

I didn't know what to fucking do, but more than that, I didn't care that I would go home smelling of booze. I poured myself another glass.

Chapter 21

Olivia

The stares were beginning to grate on me.

This was only the second time that Damien's sister could take Noah on a weekday, and from the whispers and glances toward my desk as I tried desperately to focus, it was clear that others had taken notice of my prolonged absences.

With my only other friend here, Sophie, working in Human Resources instead of project management like me, I couldn't even *ask* what had gotten around and what hadn't. She had no idea of the office gossip on floor five, and now, neither did I.

But it revolved around me. That much was obvious.

I slipped my phone from my bag and pulled up my texts with Damien. The log from this morning seemed so mundane, so normal for two people living together, that it was almost a small shock to my system to have them in front of my face again.

Do we still have eggs?

Yes, but Noah would like to clarify that we're out of cheese.

Cheese. Got it. What's the chicken nugget situation?

Dame, we have a never-ending supply of chicken nuggets.

Have you seen how many Noah can eat? He set a record the other night while you were working out. Twenty-two in a single meal. My son is a fucking machine.

I pressed the little box that brought up my keyboard and sighed. I could message him. I could tell him what was going on, but he was already dealing with so much that I wasn't sure I wanted to add another layer to that — especially when I knew damn well that he would only want to help.

But I also needed someone to talk to, and Sophie was in a meeting until three.

Me: If I tell you about how shitty my day is going, do you promise not to make it your number one priority to try to fix it?

Almost immediately, the three little dancing bubbles popped up.

Dame: That depends on if it's something I'm capable of fixing. If I can, I will.

I set my phone down on my desk in frustration, burying my face in my hands. I just wanted to complain, just wanted to vent and feel heard, and although I appreciated his willingness to solve my problems, he had enough on his plate right now.

My phone buzzed.

Dame: Is it your coworkers again?

I groaned quietly into my palms.

Dame: Tell me what's going on or I'll come down there myself.

Me: It's not my coworkers.

A lie, but hopefully it was enough to get him out of it and keep him from intervening.

Dame: Come up to my office then and we can just chat about whatever it is.

Fuck. I couldn't do that, not when this many eyes were on me, not when our... *situation* was likely the cause of it. He had to know that. He had to be testing me.

Me: I can't do that.

Dame: Because it's your coworkers.

Me: You're the worst.

Dame: You didn't think that last night.

My cheeks heated as I read back the message again, and again, and again. I definitely, absolutely, did not think that last night. I thought everything *but* that.

Dame: Tell me what's going on.

Me: Fine.

Emma, one of the chosen interns two desks down from me, snickered under her breath as she averted her gaze from me. I wanted to throw my fucking wireless mouse at her face.

Me: They keep looking at me. And people keep fucking whispering and snickering and just staring at me. It's worse than it was last week.

Me: I think they know something's going on. Idk if something slipped up in HR or if Sophie didn't shut her mouth, or maybe they're just speculating.

Damien's three little bubbles popped up again but disappeared a moment later.

Me: Maybe I shouldn't have let you drive me to work.

Me: I can just take the bus or something. It's not that big of a deal once a week.

Me: Hello?

I stared at the lack of bubbles for far too long before

putting my phone down in frustration. Either he was on a call, or he was making my situation far worse.

I tried to focus again on the PowerPoint I'd been trying to assemble. It was bare bones, just loaded with information but without any graphics or images — just plain white pages that made my eyes burn to look at. I'd at least separated everything out into their individual slides, but I almost wished I was at home instead with Noah's shows playing in the background and a beeping oven telling me it was time to take out the goddamn chicken nuggets. At least then I could actually get some work done instead of feeling like a caged animal in the zoo, only there for Emma's and Matt's and Polly's and everyone else's entertainment.

A hand came down on the backrest of my chair, and I nearly jumped out of my seat.

Turning halfway around in my now unmovable chair, Damien's hard-set jaw and full suit came into view, and all I wanted to do was strangle him.

"You can't just come down here," I hissed, my face heating, burning, *scolding*. I couldn't deny that his presence was a welcome relief, but oh my god, I wanted to kill him. *Everyone* was staring now — not just those who had been in the loop before. And I couldn't blame them. The fucking owner and CEO was in our small office, looming over an employee, looking far too attractive for his own good.

"I believe, Olivia, that I own this entire building and can go wherever I please," he grinned. "How's the project coming along?"

Being honest, telling him it was going terribly, would only raise questions with the people around me. No one in their right mind would tell the highest-up person in this company that their work was going *terribly*. But I didn't want to lie to him, either.

"Is this it?" he asked, glancing at my computer screen, one eyebrow raising at the white and black PowerPoint slide.

"Please don't do this," I breathed, keeping my voice low enough in the hopes that only he could hear me. "Just get me out of here."

He rolled his eyes and pushed himself up off my chair. "Looks great," he lied, but he sounded believable enough. "Hillary in accounting needs to see you. I was nearby anyway so I figured I'd grab you for her."

Who the fuck is Hillary in accounting? "Uh, okay," I mumbled. I pushed back in my chair and stood, smoothing out my black pencil skirt where it had wrinkled from sitting down for hours.

"Bring your things," he added.

"To accounting?" I could feel the stares lingering on me as I held his gaze, the hairs on the back of my neck prickling.

He nodded.

————

The fucking elevator went right past the floor for accounting.

"Prick," I mumbled, fidgeting with the sleeves of my cardigan as the elevator climbed and climbed.

One arm slid around my front, pulling me back against his hardened chest. "You wanted out. I got you out, princess. Be *thankful*," he purred. Something sharp grated against the top of my ear, and in the metallic reflection of us from the doors, his eyes met mine, his teeth gently holding onto my ear.

"They'll ask more questions now," I sighed.

"They won't." The elevator dinged and he released me immediately, putting a breath of healthy distance between us before the doors slid open to his floor. "I was drafting an email to your manager on my way down. If your coworkers think that their jobs are secure just because they got selected for a presentation, then they're far too naive."

He stepped around me and motioned for me to follow, crossing the threshold out into the long corridor that branched the private offices. "Damien, you can't just fire them."

"I'm not *firing* them, princess," he said quietly, his guard not as high in the empty hallway. "It'll be a warning. A warning they should have received last week when you didn't want me to intervene."

"Because I don't want you bringing more attention to the problem. It'll just make it worse."

"Not if they'll be written up for it happening again," he grinned.

He pushed the door to his office open, the natural light flooding my senses. It was so much nicer in here than it was in our small office downstairs — all we had was fluorescent lighting and dying plants, but that's where the first-year hires in project management ended up.

"You can work in here for the rest of the day," he said. "I've got a meeting in half an hour, and I'll be in and out for the rest of the afternoon. Might as well get a good amount of use."

As much as I hated him for intervening, I fucking *loved* his office. And I could actually get work done in here.

I shot him an annoyed smirk as I dropped my bag onto

the sofa and shucked my cardigan. The natural light made it warm enough that I didn't even need it — it was a *normal* temperature in here instead of the freezing one my manager was set to keep the thermostat at.

I flopped down onto the plush cushions as he watched, sprawling across the sofa and lying down in the sun. "I guess marrying the CEO has its perks," I grinned.

A little chuckle left him as he took a step toward me, shoving his hands in his pockets. "Is that why you married me, then? Not so you could feel okay about losing your virginity to someone you barely knew?"

Asshole. I tucked my lower lip between my teeth and pulled my legs up onto the couch, my pencil skirt rising just an inch, the slit in the back parting. "Don't act like *you* didn't marry *me* just to fulfill some wild fantasy of stealing a woman's virginity."

He snorted as he stepped around the glass coffee table, his wristwatch glinting as he entered the rays of the sun. "I've done that before," he said, slipping one hand from his pocket and placing it on my bent, stockings-covered knee. "But that wasn't it. Want to try again, Liv?"

His fingers made circles on the sheer tights, forcing goosebumps to erupt across my skin and my lower gut to coil. *Fuck.* "You were so drunk and horny that you'd have done anything to see me naked?"

"I saw all of you in that bathroom before we met Elvis," he drawled, the tips of his digits digging in and forcing my legs to part just a little bit more. "One more guess."

At the front of his slacks, just between his hip bones, something hard pressed against his zipper. My heartbeat thundered in my ears.

His fingers dipped lower across my inner thigh, exploring, feeling, traveling down, down, down, until they slipped beneath my skirt, until they rested against the fleshiest part of my leg, until they fisted the fragile material. Runs sprang to life across my tights, and he pulled, splintering the fabric more. "Come on, princess. Use your words."

Cool air hit the warmest part of me as the tights gave way, ripping entirely along the center seam. "You..." I swallowed, struggling to find the right words as he pushed my legs further apart, his eyes locked on me as his hand *explored.* "You wanted to fuck me and I wouldn't let you unless we were married."

His fingers ghosted across my already damp lips, forcing a whimper from me as a shiver crawled up my spine, and his eyes widened. "Jesus, Liv," he laughed, the lids of his eyes lowering as he leaned over me, one hand resting on the arm of the sofa and the other slipping against my clit. "No underwear? At *work?*"

I gasped at the sensation. "I was in a rush—"

"No, you weren't. Don't fucking lie," he smirked. One finger slipped inside of me, his thumb coming to rest against the bundle of nerves, and oh my *god*, he was going to kill me like this. "Tell me, princess. Do you like the way it feels without them? Do you like the way the seam rubs against you?"

Another finger, and a little more pressure. My back arched up off the cushions, my face heating once again.

"You went to bed last night full of *my* cum," he rasped, slowly lowering himself until he was on his knees, forcing me to open even more. "Were you hoping it would leak out while you sat at your desk? Were you hoping it would coat your fucking tights?"

His fingers curled, hitting that spot inside of me that made my head swim. "Damien," I moaned, reaching for him, snaking my hand around the back of his neck. He looked so fucking perfect in the sunlight, little specks of gray reflecting in his hair, his blue eyes shining.

"If I didn't have a goddamn meeting..." he breathed, sinking another finger into me, stretching me just enough that I lost every brain cell left.

"Don't go to it," I begged. I dug my nails into the back of his neck, tried to pull him closer. "Fuck me instead. Please."

Something akin to a growl reverberated through him as he pushed my skirt up my thighs until it settled around my hips, revealing every bit of damage he'd done to my unsalvageable tights, revealing the cords of my dampness that connected my upper thighs.

"As much as I'd love to, I don't have the time."

His mouth descended on me, his tongue replacing the work of his thumb. I could barely breathe, could barely *move*, and in an instant I could feel my release beginning to build like a finish line I didn't want to cross. I didn't want to *stop*.

"Fuck, you're close," he grunted, the words obscured from his mouthful of *me*. "Good fucking thing, too. Ethan's on his way up, and I didn't lock the door."

God fucking dammit, he knew what he was doing, what he was *saying*. Just the idea of his friend, his lawyer, walking in expecting to find Damien behind his desk and instead finding him with his mouth between my spread legs and my pussy on display, sent me spiraling at top speed toward my release.

I broke in an instant, a painful screech daring to rip through my vocal cords, but Damien's hand covered my mouth at the last possible second and dampened the sound. Pleasure invaded my system, spreading through my veins like wildfire, breaking me, mending me, *devouring* me. He kept going far past when it was too sensitive, making me squirm, making me sob for him to stop, and only then did his tongue leave me.

His fingers stayed, though. They dragged me through every aftershock.

Half drunk on pleasure and the sight of glistening wetness coating his lips and chin, words fell from me that I didn't think through. "I can't believe I get to have this for the rest of my fucking life."

He picked himself up from the floor and leaned across my spread legs to kiss me, his fingers slowly slipping out of me. "Only if you stay married to me," he joked, his breathy chuckle fanning out across my lips.

"Absolutely not," I laughed. But with my mind too full of him and not enough hesitation, sneaking thoughts drifted in. *Would it be so bad to stay married to him? Do I even want this to end?*

I shifted my hips up toward him, just narrowly missing a collision with his slacks before he pushed me back down onto the sofa. "Do *not* stain my suit right before a goddamn meeting, princess." His voice was harsh, but his half-lidded eyes and wide smile told me he wouldn't have given two shits if I had.

He kissed me again, and again, and again, his hips preventing my legs from closing or my skirt from moving back into position. He kissed me as long as he possibly could, sharing the taste of me, holding me, only making me want more from him, longer with him, everything with him. I needed to get a fucking hold of myself, but I didn't *want* to. I wanted this. I wanted this for as long as he would give it to me.

But a robotic voice from across the room sounded, and both of us paused. "Board meeting in five minutes. Board meeting in five minutes."

"I have to go," he sighed, pushing himself up off me and dragging my skirt back into position. "I'll be back in an hour or so."

I pouted but let him retreat, the realization fully sinking in that Ethan likely *wasn't* on his way up and he'd just said that to get a rise out of me. The door was unlocked though — that much had been true. But I doubted anyone in their right mind would barge in unannounced to Damien's office.

He offered me a hand, and I took it, letting him pull me back up into a seated position. "HR," he said.

What? I looked up at him, my gaze quizzical, my brows furrowing.

"I married you because I wanted to have you without breaking mine or HR's rules." He straightened his suit jacket before leaning down to press a final kiss against my lips, my mind still spinning. "Among all the other reasons."

Chapter 22

Damien

The inconsistencies of my choices had been gnawing at me for well over a week. *Stay with her for Noah's sake. Let her go for her sake. Keep both, somehow, for my sake.*

A date had been set for the court hearing. Ethan and I had two months to figure everything out, and I was going to use that to my advantage. I had time on my side. I had Olivia, still, for however long that would last. And I had Noah. For at least two more months, I had Noah.

But thinking about the potential of not having him after those two months sent me in such a downward spiral that I knew I'd lose my mind if I went too far, so I kept that tucked away, out of sight and out of mind, so that I could at least function.

But that left every other horribly stressful thing at the forefront.

Board meeting after board meeting about the financials came and went, but today's was far more important than the last few. I'd invited Olivia along, succumbing to my want for her calm in a room full of snakes and higher-ups within the company. It wasn't *just* the board today — it was everyone important. Everyone who made decisions. Managers, execs, the highest accountants, Ethan, and the board.

And I had to present my solution. Not the one that came from lawsuit after lawsuit against the companies we'd acquired, but the one that would actually gain us a net positive cash flow.

And for the first time in a long, *long* time, I was nervous to present.

I stood at the podium with the screen behind me, back in that same room where I'd announced the final intern whose proposal was chosen, back in the same room I'd been in moments before Olivia had run into the elevator. All eyes on me, everyone waiting with bated breath, binders out for note taking — a sea of professional attire and hungry capitalists.

Olivia stood at the back of the room, one hand around the wrist of her other, her legs crossed as she leaned against the wall. I knew what she was hoping for. I knew she wanted me to present her idea, the one she'd worked tirelessly on, the one she'd spent hours working on into the dead of night, falling asleep at her desk at home until I carried her to bed with me. Her proposal was solid. It was thorough.

But it wasn't the positive cash flow idea the board was begging for. No, that was what I had pre-loaded on my computer in front of me, ready to display on the screen. That was what was expected of me.

The board wanted buy-ins. They wanted Blackwood to openly back politicians who preached "A Greener Tomorrow," despite having nothing in their plans to make it happen. They wanted Blackwood to accept money in exchange for the favors. And it would work — the prices quoted were astronomical. Having a company like mine behind you brought solidarity to a political campaign.

But more than any of that, the board wanted budget cuts. The board wanted layoffs.

"Thank you for coming this afternoon," I started, loading up PowerPoint on my laptop. "As most of you know, Blackwood Energy Solutions has been having some trouble over the last few months with our financials due to a handful of companies we've acquired."

The files sat next to each other on my desktop. I swallowed.

"I appreciate your patience during this time while we work things out behind the scenes. I want to stress that no matter the solution, retaining jobs here is the utmost priority. Every decision we have made so far has been with that at the forefront," I continued.

My stomach churned. When I started Blackwood twenty years ago, I'd always said that I would never consider layoffs. And I hadn't. Not until the board started pushing.

"And we believe we've come to a solution," I swallowed.

Olivia's eyes met mine over the sea of people, her hand now pulling at the collar of her shirt, her gaze wary. I knew damn well her idea was better. I knew it in my gut, knew it with everything I had, and although we'd considered roughly ten other proposals that were decent in their right, hers stood out among the rest. But the board would fucking kill me.

Her lips pursed as she gave me a solemn nod. She already knew. I'd told her this morning. And it had hurt like a fucking bitch to rip off that bandaid for her.

I clicked on the presentation. A second later, it filled the screen behind me.

"After much negotiation, Blackwood has come to hold ownership over a new technology out of South Korea."

Olivia's eyes went wide as they locked with mine again, her collar forgotten and her hand over her mouth. There was something there, something in her gaze that looked less like dread and more like pride, and even though I was committing corporate suicide in front of the board, I knew damn well it was the right thing to do.

Especially when she was looking at me like that.

———

A much larger set of arms than what I was expecting wrapped around me the moment I stepped through the door of my home.

"Daddy's home!" Noah called from somewhere off in the distance, and my heart cracked just a little bit more as I realized that was the first time he'd called me that.

But I focused on her instead in the short window I had before Noah inevitably would take over.

"You presented my project," Liv said, her head buried in the crook of my neck, her feet dangling as I held her to me with my free hand. I could barely tell the tone in her voice, but from the way she was holding me, from the way she clung to me, I could tell her emotions were going haywire.

"I did," I chuckled. I set my briefcase on the console table by the door and wrapped my now free hand around her, squeezing her tightly and shutting the door behind me with my foot. "The board is fucking furious."

210

"Fuck the board," she mumbled.

Fuck the board, indeed. I'd stayed after for far longer than I thought I would, and even though the sun had set and it was going on eight in the evening, even though Noah wasn't in bed when he should have been, even though I'd offered to pour half of my life savings into the business in case everything crashed and burned, I didn't care. Not tonight, at least.

Noah came running around the corner from the staircase, and in an instant, Liv was slipping from me, letting me go. She took a step back, giving Noah the space he wanted with me, and as I leaned down to scoop him up, I caught sight of her.

Her eyes glistened, a touch of water pooling along the edges. They were bloodshot and raw, likely from staying up almost all night last night finishing up the presentation. She wore my gray joggers, her loose shirt tucked in and her cardigan hanging limply around her, one sleeve-covered hand covering her mouth and nose, her long auburn waves hanging wildly around her shoulders.

"Where have you *been?*" Noah griped, his arms wrapping around my neck as he squeezed me.

"I *told* you he was at work, squirt," Liv chuckled, wiping her nose with the sleeve of her cardigan.

"You should have been home hours ago," Noah said.

I opened my mouth to speak, but Liv spoke for me. "Noah," she started, putting a hand on his back. "Your dad did something really, *really* brave today. But that meant that he had to stay at work a little longer. Maybe we should be proud of him instead of upset with him, yeah?"

God, I wanted to fucking kiss her.

"You were brave?" Noah asked, rearing back as if that was the wildest thing he'd ever heard in his life. I snorted.

"I was," I laughed. "Is that a surprise to you?"

He tapped his finger against his chin, pondering the question, before shaking his head.

"Good. Glad I'm not a massive disappointment," I chuckled. "Are you all packed for your weekend at Aunt Carolines?"

Noah nodded. "Olivia helped."

"Perfect." I lowered him to the ground despite his protests. "Why don't you go get your pajamas on so we can start bedtime?"

He pouted and Liv laughed, but within a second he was racing back up the stairs, too much energy in such a small body. Something told me he wasn't going to fall asleep quickly tonight.

The moment he was out of eyeshot, I grabbed her.

With my arms around her waist and hers around my neck, I kissed her. I kissed her as if she were my wife, I kissed her as if it was the one thing in the world that I wanted at that moment, I kissed her as if no one was watching and I could have every bit of her. And all of it was true.

"They haven't kicked you out as CEO, right?" she asked, her words practically absorbed by my mouth.

"Not yet," I laughed. "I still have the majority of shares so they'd be damned if they fucking tried."

"Okay so we're not mourning your business, then," she grinned, pulling back just an inch so she could look me in the eyes.

I shook my head. "The opposite," I said. "We're fucking celebrating. With Noah taken care of for the weekend, I figured we could make the most of some alone time."

One brow raised as she eyed me with suspicion, and all I could do was beam back at her.

"You should pack a bag, too."

Chapter 23

Olivia

Tucked away in the forest of the Olympic National Park just outside of Seattle, Washington, a massive log cabin covered in solar panels and bits of moss stood tall amongst the western red cedars. A thick fog hung in the tops of the trees, and from the sounds of it, there wasn't anyone or anything else around for *miles*. I still wasn't used to being charted around on a private jet, but I felt like I'd been thrust from one weird thing to the next with the sight in front of me.

"You can't be serious," I said, staring in awe at the home, taking in every last detail from the carved wood balconies to the circular hot tub up on the second floor.

Gravel crunched behind me and Damien's arms wrapped around my body. "Why are you surprised? You're acting like I never mentioned my vacation house."

I twisted in his arms, shooting a glare up at him. "Because you *didn't*."

"Ah," he grinned. "My bad."

"We should have brought Noah. He'd love this."

"Noah is far too preoccupied with celebrating his

214

cousin's birthday," Damien laughed, releasing me and ushering me forward toward the cabin. "Is it so bad that I wanted to get away with you while we can?"

While we can. I knew what he meant, but that phrase grated on me as we walked toward the house. I didn't like what the double meaning implied, didn't like how it sat like a stone in my gut. *While we're still married. Before it ends.*

———

The stars above us were so much brighter out here than they were back in the center of San Francisco. The cool air nipped at my bare skin, but everything from the tips of my breasts down was submerged in the bubbling, warm water. Somehow, it felt almost more intimate to be naked in front of him when he *wasn't* touching me.

At least, not in that way.

His hand rested gently on my upper thigh, unmoving, unassuming. His knee knocked against mine as he sipped at his glass of red wine, his Adam's apple bobbing with each swallow.

"Are you happy?" I asked, the words slipping from my lips far too comfortably in the easy quiet.

He let out a breathy little chuckle as he looked out into the endless woodland. "You ask such interesting questions. *Have you had sex with her? Are you happy?*" He downed the rest of his glass and set it off to the side. "What exactly do you mean by *happy*, princess?"

He turned to me, his knee knocking against mine again, and I shrugged.

"I'm not happy about the custody battle. I'm not happy about the situation at work, even if I feel righteous in my decisions. I'm not happy about my level of stress, or the fact that I've missed out on over five years of Noah's life," he said, pushing a loose strand of my hair out of my face and tucking it behind my ear. "But I *am* happy. I'm happy that I have Noah. I'm happy that I'm able to spend this time with you without having to hide anything. I'm happy that I get to have you around at *all*. I'm happy with my job, I'm happy with my company, I'm happy with the way my life is going. So... yes. And no. But mostly yes."

His fingers lingered on my cheek, and I turned my head into them, letting him caress my face. "Is there anything else that you want out of your life?"

He chuckled again. "I don't know," he said. "I'd like to settle down at some point. I'd never really given too much thought to kids — Noah was a welcome surprise, and when I was with Marissa, I knew she wanted at least one, but that was me following what *she* wanted. But I think I'm happy with one. Another sounds like a nightmare. And then maybe when I get too old to run my business, I'll move out here and spend my time in these woods with whoever I'm with."

I studied the twitch in his jaw as he said the last of his words. His thumb dragged idly along my thigh, just an absent-minded touch, and I couldn't help but wonder what it would be like to be *whoever he was with*, to live out in the sticks and not have to worry about what anyone else thought. But it wouldn't be me. We had an expiration date.

"What about you, Liv?" he asked, his fingers trailing down beneath my chin and lifting it. "Is there anything else *you* want out of life? You've got so much of it left to live."

I shrugged, the water sloshing around me. Behind me,

216

the flood light turned off, and we plummeted into a shocking darkness that was only lit by the stars and the moon above us. With the moon at his back and the light from it illuminating the edges of his skin, he looked almost ethereal, and I found myself having to draw focus back to literally anything else to keep my mind from wandering.

"I don't know," I breathed. "Settle down. Keep a good job. I've never thought much about kids, either, so I guess what *whoever I end up with* wants is... good. My brother already has kids, so it's not like I *need* to. But I want to travel. I want to solve the water scarcity problem, but I know that's a big ask. And then settle down somewhere comfortable."

A little grin tugged the corners of his lips up. "Of course you want to solve that."

"Can you blame me? Two-thirds of the world's population—"

"—deal with water scarcity at least one month of the year. I know. It's atrocious, but I think your project could make a genuine difference to that."

Why was he even sexier when he was speaking on the things I was passionate about? "You can't just do that," I laughed, my cheeks heating as the bubbles stopped, leaving my nipples just barely out of the water.

"Do what, princess?"

"Talk about the things I care about when we're both fucking naked in a hot tub and you look like *that*." The wine had made it easier to speak and had loosened my tongue just a little too much, but I couldn't find it in me to be ashamed of what I was saying.

"It's not my fault we have common interests," he chuck-led. "And believe me, princess, no matter how I look, it is fucking *nothing* in comparison to you."

. . .

———

Another bottle of wine down and we were far too loose with each other.

His hands across my towel-covered stomach, he held my back against his chest, his mouth on my neck. The scent of chlorine and Damien's cologne lingered on the deck along with his towel lost somewhere behind us.

"God, you're perfect," he mumbled, his fingers pulling at the edges of my towel. My reluctance to release came only from the chill of the night air and not from stopping him from getting at what was underneath — no, I wanted that just as badly as he did.

I gasped as his teeth sunk into the soft spot just beneath my ear. My fingers fumbled with the handle on the glass door, finally catching hold and sliding it open. We tumbled into the dark space, and I couldn't remember if this was a spare room or the master suite. But it didn't matter, and the second the door slid shut, I let the towel fall away.

"*Fuck*," he groaned, spinning me to face him. "Come here."

His mouth crashed into mine, his kiss messy and chaotic, his wandering hands skating across my breasts. There was something about him that had changed since we'd arrived, something that felt more akin to the despera- tion and neediness he'd shown me two months ago in Vegas, back when we hardly knew each other, back before both of our lives changed. But I returned the fervor.

He pulled me to his chest, his length already solid and

pressing against my stomach. "Let me keep you," he mumbled against my lips, his hands sweeping down and over my rear. I didn't know what he meant, didn't understand what he was saying, but before I could question it he was lifting me up and forcing my legs around his waist.

With his cock wedged firmly between my wetness and his stomach, every step he took rubbed against my clit. A moan escaped me before my back was squarely against a polished wood wall. Arms slipped beneath my legs, hoisting them up, taking my weight along with them.

Before I could even fully work out what was happening, his body shifted, giving him just enough room to position the head of his shaft at my entrance.

"Oh, fuck," I breathed. "Dame—"

"Do you want me?" he asked, green eyes piercing through the darkness and meeting mine.

"I don't know what you mean." My chest heaved with every breath, the space between my legs heating and beginning to ache with need. "Of course I want you."

The tip of his cock pressed in, the sensation swamping my senses as little pinpricks of pain erupted. He hadn't stretched me at all — he hadn't even touched me, not really, but he didn't *need* to touch me to make me want him.

"Oh my god," I whimpered, letting my head fall back against the wall. He pushed a little further and the pain began to give way to pleasure. "Ah."

The moon broke free from behind a cloud and there he was again, painted in that fucking intense silver light. It snuck into every crevice of his body, between cords of muscle, and all I could do was watch as he sank into me fully, watch as he lost himself the moment he bottomed out.

"Fuck, Liv," he groaned, but he didn't move. "Let's just stay here. Fuck everything else. We can go get Noah and bring him up here, and we can stay away from all the bull-shit, stay away from work, stay away from Grace, away from the lawsuits and the custody shit. Just you and me."

I blinked at him. I didn't know what to say, even if it was hypothetical. Even if it was just his neediness talking, even if it was just a pipe dream. I took his face in my hands, brought him closer to me, and let him share the same air as me. "Damien."

He searched my eyes — for what, I had no idea. But the way he watched me made my chest ache alongside the need for him to thrust.

"I wish we could," I breathed. "I do."

That seemed to be enough for him.

He moved, finally, slipping nearly all the way out before settling himself back inside of me. I slipped a hand between us knowing full well both of his were occupied with holding my weight.

He kissed me. He kissed me intensely as he moved his hips, kissed me the ways I'd always imagined I'd want to be kissed, kissed me in a way that would inevitably screw me up forever. I could tell by the way it *hurt* instead of helped, but even if it made my chest ache to consider the fact that this wasn't going to be my forever, it didn't make the *now* less enjoyable.

His fingers dug into the backs of my thighs so hard I thought they'd bruise. He moaned against my lips, the sound gruff and dark and desperate, and I followed his lead, swirling my fingers across my clit, letting him fill me over and over.

What if it isn't like this with someone else?

I batted the thought away. Of course it could be. It was just sex, and that was it.

But it doesn't feel like it's just sex.

"I can't — can't stop wanting you," he rasped, his movements getting choppy, his breathing heavy. The way he spoke was erratic, as if his mind was breaking, as if he was losing himself more than he normally did. "You're, *fuck*, Liv, I need you. Need this. *Needed* this."

My release coiled in my gut, rapidly approaching, and within seconds we were both spilling over the edge, words dripping from our lips, warmth spreading out inside of me and dripping down. He kissed me again the way he had before as he released my legs, letting them fall around his hips. He stayed inside of me, his hands caressing my cheeks, my sides, my rear, anything he could touch.

I cherished every bit of it.

––––––––––

Along the rocky beach, the waves crashed and formed a low-hanging mist, twinkling in the barely-there sunshine out along the water. We'd hiked our way here despite the ache between my thighs and the slight bit of nausea that had plagued me all day, and the view was absolutely worth the journey.

He'd apologized out of nowhere this morning. He'd said he wasn't used to drinking so much wine and that it messed with his head, but I didn't mind it. I'd told him as much, and his answering, soft smile was enough to smooth it all over.

"We should have time to stop in Seattle tomorrow morning before our flight," he said, leaning back into the damp sand with his hands behind his head beside where I sat. "If you want to."

"I'd love that," I grinned. "But you should bring Noah out here. Seriously. Fuck Disney, bring him here next time you get the chance. You guys can like, make a bonfire or set traps or whatever it is guys like to do in the woods."

He laughed as he slipped one hand out from behind my hand and rested it against the small of my back instead. "And what would *you* be doing? Reading your sexy little books from the balcony?"

My cheeks heated as I looked away from him. "I'd probably be back home in San Fran."

"Don't be rid—"

Damien's phone sprang to life in his pocket, his ringtone carrying along the empty beach. He fished it out of his jacket and sat straight up.

"What's up, Carrie?"

I watched as his face morphed from excited dad and turned into something I'd never, ever seen before on him. Not when he'd come to me stressed out of his mind and asked me to watch Noah, not when he'd looked like he was about to break after the phone call in Disney.

My stomach sank and bile crept into my throat. I didn't know what it was, but fuck, it wasn't good.

"What happened, Carrie?"

He shot to his feet a second later, holding out one expectant hand for me. I took it, and he hoisted me up before turning back to the trailhead.

"Words, Carrie, I need fucking words!" he shouted, his voice warbling.

I opened my mouth to speak but decided against it as I followed his hasty footsteps.

"Where is he? Which hospital?"

Oh my god. Bile filled my mouth. I vomited next to the

sign for the beach, the act of heaving only making it happen again and again.

"Stay with him. I'm on my way."

Damien shoved his phone into his pocket as I pulled myself away from the sign. He clocked me, his eyes wide, his face *damp*, and I could see the fight in his eyes that pulled him in two directions. But he came back to me.

"We have to go. We have to *go*," he croaked, grabbing my hand and pulling me toward the woodland.

"What's happened?" I asked. I wiped my mouth with my jacket sleeve as I tried to pick up the pace. It had only been a thirty-minute hike to get out here — surely we could make it back quicker than that.

"Noah had a seizure."

Chapter 24

Damien

"Noah Blackwood," I said.

"We don't have a Noah Blackwood." The short, stout woman behind the desk looked up at me, her eyes wide, her chair squeaking as she leaned back. She looked afraid of me, and I couldn't blame her.

"Noah *Thompson*," Liv corrected.

The woman typed at her screen again before nodding. "We've got a Noah Thompson here, but only his parents are allowed in."

The smallest, tiniest bit of relief hit me for the first time in hours. "I'm his father," I said. "And this is my wife, Olivia."

"Do you have identification with the same last name?" she asked.

And there went any relief. I buried my face in my hands as I leaned against the high end of the desk. "No, I don't. He has his mother's last name."

"And the mother isn't here?" she asked, eyeing Olivia.

"His mother passed away a few months ago," Liv

offered. I wasn't sure if I was thankful or disturbed by her air of calmness, but whatever it was, it was helping the situation. The woman seemed much more up to talking to her.

"Do you have anything to prove that?"

"Um, no, but..." Liv fished in her bag for her phone and pulled it out, flipping it around to show the lady her lockscreen. "But this is Noah and I in Disney. Does that count for anything?"

If I had any bit of me that wasn't engulfed in stress, I could have cried from realizing that Noah was her fucking lockscreen. But I couldn't do that right now.

The woman sighed and sucked her teeth, weighing up her options. But then she hit a buzzer and the doors to the pediatric unit opened, and I grabbed Liv before the woman could change her mind.

"Room 208!" She called after us.

We rushed down the hallway, checking room numbers, sidestepping IV carts and abandoned beds. I gripped Liv's hand, my heart pounding in my chest, all cylinders firing on anxiety. She'd thrown up back at the reserve, and I'd felt like I was going to every second since.

The sign for Room 208 shone like a fucking beacon at the other end of the hall, and I sprinted toward it the second I clocked it.

I pushed the door open.

"Daddy!"

"Damien, thank *fuck*."

Noah sat on the bed bolt upright in a tiny hospital gown, his toy car in front of his crisscrossed legs, my sister by his side. Despite the IV port in his arm and the cannula hanging half out of his nose, he looked okay, he looked *alive*, and oh my god, I could *breathe*. I could breathe.

I pushed across the room, minding the wiring and the tubes, and pulled Noah into my chest. I could breathe, but my throat was closing, a lump forming. A sob wracked my chest and I bit it back, far too worried about concealing that from him to deal with the implications of stuffing it down.

Across the room, a nurse spoke to Liv in hushed tones, and she eyed me warily. He must have assumed she was Noah's mother.

"Where were you?" Noah asked, and I pressed a wet kiss against the top of his head.

"Don't worry about that. I'm here now. Just give me one moment." Slipping out of Noah's arms, I sidestepped my way to the doorway, pushing myself into the conversation with the nurse.

"You must be Dad," he said. "I was just explaining to Mom here that we've run some tests and nothing to suggest a reason for the seizure has come back."

"That can't be right," Liv said, her brows furrowing. "There must be a reason. Fever, epilepsy, something?"

Thank god she was composed. All I wanted to do was wring the man's neck and let his guts spill out onto his scrubs.

He shook his head. "No fever. Epilepsy is only diagnosed when two or more unexplained seizures happen, so I would suggest keeping an eye out. He was a little dehydrated but not enough that it would cause something like this, so we've got him back up to normal levels."

"I don't understand," I interjected, the words too biting, too angry. "There's not a cause? How do we know it won't happen again?"

"Dame," Liv breathed, her hand slipping back into mine and squeezing.

The nurse didn't even seem phased. "You don't," he

226

said. "It could just be a one-off. That happens sometimes. The MRI showed nothing of significance so it doesn't look like there's any damage."

"A one-off? People don't just have one-off seizures," I snapped.

Liv squeezed my hand again and pulled my attention to her. "It happens, Damien."

Her softness, her ease, put that tiny bit of calm back into me. "What do we do, then?"

The nurse sighed. "You can take him home in a few hours once we get his discharge sorted. I'd recommend keeping a close eye on him and telling him what happened. Make him feel okay about it so that if it happens when neither of you is around, he feels comfortable telling you that it happened. And if it *does* happen again, we can look at diagnosing him with epilepsy and getting him on the right medication for handling it."

"Sorry," Liv said, cutting in. "Is there a reason why we can't get him on medication now in case it happens again?"

"I wouldn't recommend it," he said. "Taking it when it could be unnecessary is likely to just give him the side effects of it without him needing them."

Liv nodded and slipped past me, leaving me to speak to the nurse alone as she gave the biggest, fakest smile to Noah and sat down at the end of his bed. Through the anxiety and the words the man was saying to me, I could hear her introduce herself to Caroline.

"The woman who brought him in, she timed his seizure," he said. "It was only about a minute and a half. That's within the normal range, so you don't need to worry about long-term effects. If it happens again, you or Mom or whoever he's with should time it. Thirty seconds to two minutes is normal, but anything over five minutes is an emergency."

"*Any* seizure is an emergency," I countered.

"For you, yes. When *we* don't know the cause then yes, of course. What I mean is — anything over five minutes means there could be serious damage," he explained.

"Okay," I sighed. "Have you checked his file? This definitely hasn't happened before, correct?"

The man rose a brow at me. "I'd assume you would know if it had happened before."

"It's a long story and I don't have the patience to explain."

He sighed and flipped open his folder, scanning the page. "The doctor noted that there were no other occurrences on file for Noah, so I would assume this is his first. I'll be back once we've got the discharge paperwork."

I let Olivia drive us home from the hospital.

My built-up anxiety had left me crashing and bleary-eyed, and she was more than happy to get behind the wheel of the rental car I'd arranged for us when we'd landed in San Francisco.

The little bandaid over Noah's already needle-bruised arm served as a constant reminder of that panic as I gathered him from his car seat. He was more exhausted than me, his eyes squinty and his excitement to be home already dampening.

I carried him inside, his head slumped over my shoulder, his legs and arms wrapped around me like a starfish. Even though I knew he was tired, it took everything in me to not assume something else was horribly wrong and rush him back to the hospital.

"Do you want some time alone with him?" Liv asked, her bloodshot eyes meeting mine across the living room.

I shook my head. "I'd rather you come up with me to put him to bed," I sighed. "If you want to."

She sniffled and nodded once. "I want to."

Together, we walked him up the stairs, our bags abandoned in the car and carrying nothing but Noah and the toy car in Liv's hand. Together, we changed him into his pajamas, careful not to brush against the bandage that he was already complaining about. Together, we read to him, taking turns doing silly voices for the characters. Together, we tucked him in far too literally, dragging a happy giggle out of him as we stuffed the covers under his legs and abdomen. Together, we handled the crash when he finally asked us where his mother was and why she wasn't there at the hospital. It had finally clicked. Together, we set up the baby monitor I'd bought on a whim, making sure that the camera was pointing directly at him just in case.

Together, we parented in the only ways two people who had never been parents knew how. And I couldn't help but want more of that, couldn't help but want her by my side when anything like this happened again, couldn't help but want to blend my professional and personal life with her seamlessly to make whatever this was *work*. And on top of that, I couldn't help but let the rage bubble up inside of me that Grace wanted to take any chance of a future with Noah away from me.

It wasn't until I'd shut the door behind me and put

enough distance between his room and me that I let myself come to terms with what happened.

"Are you okay?" Liv asked.

"No." I shut my eyes, letting the tears well up before smearing them away with the palms of my hands.

"He'll be fine," she said softly, reaching across the kitchen island and taking my hand, squeezing it.

"I know," I sighed. "It's just... all of this. *All* of it, Liv."

"I know."

"Thank you," I added. "For just... for being there. For helping me. For being a... second parent, when he needed it. When *I* needed it."

She pursed her lips, offering me a sad little reassuring smile. "Of course. I care about him too, you know."

I nodded as I moved around the edge of the edge of the counter. "I know," I said.

She released my hand and I used mine to cup her cheeks instead, to hold her in place as I pressed my lips against hers. She was a comfort I didn't deserve, but I needed it, needed her, needed the solace she brought and the idea of something more. I needed to feel, and she was one of only two people capable of giving me that — and the other was sound asleep upstairs.

"You've had a long day," I mumbled against her lips, letting my fingers push back into her hair just a touch. "I'll understand if you're not up for anything."

"I am," she breathed. "If you need it, I am. I could use an outlet, too."

"Thank fuck."

Her arms snaked around my neck as she brought her lips to mine this time, her kiss so soft, so easy.

I buried myself inside of her until every raw, aching, angry emotion I felt about the situation with Noah was overwhelmed and diminished by *her*.

In the darkness of my bedroom, I loomed over her, my length fully encompassed by her, my *everything* swarmed in her presence. Her rear rested on my knees, and with one of my hands on her hip and the other cradling her head, I thrust into her.

"God," I breathed, my lips brushing against hers, my forehead resting on the curve of her hairline. "You're perfect. Every fucking inch of you. Everything... fuck, everything about you."

Her fingers dug into my back, my neck, as she briefly pressed her lips to mine. She'd had her release twice already, and in her desperate pleas for me to give her a second to recover, she'd begged me to be inside of her at least.

"I need you," I rasped.

"I'm right here," she whispered, her voice cracking as I hit that spot inside of her that she liked so much. Her words turned to gasps. "I'm—I'm right, right here."

Using my nose, I turned her head just enough that I could kiss her jaw, her neck, the soft spot beneath her ear. "Thank you."

My thrusts grew erratic, and I shifted the hand on her hip and tucked it between us instead, drawing whimper and cries from her as I met her swollen, oversensitive bundle of nerves. She built quickly and drastically, her body locking, her breaths too fast, too desperate.

"Need this," I groaned. "I need this, Liv, fucking *always*. I...shit, I need you, need you just like this, need—"

A beep came from beside us and both of us froze, shifting only to check the baby monitor on the bedside table. Heavy breaths wracked my body as I stared at it, Noah's unmoving form lighting the screen. It was meant to alert when there was excessive movement, but all I could see was the rise and fall of his chest.

"It's okay," Liv breathed, her hand reaching out to point in the darkness toward the top of the screen. "It's the battery alert. It's okay."

I couldn't tear my gaze from it.

She took her face in my hands so fucking gently that they almost didn't register until she was softly pulling my gaze back to her. "Dame," she whispered. "He's okay. It's just the battery. *He's okay.*"

My throat closed in. I didn't deserve her, no matter what I did, no matter how many lifetimes I lived, she was too perfect to me.

"He's okay," she repeated, pushing the sweaty strings of hair that clung to my cheeks out of my face. "You're okay, and he's okay."

She kissed my lips, my jaw, my nose, both of us unmoving below our shoulders and both of us locked to each other. She comforted me, she held me, and when I needed it, needed the distraction but couldn't bring myself to do it, she moved for me, pitching and shifting her hips.

"You're okay," she said, over and over and over, interspersed with replacements of *he's* instead of *you're*. She pulled me out of the haze of panic as if she knew exactly what would work, exactly what would make me feel okay, exactly what I needed.

But she was what I needed. Her and Noah. They were

all I fucking needed. And as the temptation to speak words I hadn't said in over five years bubbled up, I found myself stuffing them down, burying them, demolishing them before they could take shape. I distracted my lips with hers. I said it in the way I moved, in the way I put her first in that moment.

I told her I needed her, and nothing else.

Chapter 25

Olivia

Having a private office, no matter how small, had improved my time at the office tenfold.

I wasn't sure if it was a silent gift from Damien or if it was simply a result of him putting pressure on my manager to curb the stares and whispers, but either way, it gave me space to escape the house and bury myself in work without worrying about whether or not Noah would get himself into trouble. But of course, even with Caroline watching him, even with the privacy to keep myself focused, and even with the pretty view out of my singular floor to ceiling window that looked out toward the Angel Island State Park, I hadn't been able to stop worrying about the possibility of Noah having another seizure, and a private office wouldn't fix *that*.

I knew deep down that it wasn't my place to worry about him as extensively as I was. I was in charge of him when Damien or Caroline or his new school weren't, but even still, I'd found it difficult to turn that off or put it out of my head. It was always there, a constant fizzling anxiety that Damien and I would need to rush to the hospital again.

Or Damien. Just Damien. I wasn't guaranteed a spot there.

I sighed and deleted the last two paragraphs I'd written in the email I was drafting. Maybe a private office out of the house wasn't the answer to all of my problems, considering I could barely fucking focus. I wanted to call Damien, wanted to ask him if he'd heard from Caroline, wanted to check up on Noah. I knew I needed to get through the emails that were piling up, but I just couldn't bring myself to shift my attention.

I spun halfway around in my office chair and plucked my purse from the table behind me. My phone sat sideways inside up against the handful of just-in-case tampons I'd shoved in there this morning, and when the screen lit up as I lifted it out, a text notification sat there unattended on my lockscreen. It couldn't have been that important if it hadn't notified me out loud — Damien's and Caroline's calls and messages would have bypassed silent mode.

The moment it recognized my face and my brother's name replaced the *Text Message* notification, though, my stomach sank.

James: What the fuck is this? Are you married? [Attach-ment: 1 Image]

Oh, fuck.

I opened up the messages and there, clear as fucking day and as nauseating as Noah controlling the spinning teacup at Disneyland, was a photo of me and Damien exiting the chapel in Vegas. I could *barely* remember him carrying me like that, like I was genuinely his *bride* — tucked up against him, an arm beneath my knees and another under my waist, my hair and makeup a mess and a cheap netted veil falling off my head. I was clutching a bottle of champagne in one hand and my heels in the other, and Damien, with the mismatched buttons on his shirt and his pocket square unfolded and hanging limp from his jacket pocket, was pressing a kiss against my temple.

If it wasn't the most horrifying evidence of what we'd done, I might have actually found it adorable. But it *was*, and my breakfast was coming back up.

I reached for the little trashcan beside my desk and nearly threw my phone across the small, enclosed space in the process, my head only barely making it over the lip of the flimsy, carbon-neutral bag. I spilled the small amount of cereal I'd managed to down this morning into it and dry heaved once before placing it back down on the ground.

I needed to text him back.

Me: Where did you find that?

Me: It was a joke. Office initiation for the new hires.

Me: James.

Me: JAMES.

Three little dots finally appeared after what felt like hours but must have only been seconds — the time on the top of my screen hadn't even changed.

James: It came up on Instagram.

A second later, a link to a post on Instagram from an obscure news site popped up. I made the horrible mistake of clicking on it.

Everyone's favorite SanFran multi-millionaire seems to have tied the knot in a drunken Vegas escapade... but who is the far younger woman he's holding? Visit the link in our bio to see more!

Oh my god.

Me: Don't tell Mom and Dad. It's not what it looks like.

James: Liv. You do realize that it's weird to do photo-ops with new hires like THAT, right?

I grabbed my purse and stood from my desk before I

could throw up again, sending the wheeled office chair careening back into the bookshelves. I didn't dare meet the eyes of anyone from my team as I stepped out my door, didn't dare to question who had seen it and who hadn't. I needed to breathe, needed a ginger ale, but more than either of those, I needed to speak to Damien.

———

That idea went up in flames the moment I found his office empty.

I shot him a text as I hurriedly made my way back to the elevator, just sending a quick *"need to talk to you ASAP. Not about Noah."* It was far too cold in the little metal box, and from the smell alone, I could tell someone had brought a banana to work before riding the elevator. The scent permeated the space, invading my nostrils, making my stomach churn all over again.

I stepped out into the less banana-heavy air of the Human Resources department. Across the wide open space filled with cubicles and hanging plants, Sophie sat at her desk, headphones in, blonde hair up in a tiny bun on top of her head. Her teeth were sinking into a fucking banana.

Instead of walking through the sea of cubicles, I shot her a text.

Me: Come here. Leave the banana.

Her brows furrowed as she glanced down at her desk.

Sophie: How do you know I have a banana?

Me: Because I'm staring at you.

Her head whipped in my direction before locking eyes

with me, her grin spreading across her cheeks. She pushed back from her chair and got up, left the banana behind on a napkin, and squeezed between cubicles and desk chairs as she made her way across the space.

"What's up? You couldn't wait until lunch to see me?" she asked, leaning against one of the structural beams that cut through the edges of the room. The happiness that sharpened her features fell as she noticed my frantic, panicked state, rounding out her face and her lips popping open. "What's wrong?"

"Some discount TMZ got ahold of a photo of us," I said, my voice far shakier than I thought it would be as I flipped my phone around to show her. "I don't know how, or why it took this long for something to come out. I don't even remember it being taken."

"Oh, fuck," she mumbled, slipping the phone from my grasp and zooming in. "I mean, AI has gotten really good. You could probably claim it was that."

"I don't think my parents have a fucking clue what AI is."

"Shit, I didn't think about that." She zoomed in on our faces, right where his lips met my temple, the crinkle of my eye as I was lost in the excitement of it all just there on the edge of the screen. "You look really cute. Really drunk, but really cute."

"That's so nice to hear when I'm panicking, Sophie," I grumbled, snatching the phone back from her.

"You don't even know if they'll see it."

"My *brother* is the one that informed me," I challenged. "I made up some lie about it being a weird initiation thing for new hires, but I don't think he believed me."

"*Initiation?*" She asked, her nose crinkling with distaste. "Damien would never do that."

"I didn't know what else to say. How the fuck do you explain something like that away?"

She sighed, her shoulders sagging. "No idea. But I don't think your lie will work, and if it does, it won't last long. I can raise it with the higher ups in PR but..."

"But what?"

"It'll draw attention to it in the meantime," she explained. "Though I guess that's bound to happen anyway if it's doing the rounds on social media. You should speak to Damien."

"He's not in his office. I know he was taking Noah to his first day of school, but maybe he got called into a meeting or something. I don't know," I sighed. "What I *should* do is call my parents and tell them what I told James before they can even see it."

She shook her head ferociously, her blonde bun nearly coming loose, and looked me dead in the eye. "No. Nope. Absolutely not, Liv. You'll raise questions and you're a terrible liar. You will wait, you will speak with Damien, and you will hope that no one else sees it. That's all you can do right now."

"But what if that news site gets its hands on a copy of our marriage certificate? What if they come out with shit I can't disprove before I can get a jump on this?" I urged, pocketing my phone with a shaky hand. My stomach was starting to twist again, and I swore I could still smell the lingering scent of banana on her. "We need this fucking annulment *now*. I don't understand what the hold up is."

She sighed and shrugged her jacketed shoulders. "I don't know. This stuff isn't always instant. You need to speak to Damien."

Chapter 26

Damien

Watching Noah be so absolutely excited to run into his new school and make new friends after what had happened last week was enough to crack my fucking chest.

He didn't even seem phased by the seizure. He was back to himself the next morning, and when I'd nervously brought up the topic of him starting at the private school I'd shelled thousands out for, he surprisingly seemed more than keen.

I'd spent hours in meetings with his teacher, the principal, and the school nurse — I wasn't about to let anything go unchecked or a single set of eyes to be off of him. Not after the seizure. If something happened, I needed to know that people would be on hand immediately.

It only helped a little bit that the school was directly next to a hospital.

"Remind me of the rules," I said, pop-quizzing him as I white-knuckled the steering wheel. My Audi, the one I barely ever drove, idled beneath us.

"Dad, I know them," Noah groaned, his head flopping back dramatically into his carseat.

I stared him down in the rearview mirror. "Then *remind me.*"

"Call you or Olivia if I need a thing," he started, his pointer fingers coming together as he started to count them off. "Don't be... what was the word?"

"*Blasé.*"

"Don't be *blasé* when I say that Mom is dead. No fighting. No back-talking Mrs. Thatch. Ask for the nurse if I feel bad and tell them to call you."

"And the sixth one?" I grinned, turning to look over my shoulder instead. He beamed back at me.

"Oh yeah! Have fun."

———

Liv's message lit up my phone in the middle of the meeting. For a split second, my heart skipped a beat at the first words: *need to talk to you ASAP.* Thank god she'd followed it with a heads up that it wasn't about Noah, because I was two seconds from leaping out of my chair and ignoring the lashing I was getting from the shareholders.

I replied to her the moment we finished up and let her know that I was heading back to my office. I'd barely made it before her — I had about enough time to sit down in my chair and open my laptop before the door clicked open and her panicked form rushed through.

"Fix this," she said, her phone in hand as she crossed the expanse of the open layout. Her wavy brown hair looked a little unkempt at the roots as if she'd been pulling at it, her eyes just a little too wide, a little too stressed. She wore one of my favorite outfit combinations of hers — a loose, flowing white button-up tucked into a pair of wide leg black slacks, cinching her in at the waist.

"Fix what?" I asked. "No *hi, how was dropping off Noah this morning?*"

She glared at me as she held her phone out. The screen was filled with a photograph, and the moment I took it from her, I realized *exactly* what photo that was. I could remember the flash of light as we left, could remember kissing her temple like that, drunkenly assuming it was a chapel photographer and not some random passerby. *Shit.* "Hi," she deadpanned, the sarcasm dripping from her tongue. "How was dropping off Noah this morning?"

"Shit. Where did you find this?" I asked, zooming in on the only evidence of what we'd done. Although it made me worried for her, I couldn't deny that it was nice to have one concrete piece of evidence that I'd liked her from the start and hadn't just wanted to fuck anything that moved. It was the *only* thing we had that wasn't a faded, drunken memory.

"My brother sent it to me," she swallowed, her voice faltering just a tad. "It was in some cheap tabloid."

"Which one?" I asked. I tried to exit the photo in the hopes that it would take me back to the website it was published on, but it just sent me back to her photo gallery, sitting there amongst the myriad of pictures of Noah eating ice cream and a handful from our trip up north. *She saved it.*

"Wealthy Watch," she scoffed. "It's some weird, off brand tabloid that apparently focuses on people like *you*. But you're missing the point."

"I'm not, Liv, I'm just trying to figure out—"

"My *brother* sent it to me. You know what my parents

242

are like. You know what I'm—what I'm *supposed* to be like."
She collapsed into one of the wingback chairs opposite my
desk, burying her face in her hands as her elbows rested on
her knees. "Fix it. Please, before I have to do more damage
control or come up with better lies. Scrub it and push Ethan
on the annulment."

I swallowed. "He's submitted the paperwork. We're just
waiting for it to clear."

"Thank fuck," she breathed. "How long does that take?"

"I'll ask him," I offered, scrolling up through her images
out of sheer curiosity and the need for a distraction. One of
them, just there at the top of the screen, was the same one
that existed on my phone, the same one she'd sent me two
days ago while I was here and she was with Noah at the
beach. He was sitting in her lap and clutching a sandwich in
his hand, and she was kissing him on the side of the head
just like I was with her in the photo she'd come in to
show me.

I didn't *want* to lose this.

"I'll call him the moment he's done at the courthouse," I
added. "He should be leaving soon."

Her lips pursed as she lifted her head from her hands.
"Okay," she nodded, taking her phone back from me as I
slid it across my desk. "Please let me know."

———

"What do you *mean* she's strengthened the fucking case?" I
gripped the underside of my desk so hard I could feel my
nails chipping as I pulled myself back to my computer.

"She found a photo." My heart sank as Ethan's hurried breaths filled the dead space of the call. From what I could tell, he was rushing back to his car after having just left the courthouse to drop off some of the forms for the custody trial. "I didn't see it, but I believe it's of you and Olivia leaving the chapel—"

"I know the photo," I ground out through my teeth. And to think this day had started on a high. "How is that related to *this*?"

"She's spinning by saying it shows that you're unruly, unpredictable, and a liability. She managed to get some statements from people who saw you that night and is able to reliably say that you drunkenly married a much younger woman in Las Vegas under dubious circumstances. She's driving home the narrative that you're unfit to be a parent," Ethan said, his car door slamming through the phone. "You're fucking lucky that the women who work at the courthouse aren't very tight-lipped. Apparently Grace and her lawyer were telling them all about it."

Shit. I was screwed. I was absolutely, positively fucked by this. My heart hammered in my chest, my mind going blank and filling with flashing images of Noah from the morning, Noah in the hospital, Noah calling me *dad* for the first time.

"As far as I know, they're still unaware of Noah ending up in the hospital, and we'll keep it that way. She has no right to his medical documents. But you need to be aware that there is a possibility of that coming into play, as well," Ethan continued, but I was hardly paying attention.

"What do we do?" I asked, cutting right to the meat of it.

"I've already told you what you should do."

"Would that even *help* still?" The anger in my voice was

rising. I couldn't hold it back, couldn't keep myself from letting it flow in the one private space I had right now. "If they're questioning the legitimacy of my marriage, would staying together do *anything*?"

"Absolutely it would," Ethan shot back. He seemed just as irritated as I was — and I hoped it was as clear to him as it was to me that neither of us were angry at the other. "They're saying that you're unpredictable. Prove them wrong. Stay married. They think it was dubious circumstances, so show them that you're in love. An annulment will only solidify the narrative they're running with. It'll show that you made a poor decision and cannot be counted on."

"Fuck," I snapped. "*Fuck.*"

"You wouldn't even have to fake anything if your *feelings* are anything to go on," he added.

"Can you please not?"

"I'm sorry. I'm just... I'm almost as angry as you about this whole thing. They're fighting dirty and this isn't my area of expertise," he explained, and I wanted to believe him, truly. But there was no way on earth he was anywhere close to my level of anger, not when it wasn't *his* child on the line. "Look, Damien, I've spoken to a few other lawyers that specialize in family law, and every single one agreed with what I've suggested. And I imagine they'd double down on that now."

The idea of doing that, of going against my word when Liv had come in here not thirty minutes ago *begging* me to dissolve our marriage, plagued me far less than I thought it would in that moment.

I couldn't think with my heart on this. I had to think with my head, had to think of Noah, had to be okay with it. I cared for her, and I cared *far* too much, far more than I thought I was capable of — but Noah had to come first. Noah would always have to come first.

"You want me to give you the green light to cancel the annulment."

"I do," he sighed. In the background, his engine whirred to life. "We can put it back through when everything is said and done. But we can still cancel it."

We can put it back through when everything is said and done.

That, *that* right there, was my saving grace. A month and a half extra was sellable. I could tell her it was a backlog of paperwork, a flaw in the system, anything. We could put it back through and she'd have no idea.

"Do it," I said, hating myself just a little bit more as the words slipped out. "Cancel the annulment."

Chapter 27

Olivia

Noah's never-ending grin the moment he stepped out of the school doors as I was there to collect him would be forever burned into my memory, but I was still in panic mode. I wasn't sure exactly what Damien had done, but the post on instagram was gone along with the article — but there were lingering effects scattered across the internet. I didn't know how long it would take to be scrubbed, and every passing second and vibration of my phone sent anxiety coursing through my veins. So when I picked up Noah and gave him the biggest bear hug I could muster outside of the school gates, only to be interrupted by the chiming phone in my back pocket... I wished that wasn't tied to the memory.

The moment I noticed that it was a text from Damien, the panic calmed just a tad.

Damien: Spoke to Ethan. He said he can't give a firm timeline, but assured me that it's in the right hands and it shouldn't be too much longer. We're still working on the photo. I'm sorry.

Another two came through a moment later.

Damien: I've got a lot to work on tonight with Ethan about the custody case. It'll be a while until I'm home.

Damien: Caroline said she was having enchilada night with Lucas. She extended an invitation to you and Noah if you want some company. I can meet you there later.

I sighed and shoved my phone back into my pocket as I hurried Noah back to the idling car. The driver stood by the backseat door, his suit and tie for once not looking out of place in a sea of rich children's drivers, and Noah practically ran to dive into his carseat.

"I made four new friends!" he said excitedly to Paul, parroting what he'd already told me. "Alex, Sarah, Muhammad, and Talon."

"Talon?" Paul asked quizzically, his gaze turning to me as one brow raised.

"Rich people." I shrugged.

———

"If I speak super fucking honestly about my life, will you tell Damien?" I asked, clutching my glass of red wine like a vice. Carrie and I sat on the back deck of her house, looking out across the rolling hills and green. It reminded me almost too much of how nice it was back up near Seattle before it all came to a shattering halt. Through the crack in the sliding glass door, a robotic voice droned on offering cake as some kind of reward, and Lucas spoke over it, explaining to Noah that the robot was lying.

"Nah. I have no problem keeping secrets from my brother," she laughed. "Unless you tell me you killed someone. Then I might need to tell someone because, you know, Noah."

I stabbed the cut off bit of shredded, Mexican style chicken encased in a tortilla, dipping it into my little pile of sour cream. "I haven't killed anyone," I chuckled, popping the bite in my mouth before following it with a sip of wine. "At least not yet. My parents are likely to keel over the moment they see that image."

She winced. I'd already explained to her how I'd been raised, how I viewed certain things, how *they* viewed everything else. And I'd shown her the image — she thought it was cute.

"I think everything is starting to hit me," I sighed, setting my fork down. "All of it. The accidental marriage. The photo. How much I care for Noah."

I paused, and she waited, as if she knew exactly what I was going to say.

"How much I care for *Damien*," I added, biting back the knot in my throat. "I don't think I could bring myself to admit it to him. But it's... there."

"It's okay to have feelings for him," she offered, her voice a little quieter, a little softer. "You've basically been flung into the thick of married life with him out of nowhere. It would happen to anyone."

Fuck, why did *that* hurt? She wasn't wrong, of course, but it felt like more than that. It felt higher than a circumstantial thing, it felt like more. "I don't think it's just because of the time we've spent together," I said.

Her mouth popped open as she quietly gave me an, "Ah."

"It's just making this all so much harder than it needs to be. This has to end, but I keep finding myself wishing that it won't," I admitted, my stomach churning again from far too

249

much honesty. "I know I'm a people pleaser. I know I do a lot of things for other people that I don't need to. I'm starting to wonder if me wanting the annulment is just another aspect of that."

"You're still going through with it?" she asked, her gaze fixing on mine as she lifted her glass to her lips.

I nodded. "I don't have much of a choice. And I thought... this sounds stupid, but I thought I was doing it for me. I thought I was going through with the annulment because I wanted it, because I couldn't see myself marrying someone just to sleep with them, because I didn't want that to be my story. But it feels more like I'm doing it so that my parents don't disown me. It feels more like I'm doing it because it's what would be expected of me. And if I had a choice here..."

"You don't know if you would?"

I pursed my lips as I thought it over. "I think I would. But I'd want to start over, do it right, and come back around. And I don't think that's on the table with him."

"Do you want my opinion?" She set her drink down on the table, and inside, Noah prattled on about whatever they were doing in their video game wouldn't be possible in real life.

I nodded.

"I think you should stay married," she sighed. "With everything going on... the custody battle, the court cases over at Blackwood, the chaos of it all... I don't know. It's just adding more stress for both of you. And in reality, as much as he probably doesn't want to say it, staying married would almost certainly help him in the custody fight."

I swallowed down another sip of wine before setting the glass on the wicker table. I'd barely had half a glass, but I just didn't want it. "I can't push the annulment back. Even if it's not what I want, the stress of it all is making me sick, literally. I need to do this the right way."

She gave me a sympathetic smile and took my hand gently. "I understand that."

"Everything is upside down." The backs of my eyes burned as I glanced in through the glass door, watching as Noah stood far too close to the television with a controller clutched in his hands. "I didn't plan on any of this for my life. And I'm not upset about it, I'm really not, because I don't even think I'd want to change what I have right now. But I don't... I don't even know if Damien feels the same. For all I know, he could be absolutely fine to drop me back at my apartment and delete my number the moment the annulment goes through."

"I don't think he'd—"

"I don't either. But I don't know how much of how he is with me is just because I'm the closest person he can pour that into." My jaw quivered as I took in a deep breath, trying desperately to steady myself. "And if he doesn't feel that way toward me, then I can't keep going like this. I'll break my own fucking heart if I do. I need the annulment, and if he wants to continue things, then we'll go from there. But for now, that has to be what I do. For myself."

Chapter 28

Damien

The quiet corner of the rooftop bar and restaurant was private enough for Ethan to discuss what he needed to with me outside of the office. If I needed to spend another hour cooped up, sitting at my desk, I was likely to lose my mind.

"Please tell me you have good news," I said, glancing over the small, leather-bound menu.

"Some." He leaned back in his seat, pushing his glasses up his nose as he lifted his briefcase up and onto the table. He pulled out four stacks of papers, each held together with binder clips, and passed them to me. "We're likely to win each of the Blackwood's lawsuits. We probably won't even need to show our faces at the hearings."

I flipped through them hesitantly, truly not understanding a word of the legal jargon that littered them, not even the highlighted phrases. "How?"

"Because what they were trying to do was technically illegal. But there is still a chance that each of the companies won't be liable for repaying what you shelled out to acquire them, so we're still working on that," he explained, passing me another, smaller set of papers that made even less sense to me. I took them regardless.

"We need that money back," I said.

"I'm aware. We're not fully out of the woods."

I put on a show of flipping through each sheet of documents for a few moments, stopping only to inform the waitress of what I was ordering. Ethan looked far too interested in the specials as she rattled them off, and for a split second, I wondered if his extensive questions about the fish of the day and its natural habitat were his idea of flirting.

When I was happy with how much I'd performed, I passed the papers back, settling into my seat with my freshly delivered glass of Lagavulin 26.

"Was that flirting?" I asked, trying my best to lighten the mood. I hadn't been able to look at him as a *friend* in what felt like weeks. He was Ethan The Lawyer lately instead of Ethan Turner, and I was beginning to feel desperate for a return to some kind of normalcy. There was just too much going on lately.

He shrugged. "I was just curious about wahoo and why they're labeled as tropical when they're also considered subtropical."

I raised a brow at him. "And you thought the *waitress* would be the right person to ask instead of, I don't know, *Google*?"

His gaze narrowed as he pushed his glasses up his nose again. "She was attractive."

"There it is."

"Oh, I'm sorry, should I do it your way and have Elvis marry us?" he questioned, pursing his lips to hide the inkling of a grin that flashed.

I snorted as I set my glass back down on the table. "See?

That's the Ethan I miss. We've been far too wrapped up in all this shit to actually talk."

He sighed as he reached back into his briefcase again. "Then we should get the biggest problem out of the way so that we can actually enjoy our lunch without it hanging over me."

I groaned in frustration as he pulled more paperwork out. I knew there had to be a catch, knew there had to be more than just somewhat-good-news. But if it meant that we could try to relax after this, then I'd deal with hearing whatever it was and knock back the rest of my whiskey to put it out of my mind.

The small stack landed in front of me. Along the top, *Application For Annulment: Notice of Acceptance* was printed in bolded letters, and it was addressed to *Damien Blackwood and Olivia Martin*.

"I couldn't cancel it," Ethan said, his voice far calmer than it had been before. It was almost sympathetic. "It's not finished. You two still need to sign and appear before a judge. But the paperwork was filed and approved."

I swallowed down the bile that was beginning to rise up my esophagus. "Fuck."

"Damien," he said softly, dragging my attention back to him. "*It's not finished.* This can't be held against you right now. A court date needs to be set, and you have sixty days to arrange that. It will only be official if the judge finalizes it. You can wait."

It's not finished.

"If I were you..." His jaw ticked as he looked between me and the heavy weight in my hands. "I would wait to set a date until after the custody case next month."

The intensity of the choice I'd made was already eating

at me, but this just made it so much worse. "She'll want the date set as soon as possible."

"I can't advise you legally to not tell her," he said, his voice so quiet I could barely hear it over the clinking of glasses and idle chatter. "But as your *friend*, I can tell you that it isn't unheard of for legal documents to take weeks to mail to their intended recipients. Do you understand what I'm saying?"

"You think I should hide it until after the custody case," I said, setting the papers beside me on the table. Those would need to come home with me regardless. "If she finds out…"

"She has no reason to."

"There's a date on it, Ethan."

"Again, cogs turn slowly in government cases," he explained. "Things can be filed and approved and printed and not mailed for ages."

"I don't want to lose her," I breathed. His jaw ticked again and my walls went up immediately, shutting down the realness I was far too ready to supply him with. He already knew it, but I didn't need to drive that home any further. "She's amazing with Noah. The kid idolizes her. And she's been putting so much time into him, so much of *herself*… She's even been helping me look for a nanny to take care of him after school for when this is settled. I don't want to break the girl."

"You don't want to break *yourself*."

"I don't want to hurt Noah, either," I sighed. "If she goes… She's been the only steady, female presence in his life since his mom died."

Ethan's eyes met mine, pointed and stressed and far too knowing. He pushed his stupid fucking glasses up his nose again, and for a split second, I wanted to break them in two. "Then you know what you need to do."

Chapter 29

Olivia

Noah's face pressed against the thick glass of the lion enclosure, his breath fogging his view. He kept swiping it away every time it became too much to see.

Ten feet behind him, Sophie and I sat on a bench in the shade, my gaze fixed wholly on Noah and hers fixed wholly on me.

"You can't be serious."

"Please don't say anything," I said quietly. "Especially not to Noah."

"I won't. But why didn't you tell me sooner?" Her lower lip jutted out in a pout, and I could just about make it out in the corner of my field of view.

Noah banged on the glass and I shifted my attention. "Noah, don't do that," I called to him. He spun on his heel and looked at me wide-eyed, his curly brown hair sticking up in funny directions from the wind. Without that, he looked so much like his father it was genuinely frightening at times. "If you were trapped in an enclosed environment, you wouldn't want someone coming up and banging on *your* glass."

He shook his head. "I would if they wanted to be friends!"

"The lion does not want to be friends with you."

"You don't know that!" he huffed, spinning back around to stare at the sleeping lion again.

I rolled my eyes and refocused my attention back on Sophie once I was positive Noah wouldn't bang on the glass again. "I'm barely capable of admitting it to myself, let alone other people."

"You haven't told him?" she asked. "Liv, you have to tell him. You can't just waltz around feeling sorry for yourself and assuming that he doesn't have feelings for you too."

I shook my head. "If I tell him, then it becomes real. And that opens a whole new can of worms that I haven't put enough thought into."

Sophie's hand motioned for me to continue, and I glanced at it quickly before turning my gaze back to Noah.

"Like, if I tell him and he feels the same about me, then we'd need to discuss what that means. We'd need to consider how confusing that is for Noah when he's probably already confused about what we are. We'd have to consider if we even wanted to go through with the annulment, and we'd have to think about the possibilities of us being long term and how that would affect both of our lives. And I'm not ready for any of those conversations yet," I explained, my throat closing in just a little. It wasn't even that emotional of a topic and I was already getting overwhelmed.

"If you love him, then you have to be okay with having those conversations," she said, her voice so fucking soft that it nearly sent me into a frenzy.

"I didn't say that I—"

"You didn't *need* to."

Tears burned at the backs of my eyes and before I could stop them, they welled up in the corners, slipping over the edges far too easily. I wiped them away, but there was no stopping her from noticing.

"Aw, Liv..."

Her arms wrapped around my shoulders from the side as she hugged me, and *fuck*, why did I want to just let myself cry at the goddamn zoo? Why did I even want to cry in the first place?

"I'm fine," I croaked. "*Fuck*, why am I crying?"

She snorted as she released me. "You on your period? You're always emotional on your period."

I shook my head. "No, it hasn't..."

Wait.

Every part of me froze. It hadn't started yet. *How long ago did I put the emergency tampons in my bag?* I thought back, days, days, days — no, *shit,* it had been a week. A fucking *week*. I'd done it a week ago after my phone had notified me that I was due to start that day.

"Liv?"

"Oh my god," I breathed.

I pulled my phone from my purse and frantically opened my period tracker. Sure enough, right there on the screen, it said I should have finished my cycle two days ago. I had never been more than a single day off since starting birth control.

"What do I do? Soph, what the *fuck* do I do?" I asked, my voice shaking, my *hands* shaking. I couldn't stop staring at it.

"Calm down," she advised, putting her hand over my phone and clicking the button to turn off the screen. "You're okay. You're fine. We can go get a test. You're on the pill right?"

I nodded, forcing myself to look back at Noah to make sure he hadn't run off. Thank god he was still staring at the lion, even if he was making roaring sounds.

"And you've been taking it correctly?"

"What do you mean?" I asked.

"You haven't missed any, right?" she asked, her hand squeezing mine.

"Maybe one or two? I just doubled up," I explained.

Her face went white as she forced herself into my field of view. "What do you mean you just doubled up? When was the last time you missed one?"

I blinked at her. "A few weeks ago?"

"Oh my god, Liv. You have to take those exactly as it says or they don't work. How do you not know that?"

My gaze bounced from Noah to her, the stone in my gut sinking rapidly. "I don't... I don't know, I got them to help with my cramps. I wasn't using them for birth control until recently."

Noah spun on the spot and started trotting back over to us as Sophie spoke again. "Your parents didn't—... Shit, no, they wouldn't have, would they?"

"Livie, why are you crying?" Noah asked, but I didn't know how to fucking answer him. He hopped up on the bench beside me and wrapped his arms around my waist, burying himself in my side. I knew he was trying to help.

"We'll go get a test. Right now," Sophie urged. Her attention turned to the five year old wrapped around me like a monkey. "Liv's not feeling very well, Noah. Are you okay if we go now?"

"But the Gor—"

Whatever look Sophie gave him was enough to calm his complaints.

———

We picked up a box of ten tests and an unhealthy amount of McNuggets on our way back to Damien's house. I hadn't checked with him regarding having Sophie over, but I didn't give a shit at this point.

Not when all of the ten tests were laid out in front of me on the bathroom counter, each one showing two bold red lines.

The faint sound of cartoons drifted in from downstairs and mixed almost harmoniously with the gasps for air through my tears. This wasn't how anything was supposed to happen, this wasn't what I'd imagined for my life. But it all made sense now — the nausea, the smells, the hormones. I was an idiot for not noticing.

"It's okay," Sophie cooed, her hand rubbing small circles on the top of my back. A string of snot slipped from my nose and fell disgustingly into the bathroom sink. I felt like I couldn't breathe.

"It's not okay," I sobbed, leaning down to put my head in my hands. "This isn't how any of this was supposed to happen. I got drunkenly married in *Vegas*, fell in fucking love with a man twice my age, and now I'm pregnant with his goddamn child when he very clearly told me he didn't want another."

I didn't care that I'd said it. It was out there, I couldn't take it back, couldn't un-speak *love* if I tried. And going off of what Sophie had said earlier, it was already obvious.

"He might change his mind once he knows," she said softly. "It's okay to do things differently than you thought you would. Things don't have to go to plan."

"I'm not telling him," I croaked.

Her hand paused. "You have to tell him."

I shook my head and wiped the bubbling snot from my nostrils. "I don't. I'll break my own fucking heart if I have to."

Her jaw hardened as her lips pressed into a thin line. "You can't do what his ex did to him, Liv. That's not fair and he's not done anything to deserve that."

She was right, and I hated it.

I couldn't hide it forever. Even if he wanted to keep seeing me, even if he felt the way I did, I couldn't conceal a baby bump. And if I told him and he agreed to stay with me, would he even be with me because he wanted to be?

Would he be with me because he felt he had to?

Chapter 30

Damien

I'd barely been able to look at her without wanting to throw myself off the Golden Gate Bridge.

The guilt was eating me alive. Olivia was everywhere, it seemed — at home, at work, in my head, in my sheets. She hadn't even been sleeping in her room anymore, and there were only so many times I could put off going to bed in the hopes that she'd be asleep when I finally joined her. As much as I wanted to spend every waking second with her and Noah, every time her eyes met mine, I couldn't stop thinking about the papers.

I felt like a monster.

And even as I sat alone in my office at home, my eyes glued to a blank screen and my mind whirring, I couldn't escape her. I could never escape her.

"Dame."

She stood in the doorway, her wavy hair tucked up into a messy bun. The shirt of mine that she wore was my old university shirt, the logo taking up the majority of the front, and it fell down just past her upper thighs, practically swallowing her. I had to battle myself not to get up from my desk and pull her into my arms.

"Are you still working?" she asked.

"Yeah," I lied, the weight of it practically cracking my chest. "I'm sorry."

She rolled her lips between her teeth. "You've been working too much lately."

"I know," I sighed. "Between the lawsuits and getting your project off the ground, it's been a lot. It should calm down here soon."

She nodded, but I wasn't sure if it was more to herself or me. A beat of silence passed between us as if she was expecting me to fill it, but I didn't know what else to say, didn't know what else I could offer that wasn't just lie after lie after goddamn lie. "I put Noah to bed. I hope that's okay."

My brows furrowed. "Why didn't you come get me? I could have done that."

"You're... busy."

I scrubbed at my face. She had a point, even if she was wrong. I'd finished work hours ago. "Yeah, you're right."

"I'll probably be up for another couple of hours," she said, one hand encompassing the other's wrist. She rubbed at it nervously. "If you've got a minute, I really need to speak with you."

She wants to ask about the papers. Avoid it. "Yeah, of course. I'll be down in a little bit," I said.

As if they were on fire, I could physically feel their presence in the drawer beside my right thigh, along with the box I kept hidden at the very back. It burned me, made me want to shrink down and bury myself inside the drawer so I could go up in flames alongside it. I'd been feeding her excuse after excuse, hiding from her, pulling myself away from her so I wouldn't have to face her asking about it. But it would come. And I'd burn.

"I *am* sorry," I repeated, hoping another apology would make both of us feel better.

She nodded again. "Have you heard from Ethan?"

Sweat broke out across every inch of my skin. "No," I lied.

"Not at all?"

"Not about the annulment," I clarified, my mouth feeling like I'd swallowed a mouthful of fucking sand. "He'll tell me the moment he gets them back. And I'll tell you."

She hesitated in the doorway, her gaze locked on mine. "Okay," she sighed.

And then she was gone.

Chapter 31

Olivia

The morning sickness was too much for me.

I'd told my manager I'd be working from home the moment I woke up. For the first time in the last week since I'd found out, I was actually relieved that Damien hadn't been in bed beside me this morning. He didn't notice how quickly I'd run to the bathroom, didn't notice the retching sounds as I spilled stomach acid into the toilet, didn't notice how pale my face had gone. I wasn't even sure if he'd made it to the bedroom at all last night.

I'd sent him a text letting him know, too, that I wouldn't be in the office today. I'd offered to get Noah after school instead of having Caroline take him for the afternoon, but Lucas and him had already made plans to finish their video game, so I let that go.

I could handle a day on my own, lost in my own head. I'd been in my head for days with Damien being so busy, anyway.

It had taken me a week to come to terms with the pregnancy and telling Damien. Sophie was right — it wasn't okay for me to keep it from him like Marissa did. I'd decided

266

I'd tell him once things settled, maybe even after the custody hearing, when another stressor on his plate wouldn't make him explode. I'd deal with the consequences then.

The whirr of the printer on the other side of my home office brought me back into my body and away from my mind. Page after page of environmental reports printed, and once I realized just how *many* pages it was, I searched for my stapler.

Odd. It should be right...there.

Where the fuck was my stapler?

I pushed my rolling chair back and popped my earbuds out. The silence of Damien's too-large house was shockingly unsettling — I was so used to having at least the steady hum of children's cartoons in the background while I worked. I couldn't remember the last time I'd stayed home without Noah around, and the more that I considered it, it might have actually been the first time.

I slipped from my chair and looked through my filing cabinet, checked my drawers, checked each shelf of the bookshelves Damien had recently installed. I couldn't remember ever opening the closet in here, but I also had pregnancy brain and wouldn't have put it past myself to forget that, so I checked there, too.

Coming up thoroughly empty-handed, I almost gave up. I could have just held the stacks together with smaller sized binder clips, but the temptation to abandon my work for a couple of minutes to get to the bottom of my mini-mystery was too tempting. I could use a break and maybe a snack, if my stomach would allow for it.

Rounding the open office door on the top floor, I made my way past useless rooms that sat unfurnished and forgotten, save for Damien's home gym. For a moment, just a fleeting, passing second, I let myself envision what I'd do with them if I lived here more than I already did. If the planets aligned and Damien wanted me *and* the clump of cells growing inside of me, and wanted me to stay...

I'd start by turning what was considered "my" room on the second floor into a nursery.

I'd move my things into Damien's room, and Noah could sleep next door to his little brother or sister, close enough that I wouldn't need to worry too much and far enough that we would still have our privacy.

As I took the stairs down to the second floor, my footsteps echoing in the eerie quiet, I considered turning one of the third floor rooms into a playroom for Noah and the baby. But the thought of us being downstairs and them being so far away seemed daunting, so my mind shifted, turning, tearing down the wall that divided the two unused rooms and redecorating it entirely. Damien's home office could move up there instead of being on the ground floor, and we could turn his office into a playroom instead. No stairs needed.

His office.

Shit, that had to be where my stapler was.

He'd been working from home in the evenings and late into the night. He must have needed my stapler and gone searching for mine, the thought not even crossing his mind to tell me or put it back.

Padding down the last set of stairs into the open living room on the ground floor, I rounded the corner, stepping into the hallway that ran opposite to the kitchen. There was only one door along it, which I'd always considered kind of odd every time I came back here — one that led directly into his office.

The scent of oak invaded my nostrils. Everything in

here was polished wood, dark paint, and matched the shadowy design of his kitchen and living room. But then the hint of lingering almonds, rum, and vanilla came swiftly after as I made my way to his desk. A last little reminder that he'd spent all night in here.

I sunk down into his office chair, doing a quick scan of the top of his desk and coming up short. He'd bought the exact same chair for my space upstairs, and although his was slightly more plush from less use overall, it was just as comfortable. His home laptop sat on his desk undisturbed and closed, and although the temptation was there, I didn't open it.

But I needed my damn stapler.

One long drawer ran along the top of the footwell, and I checked there first, but found nothing except a couple of stacks of unused post-it notes and a handful of slightly bent paperclips.

The upper drawer to my left held two stacks of paper, both some kind of legal paperwork that I didn't fully understand, but I could at least gather that they were to do with the lawsuits from Blackwood's against the four companies he'd acquired.

In the lower drawer to the left, I found nothing but a faint sheen of dust on the bottom of it and a single discarded paperclip half-lodged in the wood at the very back.

I turned to my right, hooking my finger on the handle of the upper drawer, and tugged. My breath caught.

There, on top of a stack of papers, sat my stapler. *Finally*.

I wrapped my digits around it and lifted the heavy duty stapler up onto the desk, but the moment I went to close the drawer, my vision snagged on my own name. *Damien Blackwood and Olivia Martin*.

I looked a little closer, pulling the drawer further out so I could see the entire top sheet of paper. *Application For Annulment: Notice of Acceptance* was written across the top in big bold lettering, and my fucking heart stopped beating.

What... the hell?

With shaking hands, I lifted the papers out of the drawer. The date on the top right corner was nearly two weeks ago. I scanned the page, hoping that maybe it was just a standard bit of mail to inform the two applicants that their paperwork had been *accepted* by the office but was still pending approval. But the more I read, the more my stomach churned, and the more angry I became.

It wasn't pending approval.

They were waiting for a court date to be set.

———

I wasn't sure how much time had passed when I heard the front door alarm chime.

I hadn't even moved from his office. I must have spent hours upon hours staring at those papers, reading every line, memorizing them. I vaguely remember calling the courthouse to ask whether a date had been set in the hopes that maybe he'd just recently scheduled it and hadn't had the chance to tell me, but the woman on the phone informed me that both parties need to agree to the date before it was finalized.

I'd almost thrown up on his desk after that.

Steps padded through the living room, and even in my

haze of shock and anger, even with my inability to move, I could feel myself vibrating, could feel my heart pounding against my ribcage. Part of me hoped it was Caroline, but I knew deep down in my gut that it wasn't.

The footsteps grew closer, closer, closer.

And stopped.

"Liv?"

I couldn't bring myself to tear my gaze from the papers in front of me. I couldn't bring myself to move from his chair, my knees tucked up against my chest, my toes dangling off the edge, my arms around my shins. I didn't care that I was still in what I considered pajamas when Noah wasn't around — a far too large shirt of Damien's and nothing else.

"Fuck," Damien sighed, and something leather and metal hit the ground. Had to be his briefcase.

The backs of my eyes burned, but I hadn't drank any water since I'd come downstairs and I'd cried out far too many tears. They wouldn't form — only threatened to.

"Liv—"

"Don't." My throat ached around the word. It felt raw, *sounded* raw, and I almost wished I'd had the forethought to pack my things and leave before he came home. But I couldn't do that to Noah.

"Can I explain?" he asked, a thump from his step as his legs slowly entered my field of vision.

I sniffled and wiped at my dry eyes out of instinct. "I don't want your excuses," I choked. "How long have you had them?"

He took a deep, noisy breath in before he spoke again. "A week and a half."

"You've been lying to me for a week and a—"

"No," he interjected, slowly lowering himself into the

271

leather chair that sat opposite his desk. His suit jacket, his button-up, his tie — I could see it all except his face. I didn't *want* to see that, though, didn't *want* to see whatever anguished expression he was pulling as if I was the one hurting him. "I've been lying to you for two days. I was avoiding the question before that."

"That doesn't make it better," I scoffed.

"I know that," he said, his tone far too gentle, too soft. "I do."

A heavy, charged silence fell over us. I gripped onto myself, digging my nails into my exposed skin, wishing, *wanting* to have never agreed to any of this. For a shattering second, I didn't care that it would mean I wouldn't have what was growing inside of me, and the shocking wave of guilt from that thought only drove my emotions to a peak.

For the first time in what felt like hours, I moved, but only enough to drop my forehead to my knees. I needed to breathe, needed to get a handle on myself, but I wasn't sure if I could. How much better was I when I was keeping something from him, too?

No. They aren't the same. I was keeping my secret to guard him from another overbearing stress when he had so many already.

He was keeping this from me to ensure I stayed put.

"Liv," he swallowed, the chair creaking beneath him. When he spoke again, his voice came from above, as if he'd stood up again and was leaning across his desk. "I'm so sorry. I made a horrible choice but I need you to understand that I didn't do it to hurt you. I did it—"

"I know why you did it," I sobbed. The lack of tears felt so wrong when my body was doing everything else that came with crying — the stuffy nose, the shaking breaths, the urge to crawl into myself and never come out. "That's the hardest fucking part."

For the first time since he'd started speaking, I could *hear* the pain in his voice. "I didn't know what else to do," he croaked. "Ethan said this was the only thing that would work. And you'd already made it incredibly clear that staying married to me was the last thing you wanted. But I— I couldn't risk losing him. I'm sorry, Liv. I'm so... fuck, I'm so sorry."

His heavy breathing, his steps back, forced me to lift my head, to look at him.

There, across the desk from me and a few paces away, he stared at me. The same blue eyes that I saw in his son were fixed on me, reflecting the soft golden rays of sunlight that poured in from behind me, far too glossy and damp. The fine lines across his forehead had deepened, and one hand pushed back the once-styled mess of black and gray hair atop his head. He looked genuinely frightened, and I knew exactly why I'd avoided this, why I'd kept myself from looking at him.

Seeing him like that only made me want to fix it. But I was the one who was broken here.

Still, I couldn't stop myself, couldn't hold myself back from slipping into those people pleasing tendencies that I needed to reign in desperately. "You could have *asked* me, Damien. You could have told me that was what you needed. But you *lied*."

"You would have said no and I would have been fucking screwed," he shot back, a mixture of anger and anguish in his tone. I rocked back from the blow. "Shit, Liv, I'm sorry—"

"Fuck you." His insinuation that I wouldn't have bent over backward for him was a low enough blow that it snapped me out of it. I moved again, *finally* regaining some kind of composure over myself, and forced my body up and out of the chair. "If you think for one second that I wouldn't have put my needs aside to ensure that Noah ended up with you, then you are out of your goddamn mind."

"You said—"

"You think I give a fuck what I said?" I snapped, wiping the snot from my nostrils with the back of my hand. God, my throat felt raw. "Do you understand how much I have given to you? Do you understand the lengths I have gone to, for *you?* I watched your son. I moved into your *home*."

"Liv, please—"

"I practically gave up my personal life, my time at the office, my *reputation* at the office, for *you*. I assumed the role of a fucking parent, for *you*. I gave *you* a part of myself that I vowed I wouldn't give to anyone but the person I'd spend the rest of my goddamn life with. I have kept everything bottled inside of myself, every feeling I have for you, so that *you* wouldn't have another stressor on your plate. And you're going to sit there and tell me that I wouldn't have given a shit if you needed me to stay married to you for Noah's sake? No. Absolutely not. If it came down to my personal comfort versus Noah having a stable, loving home, I would have picked the latter. And you should have known that, but you couldn't even bring yourself to ask me."

Wide blue eyes stared so intensely into mine that I thought, for a moment, that I might have broken him. Breaths came and went with at least a couple hundred heartbeats, and all I could do was stare right back.

Why the fuck didn't I leave?

"Then I'm asking you now," he rasped, his Adam's apple bobbing as he forced himself to swallow. "Stay

274

married to me, for *Noah*. We can schedule the court date right after the custody hearing."

I clenched my teeth to keep my jaw from wobbling. Every part of my body screamed to run, but my head and my heart were two blaring exceptions — they still wanted to please him. And they had the most sway. "Fine," I breathed. "But you don't fucking deserve it."

Chapter 32

Damien

E than and Eliza, the main family lawyer he'd been working with, had spent two and a half hours arguing my case to the judge as Olivia and I sat in silence beside them.

Grace sat on the other side beside two lawyers, her shoulder-length auburn hair swept up into a bun to focus all of the attention on her directly on her fucking scrubs.

She'd rather make a point of being a pediatric nurse than attend court in proper attire.

"As you can see, Mrs. Martin and Mr. Blackwood are clearly inebriated in that image. The timestamp on it is three-fifty-eight in the morning, your honor," Grace's main lawyer argued. I couldn't for the life of me remember what his name was. "Our records show that Mrs. Martin had only been signed on as a formal employee of Blackwood Energy Solutions four days before she and Mr. Blackwood set off to Las Vegas on a work trip."

"If I may," Ethan interjected, his hand reaching for the little microphone in front of him. The judge nodded to him. "I would like to reiterate that Mrs. Martin was an intern at

Blackwood Energy Solutions for five months before being signed on as an employee. Her records reflect that."

"Regardless," Grace's lawyer continued, "the timing and, if I'm being frank, *chaos* of their nuptials should be called into question. We have supplied a signed, dated, and notarized letter from the man who took that image, confirming that Mrs. Martin and Mr. Blackwood were stumbling, incoherent, slurring their words, and barely able to string sentences together. Their marriage is nothing short of a drunken night out two months ago that ended in a mistake, and shows that Mr. Blackwood is not responsible enough to look after himself, let alone his son."

I tucked my hands beneath the table to keep the evidence of my curling fists out of sight.

"Your honor, that is ludicrous," Ethan said, his demeanor utterly calm in the face of this. "My client was unaware at that time that he had a son. He married Mrs. Martin because he wanted to and he could, and at that time, a son he had no idea existed was not factoring into the decisions he made. Since then, he has been nothing short of an exemplary parent. He has provided a stable home with *two* parents, a significant income that puts any fear of the expenses of parenting to rest, and an education for his son that is among some of the best in this country. He is more than fit to have custody over Noah Thompson."

"I understand that this is a heated topic, but I would like to ask both parties to stop interjecting before they are given the green light," Judge Harrow said, her sigh blasting through the small speakers and nearly blowing them.

Grace's lawyer raised his hand, and she nodded to him. "I would like to add that Mrs. Martin has not changed her last name since their marriage took place two months ago," he said flatly. "She also still rents an apartment on the lower west side of San Francisco."

"Objection, your honor. There is no evidence of an apartment in any of the documents provided by either side," Eliza interjected.

I felt like I was going to explode.

There didn't seem to be a winner or a loser here — both sides were strong and both were weak, and there wasn't a single part of me that was certain I'd walk out of here with custody. Things were going in circles, the same talking points being brought up again and again, and I was seconds away from losing my goddamn mind and screaming at every person in this room.

But I couldn't. For Noah, I couldn't. But I could do something else.

Olivia's head turned toward me as I leaned in the opposite direction over to Ethan. "I need to say something," I whispered.

"Like fuck you do," he hissed. "I know you're stressed but you need to keep your mouth shut before you ruin the small headway we have."

Grace's lawyer began to speak again and I couldn't hear a goddamn word of it. "We'd like to call for a brief recess—"

"Your honor, I'd like to make a statement myself, if I can," I interrupted, the squeak and crunch of the shitty courtroom chair against the wood floors almost drowning out my unamplified voice.

Ethan grabbed my wrist. "Stop," he hissed.

"Mr. Blackwood," Judge Harrow responded. Her wrinkled face crinkled further, her thin, wireframe glasses shifting on her nose. "If you'd like to make a statement on the record, by all means, the floor is yours."

"Damien," Olivia whispered. My head swung around

and down toward her, and for the first time in weeks, she met my gaze and didn't flinch. "Don't."

"I'm not just going to sit here and let people who aren't involved in *this*," I motioned between us with my hand, "speak on it."

"We don't have all day, Mr. Blackwood." Judge Harrow's brows knitted together as she stared down at me over her glasses.

For a fleeting second, a look of genuine worry flickered across Olivia's features. Her lips parted, her eyes widened, her chin raised, and I knew she was thinking the same thing I was. *This could ruin my chances.*

But it could also, maybe, hopefully, solidify them.

I cleared my throat and turned to the judge. "Your honor, I don't feel comfortable with four lawyers arguing over my relationship's validity when none of them know the ins and outs of it," I started. My mind spun into overdrive in the span of a breath, words forming and being crossed out and rewritten. I should have prepared for this, but I had not. I should have seen this *coming*, but I had not. "One side is espousing theories that we were simply drunk enough to throw ourselves into a chapel for the thrill of doing something idiotic, something that we'd want to demolish the next morning when the alcohol wore off and we'd come back to ourselves. My side, however, is pushing the narrative that we were instead acting on instincts, knowing how well we meshed after a short time together and taking the plunge after weeks of seeing each other."

The too-cold air of the courtroom stung my nostrils as I forced myself to breathe in.

"Ms. Thompson's lawyers are almost entirely correct," I admitted, the heaviness of it just barely making a difference to every other weight on my shoulders.

Ethan's hand dropped from around my wrist, thunking on the table beneath him in irritation.

"They're not correct about *everything*," I clarified. "But what happened that night was not something silly we did after weeks of build-up, and we certainly weren't happy about the situation when we'd woken up half-naked and hungover the following morning. I believe I even offered an annulment to Mrs. Martin in the midst of her panic within ten minutes of us realizing what we'd done."

Why the fuck did I say that? Why did I give them more ammunition? I needed to trust my gut, but dear god, it was sending me down the wrong path.

"That was the plan, your honor. File for annulment, and pretend none of it ever happened. But before my son even entered the picture, I couldn't stop myself from seeking her out, from thinking about her, from wanting to see her again," I said. "I couldn't get her out of my head. We spent more time together, just the two of us, and I wasn't entirely sure where her head was at with it but I knew exactly where mine was. I didn't care about what we'd done — a mistake like that can be erased. But I didn't want to remove her entirely. In fact, I wanted the opposite, I wanted to see her more, I wanted to explore the possibility of *more* with her. And then I found out about my son."

"Your honor, if I may, this is irrelevant," Grace's main lawyer interjected, his voice far louder than mine as he spoke into the microphone. Ethan moved beside me. "He's admitted that it was a drunken, thoughtless decision. The rest is just nonsense."

"Let him speak," Ethan said, his curt tone halting the man in his tracks. "He has a right to speak on this. Let him."

The judge motioned for me to continue, and Grace's lawyer sunk into his rickety wooden chair.

I swallowed past the solidifying mass in my throat. "I found out about Noah, and I had to shift gears. My thoughts morphed to considering what was best for him and not for me, and what I assumed would be best for him at that time was my undivided attention. I called Mrs. Martin and told her that whatever we...*were*...needed to end. I explained my situation. And although she was upset with me, she understood. I needed to put a son that I hadn't even met yet *first*. And I did that."

Grace turned in her chair, her brown eyes boring a hole into my head.

"I was told by both my lawyer and the paperwork that was given to me that I had two weeks to prepare for Noah's arrival," I explained. "I was given a date and a time that he would be dropped off at my home, and I started to prepare. I ordered clothing, furniture, bedding, toys, simple food. I ensured that everything would come before his arrival, and Grace—sorry, Ms. Thompson went behind my back and changed the date to a week sooner. She informed my lawyer at eleven o'clock the night before when I was already in bed, and then at six in the morning, I was woken up by Grace's arrival with my very confused son. Nothing had arrived yet, I hadn't figured out childcare yet, and I was thrust into my role without the adequate time I needed."

"Objection, your honor," Grace's lawyer interrupted me. "We supplied evidence to show that the date was adjusted a few days in advance."

"And *we* supplied evidence that I was not informed of that adjustment until eleven PM the night before," Ethan challenged.

"It doesn't matter," I snapped. "What matters is that I was confused and stressed out of my skull, my sister was out of town, and I had no one to take him during my incredibly important two hour meeting that morning. And in a last ditch effort to figure out what I was going to do, I begged Mrs. Martin for her help. Being the absolutely incredible woman that she is, she agreed to watch him for me, and the two of them clicked right away."

"The two of them?" Judge Harrow asked.

"Mrs. Martin and my son, Noah," I clarified. "They clicked. And out of desperation and that inkling to still want to be around her, I asked her to watch him more. I asked her to move in while I tried to figure out childcare. She agreed, albeit incredibly reluctantly. I had *just* told her that we couldn't continue on as we were, and suddenly she was moving into my house. I understood her hesitation. There was attraction between us and I don't think either of us knew how we would handle that."

Olivia shifted in her seat, and when I glanced at her, she was already looking up at me. *Fuck, she's too beautiful.* I'd royally, horribly, disgustingly messed up with her, and every second of looking at her and interacting with her the last few weeks had only solidified that.

"But I don't think either of us expected where it would end up, either," I continued. "We tried to keep it platonic. We told ourselves that it would just be until I could find adequate childcare for Noah that met my expectations. But in truth, she set my expectations so high that I struggled to find someone that would be with Noah the way she is. She treats him like he's her own, and every second of watching that, every time I saw the photo of him on her lockscreen, the tears she didn't know I had seen when he was in the hospital, the hugs, the *love* she showed him... it only made things harder. We gave ourselves the grace to act on how we felt until we figured out what we were doing in terms of our marriage, and things spiraled."

"Your honor, he's openly admitting that it's a sham marriage," Grace's lawyer spat down the microphone, the speakers nearly blowing again.

"Let him *speak*, Mr. Allen," Judge Harrow said, "or I will have you removed."

"I found myself hoping that it wouldn't end, your honor," I continued. I couldn't bring myself to look at Olivia again, couldn't bare the idea of the anger on her face from my words. "And I think she did, too. We did what we were doing for Noah, but I think both of us, deep down, knew that it was partly for ourselves. It was both selfish and self-less, thoughtless and thoughtful. I have never been good at holding down a relationship, Judge Harrow, but with Olivia —sorry, Mrs. Martin—it seemed like the easiest thing in the world. Like breathing, or brushing your teeth, or turning on the coffee pot in the morning and being impatient for the first cup."

I swallowed again, my mouth far too dry for comfort. From the corner of my eye, I could see Olivia moving, could see her hand wiping something from her face.

"When we went out that night in Vegas, I hadn't expected to wake up the next morning with a wife. That is true. That has *always* been true. But I wouldn't go back in time and change it, I wouldn't pray to whatever is out there and ask for a different outcome. I somehow ended up with the best possible thing I could have asked for — a loving, beautiful, *smart* woman as my wife, and an incredible son that absolutely adores her. And the thought of losing either one..."

The mass in my throat doubled in size as reality began to hit.

I could lose both of them today. I was almost certainly losing one.

The breath I took in was shaky, and I couldn't hide it. The backs of my eyes burned, and although I could fight that, I couldn't stamp down what it did to my voice. "Noah loves her more than I can describe," I warbled. "And I..."

Say it. I can say it.

"I just needed that to be known."

Coward.

———

An hour passed of nonsensical back and forth between lawyers. I sat in my chair, barely hearing what was said, barely able to look at anything other than Olivia's stiff form and the empty podium in front of us. I couldn't focus. I could barely *breathe*.

I wanted to hold her hand. I wanted to apologize. I wanted to say what I nearly had, wanted to tell her that she deserved more than me, wanted to beg her to forgive me. But court hadn't been dismissed and I couldn't do that here.

Ethan's elbow collided with my arm, and I sunk back into reality.

"I want to be absolutely clear when I say that I understand both parties need for custody," Judge Harrow said. "I also understand why both parties believe the other shouldn't have that."

The older woman breathed in deeply as she adjusted her spectacles.

"But I have come to a decision," she sighed.

She lifted the papers in front of her and hit the bottoms

against her desk to align them. Nausea twisted my gut into ropes.

"In the case of custody over Noah Thompson, age five, Damien Blackwood will receive full custody with visitation allowed by Ms. Thompson. Where it is possible, Mr. Blackwood should strive to allow visitation when Ms. Thompson requests this. This decision is final and will not be up for debate unless circumstances change within the next five years, at which time Ms. Thompson, should she want to, can challenge the court's decision."

I let out a breath.

I won.

I won.

"You are dismissed," she added.

I won. I won. I won. I won—

"Thank fuck," Ethan sighed exasperatedly.

I wasn't thinking straight. I moved, and I shouldn't have, but the adrenaline was shooting through my system and I couldn't believe that I had actually *won* — I *fucking won.*

I stood from my seat. Olivia was already up.

My hands came to her cheeks, just gently, just barely holding on.

I leaned in to kiss her, and she turned away.

Chapter 33

Olivia

For a moment as I stepped through the door of Damien's home I wondered what would have happened if he had lost. Would I have had to pick up the pieces? Would I have been thrust into yet another situation where I lost agency of myself for his benefit?

"Liv, we need to talk about this."

The door shut behind him. I hadn't spoken since we'd left the courthouse and I wasn't about to start now. If I did, I'd say things I didn't mean. Or worse, things I *did* mean.

I was so entirely grateful that Noah was still at school and didn't have to be present for any of this.

My heels echoed through the quiet house as I rounded the corner opposite the kitchen, down into the short hallway.

"Liv," he tried again. He followed me, step by step, his tone almost desperate despite his big win of today. "Please."

I slipped into his office and came around his desk, wrenching the upper right drawer open. The papers felt so heavy in my hand despite being a small stack, and a second later I placed them gently on the polished wood.

286

"Olivia."

Plucking his fanciest pen out of its holder, I got to work signing my name and initials on every sheet that required it. I'd studied them for long enough the day that I found them to know exactly where each one needed to go.

The empty spots next to his name made my morning sickness morph into afternoon sickness, and before he could say my name again, I slid the papers across the desk toward him.

"Sign," I said.

His jaw wobbled as he tried to clench his teeth. "Can we please talk about this first?"

"*Sign*," I repeated, and the nausea shifted into something worse, something painful, traveling up my esophagus and cracking my chest.

He hesitated.

Reluctantly, his fingers grasped the pen from where it sat atop the papers. One by one, he signed his name and initials, following the guide I'd laid out of my signatures. Over and over, *Damien Blackwood* littered the pages. I didn't speak again until the last page was signed and dated.

"I spoke to Ethan before we left," I said flatly. I couldn't even bring myself to *feel* — I'd done too much of that in the last few weeks. "He'll set the date so we can appear before the judge."

"Please just—"

"We're done," I added, and oh, no, I still could feel. The words ripped a brand new hole in my chest, just beside the bigger, gaping one he'd dealt when he'd hidden this from me.

His gaze met mine in a flash. "We're not," he breathed.

"We are."

"I meant every fucking word I said in court," he pushed,

setting the pen down on the open papers and standing up to his full height. "I don't want to lose either of you."

"You've already lost me, Damien." I meant for it to be scathing, but it came out slightly broken, and I could see the crack in his features as that realization sunk in. "I think you knew that two weeks ago."

A beat of silence passed and the glassiness of his eyes doubled. "But you stayed," he rasped.

"For Noah. I stayed for Noah. I did *this*, for Noah," I explained, my voice warbling. I'd barely given myself space to consider how leaving both of them would affect me, and I could feel the icy tendrils of dread and despair beginning to slither inside of me. "I'll miss him. So, *so* fucking much, Damien. But I can't do this with you."

I stepped around his desk, and before I could even try to make it to the door, his hand caught me around my wrist, pulling me back, pulling me closer. "Please don't do this," he croaked. "He needs you. *I* need you. Everything I did, the lying, the hiding it from you, meeting with Ethan without your knowledge, keeping you out of the loop — I did it all for him, and it was so fucking stupid of me. I never wanted to hurt you."

"You chose to do it that way."

"I know." His hand tightened around my wrist and he pulled again, trying to bring me into him, but I held my ground. "I have never regretted anything more in my goddamn life. I care about you, Olivia. Far too much, if I'm being honest."

"Then say it," I demanded.

I'd heard him in court. I knew exactly where he was going before he changed course. I knew they were there, but I also knew he couldn't bring himself to utter the words, and if he couldn't, then it wasn't true.

"Say it, Damien."

His mouth popped open, his eyes flicking between mine with uncertainty. Hesitation, and then nothing.

"I understand why you did it," I sighed, slipping my wrist out of his grasp. "But it's done. You got what you wanted. We agreed to an expiry date, and it's here."

"I don't want a fucking expiry date," he choked. "I want *you*."

"I'll leave before Noah gets home." I swallowed, and there it was again, that splitting, aching pain in my chest that bloomed from the thought of how Noah would handle this. Or maybe it was from him saying the thing I'd been hoping he'd say before I found the papers. Either way, it burned me, leaving little left except extinguished embers. "I'm sorry, Damien. But it's done."

Chapter 34

Damien

Handing the paperwork over to Ethan might have been the hardest thing I'd ever done.

I knew it was the right thing to do. I knew there wasn't a single chance of me changing her mind, not now, probably not ever. But every part of my body had physically recoiled when Ethan's open palm faced upward, expectantly awaiting a handful of documents.

A part of me regretted giving them to him. That part of me, horrible and disgusting and thinking only with his heart and not his head, wanted to keep them and run away somewhere she'd never find me. It wanted to convince Ethan to keep her tied up in the legal system for years, wanted to cherish the only fucking thing I had left of her in privacy somewhere in the Himalayas, wanted to take Noah with me and homeschool him and lose my mind. But I wasn't *that* horrible.

I was just *very* horrible.

"You're beating a dead horse," Carrie said, her gaze locked on the flickering streetlight in the distance. The warm, dark blue hues of twilight were fading rapidly into nightfall, and the rolling hills were beginning to disappear against the horizon. She sipped at her glass of wine. "You can't undo what you did. You've fucked up, you've felt bad, now you've got to get back up."

"I can't just get back up, Carrie," I sighed. "I am the lowest of the fucking low. She did everything — *everything* I asked of her, bent over backwards, tore herself to pieces for me. And the one thing she asked of me, I avoided doing for her."

"Yeah, and you're a piece of shit for it." Her lipstick stained the edge of the glass as she held it against her lips. "I'll never let you live it down. But you've got to get yourself together for your fucking son, Dame."

She wasn't wrong. I'd won custody and then failed spectacularly at being a parent recently. Chicken nuggets for dinner every night, an endless stream of Disney movies on the television to entertain him, and shutting myself into the kitchen pantry with a couch cushion to scream into weren't exactly good parenting choices when it was nonstop. I couldn't remember the last time I'd cooked a proper meal for myself, or more importantly, Noah.

"I can't." The lip of the glass *tinked* against my teeth. "I've tried."

"You're here," she offered. "That's a start."

"I showered for the first time in a week this morning. That's not a start."

"Have you talked to her?"

I shook my head and took a sip of wine. "I tried, for the first couple of days. She didn't answer my calls or reply to my texts. I can't blame her."

She rolled her lower lip between her teeth as her fingernails plucked at the chipping red paint of her lounger.

"What is it?" I asked.

"Hmm?"

"You're worrying. You're doing that thing with your lip."

She sighed and finally tore her gaze from the distance, turning to look at me instead. "I just don't know how much I should say. I basically made a promise to her that I wouldn't blab to you about the things she told me, but I don't know how much salt that's worth anymore."

Oh, fuck. "She talked to you about me?"

"Of course she did, Dame. She was your wife."

"She's *still* my wife," I rasped. The court date wasn't for another week.

Caroline picked up the bottle of wine from the cooling bucket and poured herself another glass before topping up mine. "She had feelings for you," she said, and my jaw steeled.

"I gathered that much."

"She wasn't sure if she could tell you. She didn't say it, but I got the impression that she was scared you didn't feel the same toward her," she stated. "I think she was worried that for you, it was an opportunity to put things on someone. A weight-carrier, if you will. I think she was a lot deeper into it than you realize."

I swallowed. That didn't make me feel better. "She wasn't that to me."

"I don't think she knew that. And if she did, it wasn't until after your little speech in court."

"I will have only made that worse by doing what I did." I chugged my glass in one go before refilling it and wishing it was something stronger.

"She told me that if it wasn't for her parents, she wouldn't want the annulment," she continued. "She was struggling with that. She wanted it, but she didn't want it at all. And I think she was scared of what that meant for her, and for you, and for Noah. I think she loved you, Damien. And I think you ruined it so badly it might not be fixable."

I poured myself another serving and didn't bother with society's expectations of the max allowance in a wine glass. I filled it entirely, and downed half. "I think you're right. On all accounts."

Knowing that a part of her didn't want the annulment did nothing for battling demons inside of me that didn't want it, either. But it did give a minuscule amount of comfort to know that I wasn't the only one.

"She wanted me to say it," I said. "That I loved her. I couldn't."

"Why?"

"I don't know," I sighed. "Maybe it was because the last person I said that to in a relationship cheated on me and hid a son from me, and then *died*. Maybe it was because I was terrified to give myself to her when I have Noah to worry about. Maybe I'm not sure enough about it. Maybe it's because if I do and we're together, she has the potential to hurt not only me but also my son if she leaves. She's young, Carrie. That word doesn't hold as much weight for her."

"So you don't love her?" she asked, one brow raising.

"I didn't say that."

"You didn't *not* say it. And for her, you basically confirmed that by dodging it when she asked you."

"I know," I breathed. "I almost wish I had."

The silence that fell between was thick and weighted. The only sounds that cut through it were the gulps of wine, the sloshing of it between our teeth, and a handful of gunshots from the television inside where Lucas was showing Noah how to play Halo.

"Do you want it to work with her?" she asked.

"Of course I do. Desperately. But I've ruined—"

"Then you should try to fix it." She set her empty glass on the table and turned back to me. "I'm sure you can figure out a way. Don't let it go because you're feeling sorry for yourself and don't think there's a hope in sight."

"Car, you literally said that I've ruined it so badly it can't be fixed," I snapped. She was right then and she was wrong now.

"I said *might not be fixable*, asshat. The least you can do is try, and then if it doesn't work, tough shit. You move on for your son." She grunted as she pitched forward, her hands on her knees, and pushed herself upright until she was standing. "You need to think about whether what you're doing right now is from a lack of trying or a lack of faith. You owe it to yourself and you owe it to her."

Chapter 35

Olivia

I didn't think I'd be standing outside of his private office again, staring down the name plate and calming my nerves. But here I was.

I'd sat there for upwards of thirty minutes staring at his email, working out if there was a way I could feasibly get out of his summons. But he was the owner, he was the CEO, and I was an employee. At work, I had to play by his rules.

And his rules dictated that I come up to his office.

Swallowing my pride, I pushed the door open.

He sat behind his desk, pen and tablet in hand, his temple resting on the side of his fist, his wristwatch reflecting the downpour of sunlight through the large windows. The instant I stepped through the door, his brows rose and his eyes snapped to mine.

"Liv," he breathed.

I shut the door behind me and leaned against it. "What do you want, Damien?" I sighed, crossing my arms over my chest in an effort to feel contained.

He stood, and I couldn't stop myself from flinching. "I needed to talk to you."

"About work?"

"About us."

I stilled. I should have known. God, I should have known, should have imagined this. I'd given him the benefit of the doubt again. "There's nothing to talk about."

"There is *everything* to talk about," he pushed.

"Unless you've invented a time machine and can take it all back, there isn't."

"Liv," he sighed, coming around to the front of his desk and leaning on it. "I'm sorry. I understand that I fucked up. I understand how I made you feel when you had already done everything I'd asked for and more. You were never... You were never just there as somebody for me to use physically or emotionally."

I turned my head from him. I couldn't look at him, couldn't hear him and take him in at the same time. It made it too hard. Instead, I stared across at the sofa on the other side of the office and the smattering of plants around it, watching how the little particles of dust in the air almost glittered in the sunlight. "That doesn't matter," I said.

"*Why?*" he pressed.

"Because I can't trust you anymore, Damien. You broke that."

"I understand that. I know I fucked up. Let me build it back, please, Liv. I wanted everything with you. I still do. You, me, Noah. I want *you*, Liv, and not the things you'd do for me. I can only apologize so many times before it becomes meaningless, but I'm so—"

"It wouldn't be just you, me, and Noah," I breathed.

I almost regretted it. *Almost.* I knew it shouldn't come out like this, knew that in my fantasies I'd told him over romantic dinners or on his yacht or as we laid in bed one evening. But I couldn't do that. I didn't have the strength to do that, not when I couldn't see a future where any of those things happened again.

"What do you mean?" he asked.

I swallowed, but it did nothing to stop the rising acid in my esophagus. "I'm pregnant."

It felt like a fucking grand piano had been lifted off my shoulders. But somehow, it also felt like being hit by a semi-truck.

His silence struck me, and as much as I wanted to look away, I needed to see him. I needed to see his reaction, needed to gauge what he was feeling. I dragged myself back to him.

A steeled jaw and an averted gaze were all I got in response.

"Are you going to say something?" I asked.

"How long have you known?" The words were dark, twisted, *angry*. If I hadn't been leaning against the door, I would have taken a thousand steps back.

"I knew before I found the papers," I gulped. "I'm eight and a half weeks."

"Are you positive?"

"About the timeline? Yeah, I—"

"No, Olivia. That you're pregnant," he snapped.

The back of my head knocked against the door as I reeled back from his tone. "Yes, I took a million home tests and did a blood test."

He ran a hand through his hair, his gaze drifting to the ceiling. "*Fuck*."

My gut twisted. I knew I'd picked an inopportune moment to tell him, but this wasn't how I'd imagined he'd react. Even knowing he only wanted one child, even knowing the friction between us.

"And you want to keep it?"

Fucking nail in the coffin.

Acting on instinct, I reached for the door handle and peeled myself away from the wood. This was worse than what I'd thought two seconds ago. This was hell, this was horror, and I needed to get the fuck out, needed to run and cut him off. I needed to abandon whatever small amount of hope was still left inside of me and mourn the loss of Noah and a would-be father to the child growing inside of me. I needed to mourn what I once thought I had a shot at.

I slipped through the door before he could say another word that hurt me.

Chapter 36

Damien

Olivia stood in front of me, her chestnut waves tucked up into a ponytail, in a yellow sundress that hit her mid thigh. The shade from the redwoods that sprouted off the beaten path of the San Francisco Botanical Gardens kept us from squinting in the early autumn sun, and everything about her screamed that she was a fucking image plucked from my dreams.

But the look on her face told a different story.

"Why am I here, Damien?" she asked, her nose scrunching as she looked up at me.

"Because although I am forty-five years old, I still act like a child occasionally and you don't deserve that," I sighed.

"For fucks sake," she sighed, her arms dropping to her side as she turned. "I didn't come here to listen to another goddamn apology spew from your mouth. Goodbye."

I grabbed her by the wrist and pulled her back, making sure not to bring her too close this time. "Listen," I said. "I'm not going to sugarcoat what I've done, and I'm not going to try to justify it. I fucked up. I destroyed this. But I'm also aware that I reacted incredibly poorly when you told me you were pregnant, and I can't just let it end on that. I can't *not* apologize for that."

"You said you wanted to talk about child support," she snapped. "You lured me here—"

"I do want to discuss that. But I also need to talk about this."

"You don't, Damien," she groaned, slipping her wrist out of my grasp.

"I do," I insisted. The way she looked at me, her mouth parted and her exhausted expression, did little to help with the swirling nerves in my stomach. "I reacted fucking horribly. I panicked. I was surprised, and in my head, I'd just been picturing the three of us—"

"And I destroyed that fantasy," she said, her lips pursing together.

"No," I sighed. "You enhanced it. But I wasn't expecting it, and I thought I knew what the situation was between us. It put everything back up in the air for me."

"So you were upset because your plan to sway me back into your fucking arms went up in flames?" she laughed, but the sound wasn't the sweet chime I was used to. It *cut*. "You asked me if I was going to keep it as if it's something to throw away."

I flinched. I'd forgotten how bad that had sounded. "That wasn't how I meant it, Liv, but I completely understand that that's how it came across," I pressed. "I was asking because I wanted to be sure that you were before we discussed it further, but I was a mess. That wasn't fair of me."

She scoffed. "Yeah. Sure."

"I'm telling you now, Liv, I want this." I swallowed my pride, swallowed anything that would hinder me from speaking my mind to her. "I want you and me and Noah and the baby. I want the four of us. I want to raise it, I want to be there for the things I missed with Noah. I want to be there *with you.*"

She steeled her jaw as her arms crossed over her chest again. "You want to be there *with me?*"

"Yes." I took a step toward her, gauging her reaction. She didn't move, but she didn't stand down. "I want you. And everything that comes with that."

She pursed her lips and shook her head, her ponytail swaying from side to side. "No, Damien, you want the baby as a byproduct."

I couldn't keep doing this. I couldn't keep having this back and forth with her, this constant arguing over who I was and what I wanted. I recognized that it was my own fault, that I had caused every bit of it, but she needed to understand.

I took another step forward, closing that distance between us, and took her face in my hands. Wild green eyes met mine, her lips popping open to protest.

"Stop. Please. Stop assuming everything and just listen to me. I do not want the baby as a byproduct of wanting you. I want you both. I *need* you both, Noah needs you both. I want everything that entails, and not because it's required."

Her eyes closed.

"I have made horrible mistakes, princess, but I am trying so hard to atone for them—"

"I did so much for you, Damien, so fucking much out of empathy for you. I wanted to help. Every time you needed something, every time Noah needed something, I bent myself out of shape for you. I pulled early mornings and late nights, I put work second, I put my *life* on hold for you.

You've made me feel a lot of things, but overwhelmingly, you made me feel *needed*." Her lids lifted and a sheen of tears wicked at her lashes, turning black from her mascara. It cut like a knife to the chest. "I don't want to feel needed anymore."

I didn't know what to say to that, and the words fell flat. "What do you want, then?"

Her anger melted away and all that was left over was the shaking, the tears, the *sadness*. "I want to feel *loved*, Damien."

Fuck.

"I want to feel loved, but you can't even say it," she choked.

She took a step back out of my hold again, wiping at the tears and smudging the black across her lower lid. I wanted to follow, wanted to grab her, wanted to make this better. But I froze again. I kept *freezing*.

"Do you want to know the worst part?" she asked, something akin to a laugh or a sob wracking her small frame. "I know you didn't do all of this to hurt me. I know you had the best intentions. If you didn't, you would have twisted that knife sooner, you would have told me you loved me well before any of this. Your carelessness has led to this and nothing else."

"Liv," I pleaded. It was the only thing that I could get out of my mouth.

"Tell me you love me, Damien."

Nothing. Fucking nothing. I'd had enough time to sit on this, enough time to consider it, and I knew my answer. But it wouldn't *come*. The fear was too much, the worry that I would say it and we would be happy for five years before she left and broke not only my heart, but Noah's and the baby's too.

"It's not hard," she snapped, a bit of that anger seeping back in as she took a step toward me. "I love you. I *loved* you, Damien. See?"

My throat closed in on itself. I hadn't expected her to say it, hadn't expected a past tense tagged on at the end. I was losing her *again*, losing this, and I just needed to *say* it. My mouth opened, and nothing came out.

Her hands flew up in surrender. "I'm done," she breathed. "For the last goddamn time, I'm done. I'll send my resignation in the morning."

I took a step forward and she took two back. "Liv, please. I'm trying," I croaked. The backs of my eyes burned, and a second later the breeze through the hanging canopy of woodland felt far too cold against my cheeks. I wiped it away.

"Have Ethan sort out a custody proposal. We can handle it through him outside of court."

"I don't want that," I begged. I felt like a fucking fraud, felt like a failure of a human. I could fix this so easily but it just wouldn't come out. "I want this, no matter what that takes. I want to argue with you. I want to hold you. I want to fucking say it, Liv, I'm *trying*, please just—"

She shook her head. "No," she said. "I'll miss this and I'll miss Noah, but I can't do it. For once, Damien, I need to make a decision for myself and not for you."

It felt as if the world tilted on its fucking axis. Everything was off center, everything was *wrong*. This wasn't how we were meant to end. Brick by brick, a future I'd imagined hundreds of times, a future I'd *counted* on, crumbled.

"I hope you have a wonderful life," she choked. "And I hope you meet someone that fills every need you have."

Chapter 37

Olivia

I knew pregnancy wouldn't be easy. I knew that it would be difficult and tiresome and impede on my everyday life, but what I hadn't planned for in all of my fantasies growing up was the *loneliness*.

I hadn't imagined a life for myself where I did everything wrong. I hadn't imagined marrying a man I loved in a shitty chapel in Vegas just to feel okay about sleeping with him, or taking on the role of a mother to his child, or having an annulment verified by a judge and avoiding eye contact with my ex husband as I shuffled out of the courthouse, or ending up pregnant with no support except money and a promise to share custody.

Through Ethan, Damien had insisted on covering my lack of wages and my rent. He'd added top-ups of thousands of dollars, little notes left on the transfers that said *for whatever you want*. Every time I saw one, it brought it all back up, brought up every emotion, every ache, and as I stared down at my banking app outside of the birthing class studio, I couldn't stop myself from wishing I'd given him a little more grace.

Maybe then I wouldn't be as much of a shell of myself.

Ethan had kept me updated to an extent on Noah. Three weeks turned into three months, and Noah was off for Christmas break. Damien, Caroline, Lucas, and him were going to spend Christmas and the surrounding days up at Damien's cabin in Seattle, and I couldn't help but think about what that would be like, couldn't help but picture Noah's face when he saw the settling of snow on the ground in the middle of the forest or his excitement when he realized the cabin had a hot tub.

I missed him. I missed both of them.

I had to hope, at least in part, that by sharing custody of our daughter, she would get to experience all of the things that Noah would. I'd get to hear them through her one day, and although it would be difficult and things would be strained by having one parent who wasn't strong enough to be around the other, I hoped that the life she could have when she was with Damien would counterbalance it.

"All done for the day?"

Sophie sat in her idling beige Toyota, her window halfway down, her green jacket buttoned tight. She beamed at me as the door locks unlatched all at once.

"You good? You look like you've seen a ghost."

"I'm fine," I sighed. "Thank you for picking me up."

The dizziness of getting back up onto my swollen feet after the class still hadn't dissipated, so I placed my hand on the hood of Sophie's Toyota to steady myself as I came around the front of it. Thankfully I wasn't overly large yet, but I'd struggled to get used to the bump, struggled to come to terms with how much my body had changed in five and a half months.

I grabbed the handle on the inside of the car just above the window and lowered myself into the seat. My jacket felt almost useless — I was either running far too hot or far too cold nowadays, and as I unbuttoned it desperately because of the heat pouring out of her air vents, she looked over at me as if I was insane.

"It's freezing," she said.

"I feel like I just stepped out of *hell*," I shot back, wiggling out of my jacket and tossing it over my shoulder and into the backseat. "Excuse me for being fucking pregnant."

"Sheesh, Liv, calm down," she grumbled. The car began to move beneath us. "Bad class today?"

I pursed my lips and focused on the tarmac through the windshield. Carsickness was a new problem I was being forced to deal with, and I really didn't want to throw up in here a third time.

"I'll take that as a yes."

"Everyone brought their partners today," I sighed.

She didn't say anything, and the idle tick of the turn signal filled the empty space instead.

"It just stung a little. And I'm trying not to let it bother me, but *everything* is bothering me," I explained, my filter well and truly gone. "This seat being uncomfortable is bothering me. The heat is bothering me. The lack of snow is bothering me. Stupid Jennifer and her stupid husband with washboard abs and a wedding ring were bothering me. I can't sleep right, I can't reach my toes, I can't drink wine, I can't see Damien or Noah, I can't take a deep breath without feeling like her foot is kicking me in the diaphragm. I can't eat blue cheese and I can't have sushi. My nipples are a different color and that's starting to freak me out."

The car came to a stop at a red light and she slowly turned to look at me. "I love you, and that sucks, but I cannot fix the majority of that." She reached for the temperature dial and turned it down to sixty, and a wave of cool air finally blasted me, wicking away the thin sheen of sweat.

"Thank you," I said, letting my head fall back against the headrest.

She bit her lip as we took off again, her gaze focused on the road instead. "Do you miss him?"

"Would you think it's insane if I say I do?"

Sophie shook her head, her blonde ponytail shifting side to side. "No. I think what he did was psychotic and shit, but I think he did it with good intentions. I think he's done as good of a job as he can in supporting you without being allowed to be present. And to be honest, Liv, I think you're going to really struggle in a few months when she pops out and needs her mother close by at all times."

For a second, I let my gaze drift out the passenger window. I didn't want to see Sophie's face as she said her words, but as quick as I'd let it happen, the nausea from carsickness started to grow and I was forced to bring her into my field of vision again.

"Have you guys talked about that at all? How is he going to split custody with you if she needs her mother and you won't be in the same room as him?"

"We've had a bit of back and forth through Ethan about it," I sighed. "We haven't been able to come to an agreement."

Her turn signal popped on again, and she took a right where I wasn't expecting. Maybe there was traffic.

"He wants to be there when she's born," I added, my voice barely above a whisper. "I haven't decided if I can handle that yet."

An unexpected left, and I started to wonder if maybe she wasn't taking me home. "I know you probably don't want to hear this, but if you want my opinion, you should let him be there. It's his daughter, too. I know it will be hard for you and that will only potentially make it harder, but I think he deserves to be there."

The backs of my eyes burned for what felt like the millionth time that day. I'd been so overly emotional since getting pregnant. "I know he does."

"Why are you worried about seeing him?" Another unexpected turn.

"Because if I see him, I'll forgive him," I choked.

"And you don't want to forgive him?"

"I *do* want to forgive him." I sniffled and wiped the little droplet of snot from my nostril with the back of my hand.

"I'm struggling to see the problem here," Sophie chuckled, the first instance of a little bit of lightness in what felt like a far too heavy day. "If you want to forgive him and if you miss him, you're just hurting yourself by not allowing that to happen."

"But I'd be betraying what I want."

The car came to a stop in a turn lane, the click of her signal indicating left. *Gashouse Cove Marina* was plastered on the cement sign in swirling letters on the other side of the road. "You just said that what you *want* is to forgive him. I think you'd be betraying what you *wanted*."

My stomach turned as I realized we weren't just making a U-turn. "Sophie."

"I'm not going to apologize for this," she snorted.

"*Sophie*."

"Face your fears head on, Liv."

Chapter 38

Damien

Her warm brown hair rippled in the early winter wind. It was in the forties outside, and yet she wore only a long sleeve black shirt and a pair of black leggings, not a jacket in sight. Only the basic bits of makeup coated her skin — a little bit of mascara, something she called *bronzer,* and a smattering of blush. From the front, I could barely tell she was pregnant from the dark clothing, but the moment she turned halfway down the dock to look over her shoulder at the dry land where Sophie stood, I could see the roundness there, could see how much she'd grown since I'd last seen her at the Botanical Gardens three months ago.

She was the most beautiful thing I'd ever seen, and as I drew a shaky breath in, her gaze snapped back to me and what I stood in front of.

She paused, one hand covering her mouth, her other forearm resting just above her bump and just below her breasts. I knew she was reading it. I knew she could see the bold, curling font behind me on my yacht, could read what I'd renamed it to.

I Love You, Olivia.

She wouldn't move, so I did.

"I love you," I said, and god, it was so easy, now. I stopped in front of her, some twenty or so feet away from the boat and at least two from her. "I love you, and I'm so sorry that it took me so long to be able to say that."

She shook her head in what I could only hope was disbelief. "I don't—"

"Please, Liv, understand that I only struggled with admitting that because of Noah. The idea of cementing someone in his life like that and committing to you wholly when you had the potential to break not only me, but him as well, scared the living shit out of me. I loved you then, and I love you now, and I love our daughter and everything you've done and will do for her." The words were coming and I couldn't stop them if I wanted to. But I didn't want to, not now, not ever, not when it came to her. "I love you, and I don't deserve you."

Her glossy eyes glanced behind me at the yacht again. "What?"

A little shaking sound came from her, and the hand over her mouth made it impossible to tell if she was taking short little breaths from the buildup of tears or if it was something worse, if she was *laughing.*

"Liv?"

She uncovered her mouth, revealing a wide grin beneath it. "It's so cheesy," she snickered. "The name."

Oh, for fucks sake.

"I'm sorry, thank you for saying it, but that — that is *so* funny, Dame," she laughed. She took a step toward me, her shoulders bouncing from her breaths between cackles. "Your neighbors are going to make fun of you."

"I don't... I don't care if they make fun of me—"

Her arms wrapped around my jacketed torso, her stomach pressing against mine before the rest of her slotted in. "It's so dumb. I love it."

Her words, however silly, hit me like a punch in the fucking chest. But instead of knocking the air from me, it loosened me, it relaxed me, it opened up my airways and holy shit, I could *breathe*. She was here. She was here, and she was holding on to me, and she wasn't yelling at me or walking away.

I let myself hold her. I let myself lift her, let my fingers dig into her clothed flesh, let my myself breathe her in and keep her to me. "Hey, hey, you're not supposed to lift pregnant women!"

"Shit, sorry," I laughed, dropping her back to her feet. She pulled away and for the shortest, horrifying second, I wasn't sure how far she'd go or if she'd run off. I grabbed her and brought her back to me, cupping her face in my hands, directing her bright green eyes up at *me*. "Please don't leave."

"I wasn't," she said.

My chest fucking cracked.

"I get it, Dame." A tear slipped from her eyes and I swiped it with my thumb before it could make her colder. *Why the fuck isn't she wearing a jacket?* "Genuinely, I do. I've had a lot of time to sit on it and I think I realized a while ago that you couldn't say it because of him."

I couldn't help myself.

I pressed my lips to hers, felt the chill of them against mine. She parted for me instantly, and the second I delved into her mouth, all I could taste was the lingering flavor of a pumpkin spice latte and the rest was all her. I kissed her desperately, held her to me, wrapped my hand around the back of her neck and kept her from pulling back.

I didn't realize how much I *needed* that. It had been at least four months since she'd let me kiss her, and from the way my body reacted instinctively, I could tell that I hadn't been fixating on something that wasn't real or something I'd built in my own mind. She was here, she was real, and she was coming back to me, *finally*.

"He's going to be so fucking happy," I mumbled against her lips. "He's missed you so much. Maybe more than me, if that's possible."

She pulled her lips away and bounced up on her tiptoes, looking over my shoulder at the boat behind me. "Is he here?"

"God, no," I laughed. "He's with Carrie and Lucas. If you were receptive to this, I wanted you to myself for at least a few hours."

She beamed up at me. "I am, in fact, receptive."

"Thank fuck for that," I grinned.

———

The setting sun over the horizon set the sky on fire, shooting orange and rose colored rays across the water beneath us as we stood on the edge of the bow of the ship. We'd anchored almost an hour ago, and the moments of calm where she hadn't been telling me all about her least favorite classmate at the birthing studio and how that woman's husband shelled out multi-level-marketing smoothies, I couldn't stop thinking about how easily we slotted back into normalcy.

She hadn't been able to stop smiling, even when she was complaining. She missed cheese and wine and sushi and her usual overabundance of coffee. She missed sleeping comfortably, she missed her ankles and feet not hurting. She missed me. But she said it all while looking at me with an unmovable grin, her eyes almost twinkling, and I knew I'd done the right thing. I didn't give up.

Even when it seemed like all hope was lost. Even when I'd pulled myself together for Noah.

I wrapped my arm around her bump as I slotted myself in from behind her, careful not to put too much pressure as she leaned against the railing. The jacket I'd given her was keeping her sufficiently warm, but that left me a little too cold, a little too vulnerable in the cold air.

"I apologize if this is presumptuous," I said softly, my lips just an inch from her ear, "and you might think I'm fucking insane. But I don't want to waste another second with you after not seeing you for three months."

Her head turned, her face just slightly too close to be able to focus on. "What do you mean?"

"I mean that I am more sure about you and our future together than I have been about anything in my entire life," I said. I swallowed past the lump in my throat as I sunk my fingers into the pocket of my slacks. "I was terrified when Noah came into my life. I was terrified when you told me about *her*. But with you, Liv, it was always easy. Marrying you didn't scare me the first time."

Her eyes narrowed as I slowly pulled back just a few inches from her. She spun around, leaning her back on the railing instead. "Damien," she deadpanned.

I pulled the little wooden box from my pocket. "*Olivia*," I parroted, pressing my lips just briefly against her desperately hidden grin. I popped the lid open and held it between us, the light green, oval cut sapphire in the center reflecting and glinting off the last few rays of sunlight. Along the sides of the gem, lab-grown, circular diamonds tapered off until it was just the golden band.

Her glossy eyes flitted between mine and the ring I held in front of her.

"For the record, I bought this before Ethan gave me the papers," I said, swallowing down my pride. We hadn't brought up any of that since we'd been on the dock, and mentioning it now, in the midst of *this*, felt like a stab. But I needed to make it clear. "I told myself then that if, by some miracle, you wanted to stay married to me, I'd give it to you. I wanted to give you a proper wedding. I wanted to do it right, even though we'd started it wrong."

"Are you serious?" she croaked, her shaking fingers plucking the box from my hand.

I nodded. "I missed you every fucking second of the last three months," I rasped. "And I've loved you for longer than that. I just wasn't ready to admit it to myself."

She sniffled as she lifted the ring off of the moss-covered pillow. "I love you. Is this ethical?"

I couldn't stop the creeping laugh coming up and out of my throat. "Of course it's ethical. Who the fuck do you think I am? I didn't just waltz into a Kay Jewelers and pick the first thing I saw—"

Her lips met mine, her shaking hand resting against my cheek. "I want to see the receipt," she giggled against my lips.

"Absolutely not."

"Just for the date of purchase!"

I snorted. "Okay, fine, I'll show you that. But you don't get to see the price."

She kissed me again, and again, and again, her mouth like a saving grace or a whispered prayer for salvation against mine. I didn't want it to stop, didn't want to ever have to pull away from her, didn't want another three months or another three seconds without her touching me.

But she hadn't answered me yet. "Is that a yes?" I breathed, my lips just an inch from hers, my hand tucked against her jaw and neck just beneath her ear and my other around the small of her back.

"You haven't actually asked me, yet," she laughed. "You've just said a lot of sweet things and showed me a ring."

Oh, fuck. She was right.

I must have gotten so swept up in her reaction that I hadn't even said it.

"Marry me," I grinned, pressing my lips against hers. "Marry me again, princess."

She let out a dramatic, over-the-top sigh, her giggles only barely concealed. "I don't know, Dame, you're almost twice my age—"

"Oh, for fucks sake, Liv, I'm taking that as a yes."

———

Bare, beautiful, and strewn across my bed as the ship rocked so gently that we could barely feel it was exactly how I wanted to keep her forever.

I kissed her lips, her jaw, her neck, her collarbones. I kissed her breasts, careful not to brush over her nipples because of the soreness she'd vocalized earlier. I kissed her stomach and the roundness of it, stopped to watch in awe as I held either side of it, feeling the brief little shifts of our daughter. I kissed her thighs, and I kissed what lay between them.

I spent far too long there.

Her moans ripped through the cabin of the yacht as she came around my fingers, her hands tugging at my hair, my tongue against her clit. I tasted every drop of her that coated my hand, relished the flavor of her and the slight differences it had now. Still perfect. Still her.

But my cock was straining against the only pieces of clothing still left on my body, and although my shirt and sweater had long since disappeared, I was aching to remove everything from my lower half. I was aching to be *inside* of her.

"What's most comfortable for you?" I rasped, coming up for a mouthful of air as she twitched around my sunken fingers.

"What... what do you mean?" Her lashes fluttered as the haze of her orgasm left her slightly delirious. I couldn't help but chuckle at how easily I managed to make her undone.

"Liv," I grinned, repositioning myself above her as I slowly slid my fingers out of her. She whined her disappointment at the emptiness. "I'm going to fuck you now, princess. What position would be the most comfortable?"

A blush spread across her cheeks. "Um... shit, I don't know," she breathed, her stomach rising and falling with every intake of air. "Me on top, maybe."

"You got it."

In record time, I slipped myself out of my slacks and underwear, the sweet feeling of relief washing over me the moment my cock was set free. I wrapped one single arm around her waist and lifted her higher up the bed toward the headboard, stopping only to collapse against it myself.

She crawled to me on instinct, and somehow, impossibly, my length became even more rigid.

Her lips met mine with my back against the headboard, and lazily, desperately, she kissed me. She raised up on her knees as she settled in astride me, her hands cupping my cheeks, her head above mine. Even like this, she seemed so breakable, so fragile.

But then she was sinking down onto me, and my brain ceased to function.

Inch by inch, she adjusted to my size, her quick little breaths against my lips painting me in warm air. Slowly she sank, devouring me, pulling me in, and the moment her legs met mine and she had no more room to give, she started to move.

I could have sworn I saw stars.

"Fuck," I groaned, pushing my fingers into the deep brown waves of her hair and clutching it. "I missed this. Missed *you*."

I slid my hand into the space between us and found her swollen, sensitive clit, forcing a yelp out of her as her hips ground into me. Her walls squeezed in response to the added stimulus, and I knew there wasn't a chance in hell I'd last long. But Noah was at Carrie's for the night and we had nowhere else in the world to be, and I could do this over, and over, and over again.

Her head tipped back as I pulled a little harder on her hair, her lips breaking from mine. I kissed along her jaw, along her stretched neck, giving my attention to that space beneath her ear that drove her wild.

"Oh my god," she choked.

Her hand came to rest against the side of my cheek, and for a split second, I could see the ring she'd placed on her finger. My chest cracked just a little bit further. "I love you," I mumbled against her skin. "I love you."

Her answering giggle almost drowned out her, "I love you too."

Chapter 39

Olivia

I wasn't sure what had driven me to pick the location I had, but I couldn't deny that it was fucking hilarious to be standing outside that same stupid chapel in Vegas in the dead of the Nevada winter. I was thankful, at least, that it wasn't actually freezing outside and felt instead like a San Francisco spring day, even if it was dry.

I stood by the doors next to a fully done-up Sophie, her freshly bleached hair curled into waves and tucked up into a bun. Her mid-thigh, navy dress screamed luxury from the little details that covered every inch. Damien hadn't given me a budget, and I'd used that to my advantage since the venue itself was dirt cheap. I spared no expense on my dress, either, and had opted to have it custom made. Every option I'd seen in stores has been made to either hide the bump or accentuate it, and I didn't want either of those. I wasn't going to walk down the aisle in a grecian dress trying to conceal what we'd done, and I wasn't going to make it the center of attention.

Instead, I rushed the custom order, opting for a flowing, layered silk chiffon, with little ruffles on the off-the-shoulder

319

sleeves and embroidered flowers. It was simple, but it was *perfect*, and I felt on top of the goddamn world.

But it was still weird to be there sober.

"You ready for this?" she asked, giving me a little pat on the bump as the music inside began to play. It was the one song I'd always wanted to walk down the aisle to, the song I saw on my favorite show as a kid when the uncle got married.

I grinned at her. "Absolutely."

The woman who had taken our payment months ago opened the doors for me instead this time, and the small chapel hall was half filled instead of empty. My parents hadn't agreed to come but had given me their blessing, so James stood in their place, his white suit jacket and bow tie looking way more formal than anything I'd seen him in. Beside him, his long-term girlfriend, Erin, beamed at me, offering me a little wave.

Ethan, Carrie, and Damien's parents stood on his side. I hadn't had the chance to meet them formally yet as they had only arrived this morning, but I hoped they were as nice and cheerful about this as they seemed as they watched me stand awkwardly next to my best friend at the other end of the chapel.

And of course, at the very end of the center aisle beside The King of Rock and Roll himself, stood the two men I was most excited to see.

Damien, and almost obscured next to his father, Noah.

Elvis' dramatic, played-up scowl as The Beach Boys began to sing *Forever* nearly made me stop in my tracks and laugh. But Sophie ushered me forward, and I crossed the threshold into the sticky carpeted chapel, eyes locked on Damien and the practically vibrating Noah.

Damien's endless grin was everything I could have ever hoped for.

Let the love I have for you live in your heart and beat forever, The Beach Boys sang, and stepped past my brother, his thumbs up lost in my concentration on what was in front of me. Noah held a little pillow in his white-knuckled grip, two gold bands sitting atop it, and in a moment of haste, he held them out to me.

"Not yet, bud," Damien laughed.

"Now," Elvis said quietly, his upper lip twitching on one side. "This better be the last time I have you two in this chapel."

"Nah, I think we might come do this once a year," Damien grinned, one arm coming out to welcome me into the small space on the raised platform. He pressed a kiss against my temple, his lips hovering for just a second, and whispered, "You look just as beautiful as the day I married you the first time."

I snorted. "I was drunk as shit the first time."

Noah lifted the rings again. "Liv," he whispered. "I've got the rings. Don't worry."

"You are doing *such* a good job of looking after them, bud, just hold on to them a little bit longer—"

"Beautiful people! We are gathered here today to celebrate the endless burnin' love of Damien Blackwood and Olivia Martin," Elvis started, and all at once, my future was sealed.

Chapter 40

Damien

"Do you think I'm tall enough for space mountain yet?"

Noah's mouse-shaped ice cream melted dramatically over his hands in the early-autumn California heat. The music of Frontierland from one set of speakers blended seamlessly somehow with the bayou crickets of New Orleans Square. "There's only one way to find out," I grinned.

"Can we go there next?" he asked, bouncing up and down on the balls of his feet with excitement.

"That's all the way across the park," I laughed. "Don't you want to do Pirates? It's right there."

He pouted as he took a *bite* out of his ice cream, his wiggly front tooth shifting dramatically. He hopped up on the bench beside me, leaning dramatically over me to look at the map in my hands. "We're here," I said, pointing out our location.

"And where's space mountain?"

I moved my finger all the way across the map.

"Oh."

"Dame! Do you want anything?"

My head snapped up.

Liv stood on the opposite side of the little seating area, credit card in hand and Emily strapped on her chest, the stroller abandoned beside me. Em cooed happily as her little head turned toward me, her arms and legs dangling out the front of the carrier, and Liv beamed down at her, mumbling a little, "You see Daddy?"

"Just a water!" I shouted back.

A moment later, the two of them trotted over to me. Liv passed me a water and squatted down to put a spare one in the stroller. Em giggled and kicked, her little hands reaching out, the few little sprouts of dark hair on her mostly bald head blowing in the breeze.

"Can you take her?" Liv asked, loosening the straps on the front. "My back is killing me."

"Absolutely."

"I can carry her!" Noah practically shouted, holding out his sticky, ice cream covered hands in anticipation.

"I know you love cuddling her, bud, but it's still a little too soon to carry her around," Liv said, lifting Em out of her carrier and passing her to me. Noah pouted, but Em shrieked excitedly, her little Mickey and Minnie shirt riding up her plump tummy as I held her beneath her arms.

She happily settled into my lap.

Liv unstrapped the carrier from around herself and set it in the stroller, taking the freedom to stretch in her pretty, white sundress. Her hair was tucked up neatly into a ponytail, her makeup just barely there, and in her efforts, she forced a yawn from herself. "Please tell me we're doing an easy ride next."

"Pirates?" I offered, pressing a kiss against Emily's forehead and drawing another giggle from her. "You'll like that one, Em."

"It has *pirates* in it," Noah said to her as if that wasn't readily available information. She was also four months old and likely didn't understand a word he said, let alone what a *pirate* was.

"Can she go on pirates?" Liv asked, one brow raising.

"It says there's no height requirement. We can double check at the entrance though."

"And *then* can we go on space mountain? Please?" Noah asked, jumping off the bench and wrapping himself around Liv's thighs.

"How far is space mountain?" she asked me.

"Other side of the park."

"For f—... We'll work our way there, bud."

Em leaned forward into my chest, her little arms grasping at my shirt, and I pulled her to me, shading her with my body and holding her close. She tucked herself right in. "Think she's getting tired, princess."

"Better strap her in now, then," Liv chuckled. She passed me the carrier, her sapphire stone and two bands glinting off the overbearing sunlight, and popped a little hat on top of Emily. She helped me get it on, lifting Em just a little on my chest so she was facing me instead of outward.

"Thank you," I grinned, stretching my head up to press a kiss against her lips. She looked like fucking heaven above me — my brilliant, perfect, incredible wife, the mother to my children, the woman of my goddamn dreams. Every misplaced hair or speck of baby drool on her dress only made her that much better, and for a flickering moment, I let myself absorb how fucking lucky I was to have her, to have Emily, to have Noah. All healthy, all happy. I wouldn't trade them for the world.

She secured the last strap and gave me a kiss in return. "No problem," she chirped, patting Emily on her sleepy head. "But it looks like you'll be the one sitting out on all the fun rides."

THE END

Hey Fabulous Readers!

I hope you loved Damien and Olivia's fun and sexy romance! I'd be so grateful if you could please leave your review on Amazon on August 19th.

Thanks so much for your support. :-)

Stay sassy and fabulous.
xx
Mia

Please leave your review by clicking here.

Made in the USA
Monee, IL
21 November 2024

70830398R00181